IT'S IN HIS KISS

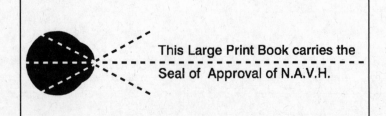

This Large Print Book carries the
Seal of Approval of N.A.V.H.

LUCKY HARBOR

IT'S IN HIS KISS

JILL SHALVIS

THORNDIKE PRESS
A part of Gale, Cengage Learning

GALE
CENGAGE Learning·

Farmington Hills, Mich • San Francisco • New York • Waterville, Maine
Meriden, Conn • Mason, Ohio • Chicago

GALE
CENGAGE Learning®

LIBRARY OF CONGRESS CATALOGING-IN-PUBLICATION DATA

Shalvis, Jill.
   It's in his kiss / Jill Shalvis. — Large print edition.
      pages cm. — (Lucky Harbor) (Thorndike Press large print romance.)
     ISBN 978-1-4104-7331-8 (hardcover) — ISBN 1-4104-7331-7 (hardcover)
     1. Large type books. I. Title.
PS3619.H3534I84 2014
813'.6—dc23   2014031076

Published in 2014 by arrangement with Grand Central Publishing, a division of Hachette Book Group, Inc.

Printed in the United States of America
1 2 3 4 5 6 7 18 17 16 15 14

IT'S IN HIS KISS

Chapter 1

"Oh, yeah," Becca Thorpe murmured with a sigh of pleasure as she wriggled her toes in the wet sand. The sensation was better than splurging on a rare pedicure. Better than finding the perfect dress on sale. Better than . . . well, she'd say orgasms, but it'd been a while and she couldn't remember for sure.

"You're perfect," she said to the Pacific Ocean, munching on the ranch-flavored popcorn she'd bought from the pier. "So perfect that I'd marry you and have your babies, if I hadn't just promised myself to this popcorn."

"Not even going to ask."

At the sound of the deep male voice behind her, Becca squeaked and whipped around.

She'd thought she was alone on the rocky beach. Alone with her thoughts, her hopes, her fears, and all her worldly possessions stuffed into her car parked in the lot behind her.

But she wasn't alone at all, because not ten feet away, between her and the pier, stood a man. He wore a rash-guard T-shirt and loose board shorts, both dripping wet and clinging to his very hot bod. He had a surfboard tucked under a biceps, and just looking at him had her pulse doing a little tap dance.

Maybe it was his unruly sun-kissed brown hair, the strands more than a little wild and blowing in his face. Maybe it was the face itself, which was striking for the features carved in granite and a set of mossy-green eyes that held her prisoner. Or maybe it was that he carried himself like he knew he was at the top of the food chain.

She took a few steps back because the wary city girl in her didn't trust anyone, not even a sexy-looking surfer dude.

The man didn't seem bothered by her retreat at all. He just gave her a short nod and left her alone.

Becca watched him stride up the pier steps. Or more correctly, she watched his very fine backside and long legs stride up the pier steps, carrying that board like it weighed nothing.

Then he vanished from sight before she

turned her attention back to the ocean.

Whitecaps flashed from the last of the day's sun, and a salty breeze blew over her as the waves crashed onto the shore. Big waves. And Sexy Surfer had just been out in that. Crazy.

Actually, *she* was the crazy one, and she let out a long, purposeful breath, and with it a lot of her tension.

But not all . . .

She wriggled her toes some more, waiting for the next wave. There were a million things running through her mind, most of them floating like dust motes through an open, sun-filled window, never quite landing. Still, a few managed to hit with surprising emphasis — such as the realization that she'd done it. She'd packed up and left home.

Her destination had been the Pacific Ocean. She'd always wanted to see it, and she could now say with one-hundred percent certainty it met her expectations. The knowledge that she'd fulfilled one of her dreams felt good, even if there were worries clouding her mind. The mess she'd left behind, for one. Staying out of the rut she'd just climbed out of, for another. And a life. She wanted — *needed* — a life. Employment would be good, too, since she was fond of eating.

But standing in this little Washington State town she'd yet to explore, those worries receded slightly. She'd get through this; she always did. After all, the name of this place nearly guaranteed it.

Lucky Harbor.

She was determined to find some *good* luck for a change.

A few minutes later, the sun finally gently touched down on the water, sending a chill through the early-July evening. Becca took one last look and turned to head back to her car. Sliding behind the wheel, she pulled out her phone and accessed the ad she'd found on Craigslist.

Cheap waterfront warehouse converted into three separate living spaces. Cheap. Furnished (sort of). Cheap. Month to month. *Cheap.*

It worked for Becca on all levels, especially the cheap part. She had the first month's rent check in her pocket, and she was meeting the landlord at the building. All she had to do was locate it. Her GPS led her from the pier to the other end of the harbor, down a narrow street lined with maybe ten warehouse buildings.

Problem number one.

None of them had numbers indicating its address. After cruising up and down the street three times, she admitted defeat and parked. She called the landlord, but she only had his office phone, and it went right to voice mail.

Problem number two. She was going to have to ask someone for help, which wasn't exactly her strong suit.

It wasn't even a suit of hers at all. She hummed a little to herself as she looked around, a nervous tic for sure, but it soothed her. Unfortunately, the only person in sight was a kid on a bike, in homeboy shorts about ten sizes too big and a knit cap, coming straight at her on the narrow sidewalk.

"Watch it, lady!" he yelled.

A city girl through and through, Becca held her ground. "*You* watch it."

The kid narrowly missed her and kept going.

"Hey, which building is Two-Oh-Three?"

"Dunno, ask Sam!" he called back over his shoulder. "He'll know, he knows everything."

Okay, perfect. She cupped her hands around her mouth so he'd hear her. "Where's Sam?"

The kid didn't answer, but he did point

toward the building off to her right.

It was a warehouse like the others, industrial, old, the siding battered by the elements and the salty air. It was built like an A-frame barn, with both of the huge front and back sliding doors open. The sign posted did give her a moment's pause.

WARNING: PRIVATE DOCK
TRESPASSERS WILL BE USED AS BAIT

She bit her lower lip and decided that, after driving all day for days on end, her need to find her place outweighed the threat. Hopefully . . .

The last of the sunlight slanted through the warehouse, highlighting everything in gold, including the guy using some sort of planer along the wood. The air itself was throbbing with the beat of the loud indie rock blaring from some unseen speakers.

From the outside, the warehouse hadn't looked like much, but as she stepped into the vast doorway, she realized the inside was a wide-open space with floor-to-rafters windows nearly three stories high. It was lined with ladders and racks of stacked wood planks and tools. Centered in the space was a wood hull, looking like a piece of art.

As did the guy working on it. His shirt was damp and clinging to his every muscle as it bunched and flexed with his movements. It was all so beautiful and intriguing — the boat, the music, the man himself, right down to the corded veins on his forearms — that it was like being at the movies during the montage of scenes that always played to a sound track.

Then she realized she recognized the board shorts, or more accurately the really excellent butt, as she'd only moments before watched it walk away from her.

Sexy Surfer.

Though he couldn't possibly have heard her over the hum of his power tool and the loud music, he turned to face her. And as she already knew, the view of him from the front was just as heart-stopping as it was from the back.

He didn't move a single muscle other than one flick of his thumb, which turned off the planer. His other hand went into his pocket and extracted a remote. With another flick, the music stopped.

"You shouldn't be in here," he said. "It's dangerous."

And just like that, the pretty montage sound track playing in her head came to a screeching halt. "Okay, sorry. I'm just —"

Just nothing, apparently, because he turned back to his work, and with another flick of his thumb the planer came back to life. And then the music.

"— Looking for someone," she finished. Not that he was listening.

On the wall right next to her, a telephone began ringing, and the bright red light attached to it began blinking in sync, clearly designed just in case the phone couldn't be heard over the tools. She could hear it, but she doubted he could. One ring, then two. Three. The guy didn't make a move toward it.

On the fourth ring, the call went to a machine, where a recorded male voice said, "Lucky Harbor Charters. We're in high gear for the summer season. Coastal tours, deep-sea fishing, scuba, name your pleasure. Leave a message at the tone, or find us at the harbor, north side."

A click indicated the caller disconnected, but the phone immediately rang again.

Sexy Surfer ignored all of this.

Becca had a hard time doing the same, and she glanced around for someone, *anyone,* but there was no one in sight. Used to having to be resourceful, she let her gaze follow the cord of the planer to an electric outlet in the floor. She walked over to it and

14

pulled it out of the wall.

The planer stopped.

So did her heart when Sexy Surfer turned his head her way. Yep, Sexy Surfer was an apt description for him. Maybe Drop-Dead Sexy. Either way, he took in the fact that she was still there and that she was holding the cord to his planer and a single brow arched. Whether it was displeasure or disbelief was hard to tell. Probably, with that bad 'tude, not many messed with him. But she was exhausted, hungry, out of her element, and a little bit pissed off. Which made her just enough of a loose cannon to forget to be afraid.

"I'm trying to find Sam," she said, moving closer to him so he could hear her over his music. "Do you know him?"

"Who's asking?"

Having come from a family of entertainers, most of them innate charmers to boot, Becca knew how to make the most of what she'd been given, so she smiled. "I'm Becca Thorpe, and I'm trying to find Two-Oh-Three Harbor Street. My GPS says I'm on Harbor Street, but the buildings don't have numbers on them."

"You're looking for the building directly to the north."

She nodded, and then shook her head

with a laugh. She could get lost trying to find her way out of a paper bag. "And north would be which way exactly?"

He let the planer slowly slide to the floor by its cord before letting go and heading toward her.

He was six-foot-plus of lean, hard muscle, with a lot of sawdust clinging to him, as rugged and tough as the boat he was working on — though only the man was exuding testosterone, a bunch of it.

Becca didn't have a lot of great experience with an overabundance of testosterone, so she found herself automatically taking a few steps back from him, until she stood in the doorway.

He slowed but didn't stop, not until he was crowded in that doorway right along with her, taking up an awful lot of space.

Actually, *all* of the space.

And though she was braced to feel threatened, the opposite happened. She felt . . . suddenly warm, and her heart began to pound. And not in a terrified way, either.

He took in her reaction, held her gaze for a moment, then pointed to the right. "The front of the building you're looking for is around the corner," he said, his voice a little softer now, like maybe he knew she was torn between an unwelcome fear and an equally unwelcome heat.

She really hoped the heat was mutual, because it would be embarrassing to be caught in Lustville by herself. "Around the corner," she repeated. Did he know he smelled good, like fresh wood and something citrusy, and also heated male? She wondered if she smelled good, too, or if all she was giving off was the scent of confused female and ranch-flavored popcorn.

"What do you need with that place?" he asked.

"I'm the new tenant there. Or one of them anyway."

His expression was unfathomable. "I take it you haven't seen it yet."

"Not in person," she said. "Why? Is it that bad?"

"Depends on how long you're staying," he said. "More than five minutes?"

Oh, boy. "I don't actually know," she said. "It's a month-to-month rental. Lucky Harbor is sort of a pit stop for me at the moment."

His gaze searched hers. Then he nodded and moved back to his work. He plugged the planer in and flicked it on again.

Guess their conversation was over. She was on her own. And if that thought caused a little pang of loneliness inside her still-hurting heart, she shoved it deep and ignored it, because now wasn't the time to give in to the magnitude of what she'd done. Leaving the warehouse, she turned right.

To her new place.

To a new beginning.

CHAPTER 2

Sam Brody lifted his head from the boat he was building and let his gaze drift to the north-facing window. The sky was a kaleidoscope of colors as the sun vanished, but he could still see the quiet, industrial street, and the backside of Tough Girl as she walked off.

And walking off was just as he wanted her, too. He turned his concentration back to the hull. He was good at concentrating. If his childhood hadn't drilled it into him, then working on an oil rig for seven years — where paying attention meant the difference between life and death — had certainly done so.

But damn if not two seconds later his gaze flickered to the window again.

Yep, she and her sweet bod were gone. She had a backbone, but she also had those warm, soulful brown eyes, and one of those smiles that could draw a man right in.

19

And a sassiness that could hold him there . . .

And she was going to be right next door. Not good news. The warehouse she'd rented was a complete piece of shit, cold in the winter, hot in the summer, not easily secured or safe. Not his call, of course, but he didn't like that the landlord had put her in there, alone. Lyons should've known better. The place had been up for sale for years now, but no one in Lucky Harbor was stupid enough to sink any equity into that money pit. Still, Sam should've bought the thing himself just to keep it empty.

Empty, and quiet.

The phone rang again, and the accompanying red lights gave him an eye twitch. He'd been ignoring the calls while trying to work, figuring one of the guys would get the hint and pick up. But neither Cole nor Tanner was good at hints. No, for his two partners to get something, they had to be hit over the head with it. Besides, Sam knew damn well it amused the hell out of them to make him answer the phone.

Finally he snatched the phone just to shut it up and snarled, "Lucky Harbor Charters."

There was a brief pause, a hesitation that made him feel like a jackass as his gaze skimmed the big sign that Cole had taped above the phone for Sam's benefit alone. It read:

Smile.
Be friendly.
Ask "Can I help you?" in a tone that suggests you actually mean it, and not that you'd like to rip the head off whoever's interrupting you.
(You smiling yet?)

Refusing to smile on principle, Sam did make the effort to sound friendly as he spoke into the silence. "Can I help you?"

"Sammy? That you?"

Sam closed his eyes. "Yeah, Dad. It's me."

"Oh, good." Mark Brody laughed a little sheepishly. "I remembered the number right this time. So . . . how's it going?"

This wasn't the question his dad really wanted to ask, but at least the guy had become self-aware enough to feign interest. In the past, his dad would've gotten right to it. *Got a little extra for your good old dad? Thanks, love ya.*

"Sammy? You there?"

Sam scrubbed a hand down his face. Yeah. He was here. He was always here, from all those crazy years when Mark hadn't had it together enough to keep Sam from landing

21

in foster care, to now, when Mark still didn't have it together. "How much you need?" Sam asked.

"Uh . . ." His dad laughed again, guilt heavy in the sound. He'd spent a total of maybe ten minutes being a dad, so he'd never really gotten the hang of it. "That's not why I called."

Yeah, it was. Of course it was. They had a routine. Sam would call his dad to check in every week, never getting a return call until Mark ran out of money, which happened every few months or so. "It's okay, Dad. Just tell me."

"A grand."

Sam opened his eyes and stared at the sign.

Smile.

Be friendly.

"A grand," he repeated.

"Carrie needs to buy stuff for the baby, and —"

"Got it," Sam said, not wanting to hear about the demands of Mark's latest woman. Or the baby that'd be Sam's half sister when it arrived in a few months.

A baby sister.

It didn't defy the odds any more than picturing his dad trying to be a real dad . . . "Did you ask for the paternity test like we talked about?"

"Well . . ."

"Dad —"

"She'd kill me, son. You have no idea how touchy pregnant women are."

Sam bit back anything he might have said because there was no point. His father had made a career out of getting ripped off by women. "You need to find a way to try," Sam said.

"I will."

Sam blew out a breath. He wouldn't try. "So a grand, then. To the usual bank account?"

"Uh, no," Mark said, back to sheepish. "I closed that one out."

More likely, the bank had kicked him out for repeatedly overdrawing his funds.

"I'll email you the new info," his dad said. "Thanks, son. Love ya."

The *love ya* was so rote that Sam wondered if Mark even realized he was saying it. Not that it mattered. Nor did his response, as his dad had already disconnected.

The phone immediately rang again. Resisting the urge to throw it out the window, he yanked it back up, wondering what his dad could have possibly forgotten. "Yeah?"

"Hi, um . . . is this Lucky Harbor Charters?" a female voice asked, sounding uncertain.

Shit. Sam glanced at the sign. He still didn't have a smile in him so once again he attempted friendly. "Yes, you've reached LHC."

"Oh, good. I'd like to book a deep-sea fishing trip for a family reunion. It's our first big reunion in five years and we're all so excited. There's going to be my dad, my grandfather, my two brothers, my uncle —"

"Okay, great. Hold please," Sam said, and punched the HOLD button. He took a deep breath and strode out of the warehouse and to their "yard." This led to the waterfront. There they had a dock, where their fifty-foot Wright Sport was moored.

Hours ago, Tanner — their scuba diving instructor and communications expert — had texted Sam that he was working on their radio system.

"Hey," Sam called out to him. "How about answering a damn phone call once in a while?"

"You're the one inside," Tanner said, not stopping what he was doing, which didn't look to be work so much as sunbathing. Not that he needed it with the mocha skin he'd inherited from his mother's Brazilian roots. He'd stripped to a pair of board shorts, a

24

backward baseball cap, and reflective aviator sunglasses, and was sprawled out on his back, face tilted up to the sun.

"Busy, are you?" Sam asked drily.

"Cole and I chartered the midnight cruise last night and didn't moor until three a.m."

"And you slept until two p.m., so what's your point?"

Tanner lifted a middle finger.

Sam gave up and strode up to the smaller building — a hut really — that they used as their front office and greeting area. The rolling door was up when they were open for business and shut when they weren't.

It was up now, and Cole was sitting behind the front counter. He was their captain, chief navigator, and mechanic, and was currently hunt-and-pecking at the keyboard of his laptop. The fingers stopped when Sam reached into the bucket beside the counter and pulled out one of their water guns. The thing had been touted as a squirt gun, but the more apt term would have been *cannon*. Sam weighed it in his hands, decided it was loaded enough, and turned back to the door.

"What the hell are you doing?" Cole asked.

"Going to spray the hell out of Tanner."

"Nice," Cole said, fingers already back to

hunt-and-pecking. "Carry on."

Sam stopped in the doorway and stared at him in surprise. Cole was their resident techno-geek. He wore cargo pants with handy pockets and could fix just about anything at any time with the ingenuity of a modern-day MacGyver. And he always, *always,* objected to fighting among their ranks. "What's up?" Sam asked him.

"Trying to work. Go away."

"If you're working so damn hard, why aren't *you* answering the phones?"

Cole lifted his head and blinked innocently. "Phones? What phones? I didn't hear any phones."

Sam shook his head. "We need to get that damn ad in the paper."

Cole's fingers clicked one last key with dramatic flair. "Done," he declared. "Ad placed."

"What does it say?" Sam asked.

Cole hit a few more keys. "Looking for self-motivated admin to answer phones, work a schedule, greet customers with a friendly attitude, and be able to handle grumpy-ass bosses named Sam."

Sam arched a brow. "You'd push the buttons of a guy holding a loaded water cannon?"

Not looking worried in the slightest, Cole

26

smiled and reached down beneath the counter, coming up with his own loaded cannon, which he casually aimed at Sam. "You forget who bought these."

"Shit." He turned to go.

"You're forgetting something else," Cole said.

Sam looked back.

"Tanner's ex-profession as a Navy SEAL."

"Shit," Sam said again, lowering the cannon. He was pissed, not stupid.

"Good choice."

"Line one's for you," Sam said.

Becca wasn't much for regrets so she decided not to stress over the fact that she'd rented a third of a dilapidated warehouse sight unseen. Thanks to Sexy *Grumpy* Surfer's warning — *I take it you haven't seen it yet* — she'd been braced.

But not braced enough.

The building was similar to Sam's in that they were both converted warehouses, and had the same floor-to-rafter windows. But that's where the similarities ended. Her warehouse hadn't been nearly so well taken care of. According to the landlord — an old guy named Lyons — the place had once been a cannery. Then an arcade. Then a saltwater taffy manufacturer with a gift shop. And finally a boardinghouse, which had last been used for a bunch of carnies in town for a long-ago summer, and they hadn't been kind.

At the moment the entire warehouse was a wide-open space divided into three units by questionably thin walls. Each apartment had a rudimentary galley kitchen and bathroom and was filled with a variety of leftover dust and crap from the previous renters — hence the *furnished (sort of)* part of the ad. In addition to beds and tables, this included some odd-looking carnival equipment and a saltwater taffy pull.

Or possibly a torture device . . .

Becca and Mr. Lyons walked through each of the apartments. The first unit was cheapest since it was the smallest, and also the coldest, as it got the least sun exposure.

Since cheap was right up her alley, and she didn't have to worry about cold for another six months, she'd handed over her check.

"If you need anything," Mr. Lyons said, "yell for the guys across the alley. Tanner's almost always on the dock or their boat, but he's a real tough nut to crack. Cole's good for fixing just about anything. But Sam knows all there's to know about these old warehouses. He's your man if you need anything."

Sam again. But she decided she'd need his help *never.* "Got it, thanks."

"He's not exactly shy, so don't you be," Lyons said. "Just don't try to date any of them. They're pretty much ex-hell-raisers these days, but still heartbreakers, each and every one of them."

"I'll keep that in mind," Becca said, knowing she could and had handled just about anything a woman could face. She absolutely wouldn't be needing help.

Not an hour later, she was in the bathroom washing her hands when she found a huge, black, hairy spider in her sink staring at her with eight beady eyes. She went screaming into the alley, jumping up and down, shaking out her hair, and jerking her limbs like a complete moron.

"You lost again?"

She let out another scream and whirled around to face — oh, perfect — Sexy Grumpy Surfer. He was in faded jeans, a white T-shirt, and mirrored glasses, looking movie-star cool and sexy hot.

He arched a single brow.

"There's a spider in my bathroom sink," she said, still gasping for breath.

"That explains the dance moves."

Ignoring this *and* him, she checked herself

29

over again, still not convinced she was spider-free.

"Need help?" he asked.

"No."

He shrugged and turned to walk away.

"Okay, yes," she admitted. Damn it. "I need help." She pointed to the offending building. "First apartment, door's wide open. The evil culprit is in the bathroom sink."

With a salute, he vanished inside her building.

She did not follow. She couldn't follow; her feet had turned into two concrete blocks. And if he came out without having caught the spider, she was going to have to move out. Immediately.

Two minutes later, Sexy Grumpy Surfer reappeared, the smirk still in place. She wasn't going to ask. She refused to ask. But her brain didn't get the message to her mouth. "You get it?" she demanded, and was rattled enough not to care that her voice shook a little bit.

"Got it," he said.

"Sure?"

He gave her a head tilt. "Do you want me to swear on a stack of Bibles, or my mother's grave?"

His mother was in a grave. That was sad

and tragic, and she knew later she'd think about it and mourn for them. But for right now, she wanted assurances. "Your word will do."

"I'm sure I got the spider."

Whew. She sagged in relief. "Okay, then. Thank you."

"I don't suppose you'd do those moves again."

Was he laughing at her? She narrowed her eyes at him because yeah, he was laughing at her. "I don't suppose."

"Shame," he said, and then he was gone.

Becca went cautiously back inside. She glared at her bathroom mirror for a few minutes and told herself she was fine, move on.

She was really good at that, moving on. She stood in the center of the drafty space with her two suitcases, her portable piano keyboard, and her pride. There were a few other things, too. Fear. Nerves. Worry. But she'd done it, she'd made the move to reclaim her life, and at the realization a new feeling settled into her chest, pushing out some of the anxiety.

Hope.

Nightfall hit in earnest, and she had nothing to do with herself. No WiFi, no cable. Just her imagination. When it kicked in gear, picturing the relatives of the doomed spider creeping out of the woodwork to stalk her, she hurriedly pulled out her e-reader to distract herself. It was an older model, and she had to hold up a flashlight to read by. She could've left an overhead light on, but then she'd have to get out of bed later to turn it off. This wasn't a new problem. She couldn't have said how many times in the past she'd dropped the flashlight and e-reader on her face while trying to read in bed, and sure enough, twenty minutes in, she dropped the flashlight and e-reader on her face.

Giving up, she drove into town, found a local bar and grill named, of all things, the Love Shack. She ordered a pizza, took it back to her place, and ate alone staring out the huge windows.

The view was an inky black sky, a slice of equally inky black ocean, and the alley that ran perpendicular from the street between the other warehouses.

Three guys were carrying what looked like scuba gear into Sexy Grumpy Surfer's warehouse. Three *hot* guys, one of them Sexy Grumpy Surfer himself. They were laughing and talking as they made several trips.

Interesting. Sexy Grumpy Surfer could

laugh . . .

She watched while eating her pizza and thought maybe she didn't need cable after all.

It was quiet when, an hour later, she walked outside with the empty pizza box, down the dark alley to the Dumpster. Real dark. There was no sign of a single soul now, and Becca hummed a little tune to herself to keep from freaking out, one of her own.

Not that it helped. A sound startled her, and she nearly jumped right out of her skin.

About five feet ahead, three sets of glowing eyes turned her way.

Raccoons.

They were sitting on the Dumpster, having a feast. She laughed at herself, but swallowed her amusement when the six eyes narrowed on her, all accusatory-like. "Sorry," she said. "But I'm pretty sure you're not supposed to be foraging around back here."

The raccoon closest to her growled.

Yikes. Becca lifted her hands. "You know what? None of my business. Carry on." Whirling to leave, she had taken one step when she suddenly found herself pinned against the wall by a big, hard, sculpted, warm body, two big hands at either side of her face. She gasped in shock, and at the sound, her captor went still as well. Then his thumbs were at her jaw, forcing her to look up at him.

"It's you," he said, and she recognized his voice. Sexy Grumpy Surfer. As fast as she'd been pinned, she was unpinned. "What are you doing?" he wanted to know.

Her mouth dropped open. "What am *I* doing? How about what are *you* doing? You scared me half to death."

"I thought you were following me."

"No." But okay, she *had* been watching him earlier — two entirely different things, she told herself. "I was just talking to the raccoons —" She gestured to where they'd been rifling through the trash, but they were long gone, the traitors. Shakily she started to bend to pick up her fallen pizza box, but he retrieved it for her, tossing it into the Dumpster.

"You need to be careful," he said.

She gaped at him, her fear turning to temper. "The only danger I was in came from you!"

"Lucky Harbor might be a small town," he said, "but bad shit can happen anywhere."

"I know that," she said. And she did. She knew far more than she should.

He was in a pair of loose black sweats,

battered athletic shoes, and a T-shirt that was plastered to his flat abs and broad chest with perspiration. She realized he'd been running, hard by the look of him, though he wasn't breathing all that heavily. If she hadn't been feeling so defensive, she might have thought about how sexy he looked. But she *was* feeling defensive, so she refused to notice.

Much.

"You okay?" he asked.

Well, now was a fine time for him to ask, *after* he'd nearly given her a heart attack. "Yeah, I'm okay," she said. "I'm totally okay." Because saying it twice made it so.

"It's late," he said. "You should go inside."

Becca wasn't real good at following nicely uttered requests, much less an out-and-out order. "Maybe I was going somewhere," she said.

He crossed his arms over his chest. "Were you?"

He wasn't going to intimidate her. She no longer let herself get intimidated. But it wasn't really intimidation she was feeling, not with the interesting heat churning in her belly from his nearness. Then he stepped even closer, and she forgot how to breathe, even more so when he cupped her face and tilted it up so he could study her. With a gentleness that surprised her, he stroked the pad of his thumb beneath her left eye.

"You've got a bruise on your face," he said.

She pushed his hand away. "No, I don't."

"You do." Those intensely green eyes held hers prisoner. "What happened?"

She reached up and touched the tender spot. "I was reading in bed and smacked myself with my flashlight and e-reader."

He stared at her. "Is that your version of *I ran into a door*?"

She let out a mirthless laugh, which made his frown deepen. Apparently laughing in the face of an overprotective alpha wasn't the right move. "Seriously," she said. "I did this one all on my own."

"This one?"

Well, shit. An overprotective, *sharp* alpha. "Have you ever tried to read in bed?" she asked, feeling contrary. "You hold the flashlight and e-reader above your head and if you start to fall asleep or relax, it's *smack*."

He gave one slow blink. "Maybe you should sit up when you read."

"Maybe." But she wouldn't. She loved to read while lying down in bed. Which meant that she'd be hitting herself in the face again real soon.

Sexy Grumpy Surfer didn't move, nary an

inch. Then he told her why. "I'm not going anywhere until you go back inside," he said.

"Why?"

He just looked at her, and she realized that he was still in protective mode.

"Fine," she said. "Be all silent and mysterious. I'm going in." She pointed at him. "But *not* because you told me to."

His mouth twitched, but he said nothing.

"Has anyone ever told you that you have a strange sense of humor?" she asked.

"Yeah," he said. "I've heard."

CHAPTER 3

There was still the night's chill on the air when Becca woke up the next morning. Early sun rays were doing their best to beat back the dark shadows of the night, stabbing through the cloud layer with hints of soft yellow and orange.

She rolled the kink out of her neck from sleeping on the floor. Today was the day she further depleted her savings by buying furniture.

And other essentials, such as food.

Today was also the day that she got her act together. She stared at the portable piano keyboard leaning so deceptively casual-like against one of her suitcases.

As a jingle writer, all she had to do was write a catchy tune for a given product. That was it. Write a jingle, sell it to the ad agency that had her on retainer, and accept their thanks in the form of a check.

Except she'd been having trouble for a

year now. Her muse had shriveled up on her, and she was eking out only the barest minimum to keep her agency interested. Her latest assignment was simple — come up with something catchy for Cushy toilet paper. A relatively easy and insignificant enough assignment, right?

Right.

With a sigh, she grabbed a roll of the toilet paper that the company had sent her, shoved it in her tote bag, and headed out. The first person she came across was the same boy on the bike who'd nearly hit her the other day. "Hey," she said, flagging him down.

He slowed. "Sam's probably in his warehouse —"

"No, this question's for you." She pulled out the roll of toilet paper. "Feel this. What does it make you think of?"

He blinked.

"I'm writing a commercial for it," she told him.

"That's weird," he said, but he reached out and took it. Considered. "I guess it feels nice to squeeze," he finally said.

"Good, but unfortunately, that commercial's already been done," she said. "Give me something else."

"Okay . . ." The kid scratched his head.

"It's . . . soft?"

"Soft," she said.

"Yeah. You know, cushy."

She blew out a breath. "Thanks."

"I wasn't any help at all, was I?" the kid asked.

"You were great," she told him, and waved as he rode off.

She walked to the pier for more ranch-flavored popcorn, which she'd bought at the ice cream stand. The same twenty-something-year-old guy was there today.

"You're back," he said.

"Yep. You give good popcorn."

He smiled. "I know. I'm Lance, by the way."

"Becca," she said. "I'm new to town." Lance was small, painfully thin, and had an odd sound to his voice, like his chest was hollow. She glanced at the jar on the counter, with a DONATE TO CYSTIC FIBROSIS RESEARCH poster taped to it, and felt a pang of worry and empathy for him.

"So what'll it be, Becca New to Town?" he asked.

She smiled. "Ranch-flavored popcorn." She paused. "And a single chocolate scoop."

"Living large," he said. "I like it."

When he brought the popcorn and ice cream to her, she held up the roll of toilet

40

paper. "Question," she said. "What does this make you think of?"

He laughed. "That's going to cost you a double scoop, at least." But he squeezed the roll of toilet paper. "Tell me why I'm humoring the crazy lady?"

"Because she writes the songs for commercials," Becca said. *Sometimes. If she's very lucky.* "And I need one for Cushy toilet paper. Only I'm stuck."

"So your brain's . . . plugged?" he asked playfully. "Your brain's got a big . . . load?"

She laughed. "Don't quit your day job."

He squeezed the roll again. "You know," he said casually. "I get sick a lot."

Her heart pinched. "I'm sorry."

"It's okay. But I use this brand for blowing my nose. It's softer and more gentle than tissues."

She smiled and handed back the ice cream cone she hadn't yet licked. "Okay, now *that's* worth a double."

He made it a triple.

A million calories later, she was back in her place, and she managed to come up with a little — emphasis on little — jingle for Cushy. She sent it off to her agency, fingers crossed.

Standing up, she moved to the window and took in a most mesmerizing sight.

41

Not the ocean, though that was pretty damn fine, too.

But Sexy Grumpy Surfer — SGS for short, she'd decided — side by side with one of the other guys from last night, the two of them doing pull-ups on some metal bar. Given their easy, economical speed and the way they kept turning to eyeball each other, they were competing and not for the first time. They were shirtless, their toned bodies gleaming with sweat in the early-morning sun, definitely outshining the Pacific Ocean.

"Wow," she whispered. She had no idea how long she stood there, or how many impossibly difficult pull-ups the two men did before they both dropped lithely to the ground, straightened, and gave each other a shove.

Their laughter drifted to her ears and she found herself smiling along with them. A sweaty tie then, she decided, and realized she was a little hot herself.

Hot *and* bothered.

Sexy Grumpy Surfer looked damn good laughing. The other guy moved off, back toward the small building between the street and beach, but SGS remained. Turning only his head, he unerringly met Becca's gaze.

Crap. She dropped like a stone to the floor

and lay flat. He hadn't seen her, she thought. He totally hadn't. The glare on the window had blocked his view. Yeah, for sure he'd missed her . . .

Slowly, she rose up on her knees to take a quick peek and winced.

He was still there, hands on hips, looking right at her.

He'd missed exactly *nothing,* and she suspected he rarely did.

Then the clouds shifted, and suddenly the sun was shining right on him, like he was the best of God's glory. Since the sun was also bright, making seeing details difficult, it was probably — hopefully — her imagination that his mouth quirked in a barely there smile as he shook his head at her.

Her stomach quivering, she ducked again.

And then from her position prone on the floor, she forbid herself from looking out the window ever again.

Ever.

Crawling to her suitcases in the center of the loft, she sat cross-legged, pulled out her list of Must-Buys, and added curtains. Curtains would keep her from being distracted by her view. Curtains would keep her on task.

And away from further embarrassment.

She showered, dressed, and left the warehouse, sending a cautious look down the alley.

Empty.

Relieved, she left. Several hours later she was back, followed by Eddie, the kid on the bike, whom she'd paid to help lug her loot. Thankfully he came with an older brother who had a truck, and equally thankfully, Lucky Harbor had a "vintage" shop, a really great one. She'd found everything she'd needed there, including gently used sheets that she bought for curtains.

In far less time than it'd taken to shop, she had curtains up and the bed made, and she was sitting on it, staring at an email from her ad agency.

Becca,
   The Cushy jingle works. I've sent accounting a request to get you payment. Next up is Diaxsis, the new erectile dysfunction medicine. Details and deadline info attached, if you're interested.

Not *Great job, Becca.* Not *You're back, Becca.* Not *We've put you back on our top tier, Becca.*

But neither was it *You're fired, Becca,* so she'd take it. But Diaxsis? She blew out a breath and hit REPLY:

I'm interested.

The next morning, Becca opened her eyes and let out a happy breath. She'd actually slept, and if there'd been bad dreams, she didn't remember them. Turning her head, she stared at the curtains where a weak daylight poked in around the edges.

The insulation in her building was either poor or nonexistent. She could hear every single time the back door of the building next to hers opened.

It opened now.

Don't do it, she told herself. *Don't go look. You're stronger than this. You don't need the distraction . . .*

But like Pavlov's dog, she got up and peeked through the curtains.

It was foggy out, but the bigger news was that Sexy Grumpy Surfer was back. It looked chilly, and yet he was in another pair of board shorts and a T-shirt that hugged the width of his shoulders as they flexed enticingly while he dumped the contents of a shop vac into the trash bin.

Sex on a stick.

He didn't look up this time, and Becca forced herself away from the window. She showered, ate the leftover ranch-flavored popcorn — breakfast of champions — and

45

gave her keyboard a long, hard look. "To-day," she told it. "Today, you give me something better than *It works.*"

Sitting on the bed, leaning back against the wall, she pulled the keyboard onto her lap.

A year. A year since she'd composed jingles for the best national brands, and the reasons why were complicated. She'd lost her muse, and her footing. On life. That had to change. Hence the across-the-country move. A new venue, a new beginning. But she still needed to prove herself, if only to the woman in the mirror.

Her parents wouldn't ask her to prove herself, she knew this. Growing up, they'd never asked anything of her, other than to take care of her brother while they worked crazy hours in the jazz clubs of New Orleans. *Watch Jase,* that's all they'd ever expected her to do.

Though only two years separated her and her brother, Becca felt far older, always had. She'd done her best to take care of him, succeeding better at some moments than others. But at least the promise of his talent had been fulfilled. He was a wonderful concert pianist.

Now she wanted, *needed,* to be wonderful at something, too.

And yeah, yeah, being worthy shouldn't be tied up in financial success — or lack thereof — blah blah. But whoever had said that had clearly never had to pay their rent on time.

Her cell phone vibrated. The screen said *Jase calling.*

Until recently, they'd been close, and had talked frequently. Except, just like her early — and short-lived — success with jingle writing, this too had turned out to be an illusion. A glossy veneer shown to the world, while the truth was hidden deep inside them both.

She stared at the phone until it went to voice mail.

Two seconds later came a text. *You okay?*

Completely okay, she texted back. Liar, liar, pants on fire . . .

But hell if she'd give anyone she cared about more stress to deal with. She turned her phone off, ignored the guilt, and spent the rest of the day alternating between nesting in her new place and trying to work a jingle about the male erection.

And maybe, also, looking out her windows a little bit. She told herself it was the ocean that drew her, but mostly her gaze was drawn to the alley. In addition to the pull-ups, she'd now seen Sexy Grumpy Surfer

47

carrying a large duffel bag to the boat moored at the dock, washing down said boat with the same two other guys she'd seen before, and taking a hard, brutally fast run along the beach with yet a third guy.

Seemed like maybe Lucky Harbor was a hot-guy magnet.

By the end of the day, Becca needed sustenance and a change of scenery, so she headed into town. She could've gone to the diner Eat Me, but instead she walked a block farther, past the pier, to go back to the Love Shack.

She told herself it was the atmosphere. The place was done up like an Old West saloon, with walls lined with old mining tools, tables made from antique wood doors. Lanterns hung from the exposed beam ceiling, and the air was filled with laughter, talking, and music from the juke-box in the corner.

She ordered a burger and sat by herself to eyeball the *real* reason she'd come back here — the baby grand piano in the far corner. It was old, and had clearly been around the block decades ago, but it called to her. She stared at it, torn between wanting to stroke it, and wanting to run like hell.

Jase might the real talent of the Thorpe family, but there'd been a time when the two of them had been a duo. Maybe she'd never been quite as good as he was — not that her parents had ever said so, they didn't have to — but she'd been good enough to boost Jase's talent. The press latched on to them early, and they'd even become pseudo-celebrities.

Things had been good, until she'd turned seventeen. With that age had come some self-awareness, and a serious case of the awkwards. Besides the headaches and bone aches that had come with a late, fast growth spurt, she'd lost all coordination, including her fingertips. Practically overnight she'd turned into the Graceless Ugly Duckling, exemplified.

The following month, their manager had gotten them invited to compete at the prestigious Walt Disney Concert Hall in Los Angeles. The place had been filled with people — more than two thousand — and all Becca remembered was being struck by sheer, heart-stopping panic.

She'd tanked, and the press had ripped them to shreds.

Shaking off the memory, Becca paid for her food at the bar and took in the sign at the register that said: HELP WANTED. She glanced at the piano and gnawed her lower lip. Then she gestured for the bartender.

"Who do I talk to about the job?"

"Me," he said with a smile as he set aside the glass he'd been drying to shake her hand. "I'm Jax Cullen, one of the owners."

"Is it a hostess position?" she asked hopefully.

"Waitressing," he said. "You interested?"

Was she? She glanced at the piano and *ached*. And she knew she was *very* interested, skills or not. And there were no skills. None. "I am if you are," she said.

Jax lost his smile. "Shit. You don't have any experience."

"No," she admitted. "But I'm a real quick learner."

He studied her, and Becca did her best to look like someone who was one hundred percent capable of doing anything — except, of course, handling her own life. She flashed him her most charming smile, her "showtime" smile, and hoped for the best.

Jax chuckled. "You're spunky," he said. "I'll give you that."

"I'm more than spunky," she promised. "I bet you by the end of my first night, you'll want to keep me."

He held her gaze a moment, considering. "All right, I'll take that bet. How about a trial by fire starting now?"

She eyed the room. Not full. Not even

50

close. "Who else is working?"

"Usually on a night like this, two others. But both my girls are out sick tonight and I'm on my own, so you're looking like good timing to me. If you're any good."

The piano in the far corner was still calling to her, making her braver than usual. "I'm in," she said.

Jax gave her an apron and a quick rundown of what was expected. He told her that here in Lucky Harbor, familiarity was key. Everyone knew everyone, and the trick to good service — and good tips — was friendliness.

Then he threw her to the wolves.

The first half hour remained thankfully slow, but every time she walked by the baby grand, she faltered.

Play me, Becca . . .

At about the twentieth pass, she paused and glanced around. Not a soul was looking at her. She eyed the piano again, sitting there so innocuously, looking gorgeous. Damn. She'd played on her keyboard, but not a piano. Not since two years ago when she'd quit. She'd had a near miss with going back to playing a year ago, but then things had gone to all sorts of hell, reinforcing her stage fright and giving her a wicked case of claustrophobia to boot.

Play me, Becca . . .

Fine. Since fighting the urge was like trying not to need air, she sat. Her heart sped up, but she was still breathing. So far so good. She set her fingertips on the cool keys.

Still good.

And almost before she realized it, she'd begun playing a little piece she'd written for Jase years ago. It flowed out of her with shocking ease, and when she finished, she blinked like she was waking from a trance. Then she looked around.

Jax was smiling at her from behind the bar and when he caught her eye, he gave her a thumbs-up. Oh, God. Breaking out in a sweat, she jumped up and raced into the bathroom to stare at herself in the mirror. Flushed. Shaky. She thought about throwing up, but then someone came in to use the facilities and she decided she couldn't throw up with an audience. So she splashed cold water on her hot face, told herself she was totally fine, and then got back to work to prove it.

Luckily, the dinner crowd hit and she got too busy to think. She worked the friendliness as best she could. But she quickly discovered it wasn't a substitute for talent. In the first hour, she spilled a pitcher of beer down herself, mixed up two orders — and in doing so nearly poisoned someone when she gave the cashew-allergic customer a cashew chicken salad — and then undercharged a large group by thirty bucks.

Jax stepped in to help her, but by then she was frazzled beyond repair. "Listen," he said very kindly, considering, "maybe you should stick with playing. You're amazing on the piano. Can you sing?"

"No," she said, and grimaced. "Well, yes." But she *couldn't* stick with playing, because she couldn't play in front of an audience without having heart failure. "I really can do this waitressing thing," she said.

Jax shook his head but kept his voice very gentle. "You're not cut out for this job, Becca. And there's nothing wrong with that."

She was beginning to think she wasn't cut out for her life, but she met his gaze evenly, her own determined. "I bet you, remember? By the end of the night, you'll see. Please? One more try?"

He looked at her for a long moment and then sighed. "Okay, then. One more try."

A group of three guys walked in the door and took a table. Fortifying her courage, Becca gathered menus and strode over there with a ready-made smile, which congealed when she saw who it was.

Sexy Grumpy Surfer and his two cohorts. Bolstering herself, she set the menus on the table. "Welcome, gentlemen."

SGS was sprawled back in his chair, long legs stretched out in front of him crossed at the ankles, his sun-streaked hair unruly as ever, looking like sin personified as he took her in. She did her best to smile, ignoring the butterflies suddenly fluttering low in her belly. "What can I get you to start?"

"Pitcher of beer. And you're new," one of them said, the one with the sweetest smile and the bluest eyes she'd ever seen. He had short brown hair he'd forgotten to comb, some scruff on a square jaw, and was wearing cargo pants and a polo shirt with a small screwdriver sticking out of the breast pocket. "I'm Cole," he told her, "and this big lug here . . ." He gestured to the dark-haired, dark-eyed, darkly dangerously good-looking guy next to him. "Tanner." Then he jerked his chin toward SGS. "You apparently already know this one."

"Yes," Becca said. "SGS."

They all just looked at her.

"Sexy Grumpy Surfer," she clarified.

Cole and Tanner burst out laughing.

SGS just gave her a long, steady, paybacks-are-a-bitch smile.

"Or Grandpa," Cole offered. "That's what

we call him because he always seems to know the weirdest shit."

"And Grandma works, too," Tanner said. "When he's being a chick. No offense."

Sam sent them each a look that would've had Becca peeing her pants, but neither man looked particularly worried.

"And your name?" Cole asked Becca.

She opened her mouth, but before she could answer Sam spoke for her. "Peeper," he said. "Her name is Peeper."

His steely but amused gaze held hers as he said this, which is how Becca finally saw him smile. It transformed his face, softening it, and though he was already ridiculously attractive, the smile — trouble-filled as it was — only made him all the more so. It gave her a little quiver in her tummy, which, as she couldn't attribute it to either hunger or nerves, was not a good sign.

"Peeper," Tanner repeated slowly, testing it on his tongue. "That's unusual."

Still holding Becca's gaze, Sam said, "It's a nickname, because she —"

"It's my big eyes," Becca broke in with before he could tell his friends that she'd been caught red-handed watching them like a . . . well, peeper. "Yeah," she said. "I've bowled him over with my . . . peepers."

Sam startled her by laughing, and the

sound did something odd and wonderful and horrifying deep inside her, all at the same time. Unbelievably, she could feel herself standing on the precipice of a crush on this guy. She'd been attracted before, of course, plenty of times, but it'd been a while since she'd taken the plunge.

A long while.

She hoped the water was nice, because she could feel the pull of it and knew she was going in.

CHAPTER 4

When Becca was called to the bar, Sam watched her go, sass in every step. She was in one of those flimsy, gauzy skirts that flirted with a woman's thighs, and a stretchy white top. Her hair was piled on top of her head, but strands had escaped, flying around her flushed face and clinging to her neck. She'd clearly had a rough night because she appeared to be wearing both beer and barbecue sauce.

"Cute," Tanner said, also watching.

"She's off limits," Sam said, and when they both looked at him in surprise, he shrugged. "We're concentrating on business right now."

Tanner coughed and said "bullshit" at the same time.

"It does feel like Grandma here's holding out on us," Cole said, still watching Sam.

Sam didn't want to get into the real reason, which he told himself was that clearly Becca was trying to get her footing, and yeah, she put off a tough, I've-got-this vibe, but there was something about her that told him it was a facade. "She's new to town," he said. "Let her settle before you start sniffing around her."

"I will if you will," Tanner said with a smile. It faded when he caught Sam's long look. "Kidding," he said. "Jesus. Hands off your Peeper, got it."

The nickname of course had jackshit to do with her eyes — though they were indeed big and luminous. They were also a warm, melted milk chocolate, and filled with more than a little trouble.

Sam wasn't opposed to trouble. In fact, he was absolutely all for it.

When *he* was the one causing it.

But this woman was trouble in her own right. He'd been amused at catching her watching him from her window — several times — but it wasn't amusement he felt now. Because this was the second time he'd been within touching distance, and it was now two for two that she'd sucked him in. It wasn't her looks, though she was pretty in a girl-next-door way. Nor was it her feistiness and ability to laugh at herself.

Instead it was something else, something he suspected had to do with the singular flash of vulnerability he'd caught in her eyes.

She wasn't quite as tough as she wanted the world to believe.

And hell. *That* drew him. Because Sam knew all too well what it was like to not be nearly as tough as you needed to be. Something he didn't like to think about. "We doing this or what?" he asked the guys. "We have shit to decide."

"Anyone ever tell you that you're a fun sucker?" Tanner asked.

Sam slid him a look, and Tanner blew out a breath. "Shit. Yeah, we're doing this."

Cole lifted a shoulder and nodded.

Neither of them liked these weekly business meetings, but if they didn't have them, then all the hard decisions were left to Sam. He was good at making hard decisions in his life — he'd had to be — but this was about the three of them, equal partners. "So we agree," he said. "We're hiring someone to take over the crap none of us wants to do."

"Told you," Cole said. "Ad's in the paper."

"You get any calls yet?"

"Yes," Cole said. "Lucille."

Lucille was a thousand years old and the local gossip queen. She had a heart of gold, but a nose made for butting into other people's business. "No," Sam said. Hell no.

"Way ahead of you," Cole told him. "Especially after she said she couldn't wait to sit on the beach and take pics of us on and off the boat for her Pinterest Sexy Guys page. She thought she could manage our phones and scheduling in between her photography. She said something about hoping we go shirtless, and us signing something that allows her to use our images for — and I'm quoting here — the good of women's mental health everywhere."

"Christ," Tanner muttered.

"I told her we had an age requirement," Cole said, "and that our new admin had to be under the age of seventy."

"How did she take that?" Sam asked.

"She was bummed, said even her fake ID showed seventy-five, but that she understood."

Becca arrived with their pitcher of beer, except it wasn't beer at all; it looked like . . . strawberry margaritas.

"You all decide on your order?" she asked, setting down three glasses.

"New Orleans," Cole said, watching Tanner pour himself a strawberry margarita.

Becca looked startled. "What?"

"You're originally from New Orleans," Cole said.

She stared at him. "How did you know that?"

"You're good, but I'm better," Cole said. "I can hear it real faint in your voice."

"Ignore him," Tanner said, toasting her with his glass. "He's a freak."

"A freak who knows we didn't order a chick drink," Cole said as Tanner sipped at his strawberry margarita.

Becca gasped. "Oh, crap. This isn't yours." She nabbed the glass right out of Tanner's hand. "I'm sorry. Don't move."

She snatched the pitcher as well and vanished.

"She *is* cute," Cole said. "Not much of a waitress, though."

"She's not as bad as Tanya," Tanner said. "She stole from you."

"Borrowed," Cole corrected. "I let her *borrow* some money for her mom, who was going to lose her home in Atlanta."

"Did you ever get your money back?" Tanner asked mildly.

Cole pulled out his phone and eyed the dark screen as if wishing for a call.

Tanner rolled his eyes. "You didn't. You let her walk with three grand of your hard-earned money. Oh, and by the way, I've got some land to sell you. Swamp land. It's on sale, just for you."

Sam shoved his iPad under their noses before a fight could break out. He didn't mind a good fight now and then, but Jax and Ford, the owners of the Love Shack, frowned on it happening inside their bar. "If you two idiots are done, we're in the middle of a financial meeting here."

"You're right," Tanner said, and straightened in his seat. "Give it to us, Grandma."

Sam gave him a long look. "It's a good thing I'm too hungry to kick your ass."

He'd been in charge of their money since their rig days. Back then, there'd been four of them: himself, Tanner, Cole, and Gil, the lot of them pretty much penniless. But thanks to his dad's unique ability to squander his every last penny, Sam had learned to handle money by the age of ten. He'd been tight-fisted with their earnings, squirreling them away — earning him that *Grandma* moniker. He'd shut his friends up when, at the end of the first year, he'd shown them their savings balance.

They'd had a goal, their dream — the charter company, and their seven years at sea had been extremely profitable.

And deadly.

They'd lost Gil. Just the thought brought the low, dull ache of his passing back as a fresh knife stab, and Sam drew a breath until it passed.

They'd nearly lost Tanner in that rig fire as well. Tanner still limped and was damn lucky to have his leg at all, something Sam tried not to think about. "We talked about expanding," he said, "hiring on more people and buying a new boat."

"When we have the money for it," Tanner said. He was their resident pessimist. Never met a situation he liked. "We said we'd revisit the issue when we were ready. No loan payments."

Sam hadn't been the only one to grow up on the wrong side of the poverty line. "No loans," he said.

Cole hadn't taken his eyes off Sam. "You already spend all your time bitching and moaning about not having enough hours in the day to make your boats," he reminded him. "You'd have heart failure if we expanded our business right now. Have you updated your will? You left everything to me, right?"

"We start with more staff," Sam said, ignoring him. "Office help first, then hire on an additional crew." He pointed at both Cole and Tanner. "You guys are in charge of that."

"Why us?" Tanner asked.

"Because I'm busy making you rich," Sam said.

Becca was back, with a pitcher of beer this time, and a huge plate of nachos, chicken wings, and pesto chips. "Your order," she said.

The guys all looked at each other, and Becca paused. "What?" she asked.

"We didn't order yet," Sam said.

"Oh for the love of —" She slapped Tanner's hand before he could snatch a nacho, picked up the platter *and* the beers, and once again vanished.

She was back a breathless moment later, looking flushed as she held her order pad. "Okay, let's start over. I'm Becca, your server for tonight."

"You sure?" Sam asked.

She let out a theatrical sigh. "Listen, I'm not exactly in my natural habitat here." Suddenly she straightened and gave them a dazzling smile as she spoke out of the corner of her mouth. "Quick, everyone look happy with your service. My hopefully new boss is watching. I made a bet with him that I could handle this job and I have tonight to prove it."

Sam craned his neck and saw Jax at the bar, watching Becca. "It'd help if you were actually serving," he said.

"Working on that," she said, and vanished.

The three of them watched her go for a moment. She went straight to the bar, smiled at Jax, grabbed a tray of drinks, and then brought them to a table. That she had to take drinks right out of a few people's hand and switch them to someone else's made Cole and Tanner chuckle.

"She can't serve worth shit," Tanner said. "But she does have a great smile. And those eyes. Man, it's like when she looks at you, you're the only one she sees."

Sam watched her take an order from the table. One of the customers said something and she tossed her head back and laughed. Not a fake I-want-your-tips laugh, but a genuine, contagious one that made everyone at the table join her.

Cole and Tanner were right. She *was* cute. And as he already knew from catching her staring at him several times now, she absolutely had a way of making a guy feel like he was the only one she saw.

She left the table and vanished into the back, coming out a moment later with a tray laden with plates of food. The muscles in her shoulders and arms strained as she moved, and Sam found himself holding his breath. Maybe she did suck as a waitress, but no one could deny that she was working her tail off. She got all the way to the back table before she dumped the tray.

Down the front of herself.

The man closest to her must have gotten sprayed because he flew to his feet and held his shirt out from his body, jaw tight. He said something low and undoubtedly harsh given the look on Becca's face as she bent to clean up the mess. Grabbing her elbow, he gave her a little shake, and before Sam gave it a second thought, he was on his feet and at Becca's back.

"You're the worst waitress I've ever seen," the guy was yelling. "You are nowhere near good enough for this job."

The barb hit. Sam could tell by the way Becca took a step back as if slapped, bumping right into him.

"You're going to pay for the dry cleaning of this shirt, do you hear me?" the guy went on.

"Hard not to," Sam said, steadying Becca. "Since you're braying like a jackass."

Becca slid Sam a look that said she could handle this. When he didn't budge, she made a sound of annoyance and turned back to the pissed-off customer. "I'm sorry," she said. "And of course I'll pay for your dry cleaning." Then she bent again to clean up.

Sam crouched down to help her scoop the fallen plates onto the tray, but she pushed at him. "I've got this," she whispered. But she was trembling, and her breath hitched. "Stop, Sam. I don't need you to help," she insisted when he kept doing just that.

He'd disagree with her, but that would only back her into a corner. So he continued on in silence, and then when she vanished into the kitchen, he went back to his table.

Tanner and Cole were grinning at him.

"What?"

"You tell us what," Cole said.

"I was just helping."

"No, helping would be going into the kitchen and wrangling us up some burgers," Tanner said, rubbing his belly. "I'm starving."

Sam shook his head and turned on his iPad again. "Where were we?"

"You were playing hero," Tanner said.

Sam ignored this. "Our boat fund will hit its projected mark this year," he said.

Both Cole and Tanner blinked at him.

"You're serious," Tanner finally said. "You really did manage to pay us and save a mint while you were at it."

"Do I ever joke about money?" Sam asked.

"Holy shit," Cole said. "Just how much are we making anyway?"

Sam thumbed through the iPad, brought up their receivables, and shoved the screen across the table.

They all stared at the numbers and Tanner let out a low whistle.

"Why the hell are you so surprised?" Sam asked, starting to get insulted. "I send you both weekly updates. Between all the chartering and the profits from the boats I've been building, we're doing good."

Both Cole and Tanner still just stared at him, and Sam shook his head in disgust. "I could be ripping you guys off, you ever think of that?"

"Yeah," Cole said. "Except you're a terrible liar and you're not nearly greedy enough."

Needing the beer Becca had taken away, Sam went to the bar for a pitcher. The bar was crazier than usual, and Sam realized he saw only a hungry crowd and no sign of Becca at all. He took the pitcher back to his table and poured.

"To Gil," Cole said, and as they always did, they drank to Gil's memory.

A few minutes later, wondering if maybe Becca had gotten her sweet ass fired, Sam stepped into the hall and found her standing there with her back to him, hugging herself with one arm, the other hand holding her cell phone to her ear.

"No, I can't come play at your concert," she was saying. "I'm — They're paying *how* much?" She paused. "Wow, but no. I can't — Yeah, I'm fine. In fact, I've got my toes in the sand right this very minute, so you just concentrate on you, okay?" She paused. "The noise? Uh . . . it's the waves. It's high tide."

This was when she turned and caught sight of Sam standing there. Flushing a deep red, she held his gaze. "Gotta go, Jase. The whitecaps are kicking up and it's making my muse kick into gear." She lowered her voice and covered her mouth and the phone, but Sam heard her whisper, "And *don't* come out here. Okay? I'm good. Really, really good. So just stay where you are." She disconnected and made herself busy stuffing the phone into her pocket before flashing Sam her waitress smile. "I think your order's almost up."

"How would you know? You've got your toes in the sand."

She drooped a little. "Yeah. I'm probably going to hell for that one."

"Jase?" he asked.

"My brother." She sighed. "You know families."

Yeah, Sam knew families. He knew families weren't necessarily worth shit, at least not blood families. He wondered what her story was, but before he could ask, she sent him one last shaky smile and walked away.

CHAPTER 5

It was two-thirty in the morning when the bar finally got quiet. Becca was cleaning up, or supposed to be, but really she was staring at the piano again.

It was always like this. She'd be drawn by the scent of the gleaming wood, the keys, the beauty of losing herself in the music.

And then she'd sit and the anxiety would nearly suffocate her.

It'd taken her ten years of playing, from age seventeen to twenty-seven, ten years of needing anxiety meds to get on stage, before she'd admitted she didn't have the heart for that life. She might have said so sooner but her brother had needed her, and her parents had depended on her being there for him. A painful crush on their manager Nathan had only added to the pressure. The crush had eventually evolved into a relationship, but when that had failed, she'd walked away from the life.

That had been two years ago.

She'd been working at an ad agency ever since, writing jingles for commercials. Behind the scenes really worked for her, though about a year ago, Jase had hit rock bottom and Nathan had come to her, pressuring her to give their world another go.

She'd refused, but the aftermath from that confrontation had killed off her muse but good.

Becca had promised herself that she'd never again duet in any capacity. Especially relationships.

Now, at age twenty-nine, she decided she was all the wiser for that decision, and not missing anything.

Play me, Becca . . .

Once again she looked around, and when she saw no one watching, she allowed herself to sit. Before she knew it, her fingers were moving, this time playing one of the first songs she'd ever learned, "Für Elise" by Beethoven. She'd been twelve and had eavesdropped on Jase's lessons. He'd hated practicing, but not Becca. She'd been happy practicing for hours.

When she finished, she sat there a moment, alone in the bar, and smiled. No urge to throw up! Progress! Getting up, she grabbed her things from the back, turned to go, and found Jax standing there.

"You going to freak out again if I tell you that you're really good?" he asked quietly.

"At waitressing?" she asked hopefully.

"No, you suck at that."

She sighed.

He smiled and handed her an envelope. "The night's pay."

She looked down at it, then back at his face. "I'm not invited back, am I?"

He gave her a small smile. "Did you really want to be?"

She blew out a breath. "No."

His smile widened, and he gently tugged at a loose strand of her hair. "Come play piano anytime you want. You'll make bank in tips." He looked at her. "Breathe, Becca."

She sucked in a few breaths. "I'm not ready for that."

His eyes were warm and understanding. "When you are then."

She laughed softly, unable to imagine when that might be. "Thanks, Jax."

"You going to be okay?" he asked.

A lot of people asked that question, but few really wanted to hear an honest answer. She could tell Jax genuinely did. But being okay was her motto, so she mustered a smile. "Always," she said.

She walked home, let herself into her

building, and then stopped short when she realized that the middle apartment, the one next to hers, was open. The front door was thrown wide, and from inside came a bunch of colorful swearing in a frustrated female voice.

Becca tiptoed past her own door and peeked inside the middle unit. There were lights blaring, boxes stacked everywhere, and in the center of the mess stood a young woman about her own age, hands on hips, surveying the chaos.

"Hi," Becca said, knocking on the doorjamb. "You okay?"

The woman whipped around to face Becca, a baseball bat in her hands before Becca could so much as blink. She took one look at Becca, let out a short breath, and lowered the bat. "Who are you?" she demanded.

Becca let out her own shaky breath. She was good with a bat, too, but it was one thing to have it in your hands, say at a softball game. It was another thing entirely to be in danger of having it wielded at your head. "I'm Becca Thorpe," she said. "Your neighbor. And I recognize you. You were working at the vintage store where I spent a fortune the other day."

"Oh. Yeah." The woman grimaced and set

the bat aside. She was petite, with dark hair and dark eyes. Caucasian features but she looked somehow exotic as well. Beautiful. And wary. She was wearing low-slung jeans, a halter top, and a bad attitude as she dropped the bat. "Sorry if I woke you."

"You didn't," Becca said. "I'm just getting home from being fired from my first day on the job at the bar." She smiled, thinking that she would get one in return, but she didn't.

"Olivia Bentley," the woman said. "Sorry about the job, I'll try to keep it down in here."

"It's okay. I just moved in, too. Need some help?"

"No."

"You sure?" Becca asked. "Because I —"

"No," Olivia repeated, and then sighed. "But thank you," she added as she moved toward the door in a not-so-subtle invite for Becca to leave.

"Okay then." Becca took one step backward, out of the doorway and into the hall. "Well, good —"

The door shut on her face.

"— Night," she finished. Apparently, she wasn't the only one having a rough day.

Sam told himself he was too busy to be curious about Becca over the next few days. He and the guys took a client for an overnight deep-sea fishing trip. They also had two scuba trips. They were running ragged, but that was the nature of the beast for the summer season.

Not much of a sleeper, he tended to stay up late, which is when he did the paperwork required for the business, and his boatbuilding. He liked to do both alone. In fact, he liked to *be* alone.

He'd noticed that there were now curtains on the lower windows of the building kitty-corner to his. And that sometimes, he could hear the strains of a piano playing. The classical music wasn't something he'd have thought was his type, but he found himself keeping his own music off in order to hear more of it.

He also noted that when he ate at the bar and grill, there were no pretty, curvy, charismatic brunette waitresses spilling beer and mixing up orders.

Telling himself to stop noticing such things at all, he was in the office of his shop working on his laptop on finances. His own, and the few others he took care of. One of those very people walked in about an hour later.

Amelia Donovan had her latest investment statements in hand.

"I need an English translation," she said, and tossed the statements onto his desk.

Amelia was Cole's mom. And in some ways, maybe the best of ways, she was also Sam's. He'd landed with her one of the times that his dad had screwed up enough that social services had stepped in. Once Amelia had gotten him, she'd made sure she was his only foster care after that, which meant that for most of Sam's trouble-filled teenage years, he'd seesawed between his dad's place and Cole's.

Sam hadn't been easy.

Actually, he'd been the opposite of easy.

But Amelia had accepted him in her house without fuss up until age seventeen, when he'd left to go work on the rigs in the Gulf. She'd even forgiven him when Cole had given up a promising college baseball career to follow him. She was a born caretaker, handling her large family with the perfect mixture of drill-sergeant and mama-bear instincts. She easily kept track of everyone, from their birthdays, to their coming and goings, to whom they were dating. She always knew if her little chicks were bored, happy, upset, or hurting.

What she couldn't ever seem to do was balance her own checkbook.

Cole's dad had passed away the previous

year from a heart attack, and Sam had been doing the banking for Amelia, handling all her other finances as well. But the reality was, he'd been doing that for years anyway. She'd retired from her high school teaching job and was still doing okay, a feat she attributed entirely to Sam, always saying that she owed him.

She didn't owe him shit.

Sam didn't care how much money he'd made her in investments, he could never repay the debt of having her watch out for him and keep him on the straight and narrow.

Or at least as straight and narrow as he got . . .

He picked up the statements and looked at her. "It's late. You okay?"

"Yes. I just got held up watching *The Voice.*" A natural beauty, Amelia had turned fifty last year, but looked a decade younger. Cole had gotten all of his charm and easy charisma from her. She was barely five feet tall, of Irish descent, and had the temperament to go with it.

And a backbone of pure steel.

Sam handed her back the statements. "The English version is that you made a shitload of money this quarter, so no worries."

She nodded, but didn't smile as he'd intended.

"What?" he asked.

"Nothing." But she was clearly biting her tongue about something.

He knew her well and braced himself, because that look meant she had something on her mind and there'd be no peace until it came out. "Just say it," he said.

"I heard that your father called you." Her sweet blue gaze was filled with worry. "Is it true?"

Well, shit. There was no love lost between Amelia and Mark, mostly because Amelia had always had to clean up Mark's mess — that mess being Sam. It didn't matter that he and his dad had lived in Seattle. She'd made the two-hour drive and claimed him whenever he'd needed her.

"Sam," she said. "Is it true? Did Mark call you?"

"Listen, it's late," he said, trying to head off a discussion he didn't want to have. "Let me walk you out —"

"It's a simple enough question, Samuel."

He grimaced at his full name, the one only *she* used. Pulling in the big guns. "Yeah, he called. I call him, too, you know that."

Her eyes went from worried mom to very serious mom. "Honey, I need you to tell me

79

you weren't stupid enough to give him another penny."

"You know, it lowers a person's self-esteem to call them stupid," he said with mock seriousness.

"Damn it!" Amelia stalked to the door that led to a hallway and into the small kitchen.

Against his better judgment, Sam followed, watching as she bypassed the fridge, going straight for the freezer, exclaiming wordlessly when she found it empty.

"You used to always keep vodka around," she muttered. "Where's the vodka?" She turned to him, hands on hips. "Sometimes a woman needs a damn vodka, Sam."

He knew that. He also knew that sometimes a man needed a damn vodka. For a long time after Gil's death, vodka had soothed his pain. Too much. When he'd realized that, he'd cut it off cold turkey. It'd sucked.

These days, he stuck with the occasional beer and did his best not to think too much. "I've got soda," he said. "Chips. Cookies. Name your poison."

"Vodka."

He sighed and strode over to her, shutting the freezer, pulling her from it and enveloping her in his arms. "I'm okay. You know that, right?"

She tipped her head back to look up into his face. "Does it happen often?"

"Me being okay? Yes."

She smacked him on the chest. "I meant your dad. Does he call you often then?"

"I call him every week," Sam said.

Her gaze said she got the distinction, and the fact that Sam was usually the instigator didn't make her any happier. "And do you give him money?" she asked.

"When he needs it."

She gave a troubled sigh. "Oh, Sam."

"Look, he's getting older and he's feeling his mortality," he said. "He's got a silly, frivolous woman, and a baby coming —"

"Which is ridiculous —"

"— And he realizes he fucked up with his first kid."

"You think?" She cupped his face. "Sam, I don't like this. I don't like him taking from you. He's done nothing but take from you, and I know damn well it affects your relationships. Because of him, you let women in your life here and there, but you don't let yourself fully rely on anyone, ever. That isn't healthy, Sam. Is Becca any different?"

He thought of the only woman who'd caught his eye lately. Becca. She certainly wasn't the type of woman to rely on anyone.

"I think she might be," he said.

"But will you be able to rely on her? That's what a woman will want, Sam. For you to do the same."

He gave a short laugh. "You're way ahead of yourself."

"Well, I worry about you," she said. "All of you."

"Marry off all those crazy daughters of yours, and then we'll talk," Sam told her.

"You're changing the subject on me."

"Trying." He sighed at the dark look she shot him. "Look, I don't like that he's getting older and feeling regrets. Or that he doesn't have enough money to support that kid. He's my dad. What would you have me do?"

Amelia sighed and shook her head. Then she went up on tiptoe and kissed his cheek. "I know better than to argue with you. I'd do better bashing my head up against the wall."

He smiled, as this was true. "So you'll leave me alone about it?"

"No." She kissed his other cheek. "But I'll give you some peace. For now."

It was nearly midnight when she left, with one last long hug that Sam endured. When he was alone, he shut the laptop and hit the lights. Bed was the smart decision but he was far from tired. Thinking about his dad had dredged up some shit he didn't want dredged.

He needed to expel his pent-up energy. Usually he did this by running with Ben, a longtime friend from town. Like Sam, Ben appreciated the art of not talking much, which meant they were well suited as running partners, but Ben wasn't sleeping alone these days, and it was too late to call. So, restless and edgy, Sam hit the beach by himself, pushing himself hard. He tried to clear his mind, but things kept popping into his head.

Love ya, son.

It drove him crazy how his dad threw around the words like they meant nothing. Love, real love, would have protected him from being taken from their home due to neglect. Real love would have forgotten the stupid get-rich-quick schemes that never came through and attempted to keep a job so they had a roof over their heads and food in their kitchen.

Sam shook off the bleak memories and kept running. The past didn't matter. The here and now mattered. Building boats. Running the charter business. Coming through for Cole and Tanner the way they'd always come through for him.

But the past was a sneaky bitch, and for some reason, tonight he couldn't escape her. Not even an hour later when he was back where he started, standing on the sand in front of their hut, breathing heavily.

A sliver of a moon cast the beach in a blue glow, allowing him to see the small shadow sitting on the sand a few feet away.

Becca.

CHAPTER 6

Sam stood still for a beat, thinking that if he was smart, he'd turn and get the hell off the beach without saying a word. Not when he was this wild on the inside, this edgy.

But apparently he wasn't smart at all because his feet didn't budge.

She wore an oversized sweatshirt and flannel PJ bottoms, her arms wrapped around her legs, a tiny little gold ring encircling one of her bare toes. Under her tough-girl exterior, she was soft and sweet, and had a smile that moved him.

Her body moved him, too, and again he told himself to keep going and not look back.

And again, he didn't budge. She looked like a quiet, calm, sexy-as-hell oasis, and she was drawing him in without even trying. "Thought Lucky Harbor was just a pit stop," he said over the sound of the surf hitting the sand. "But you're still here."

Becca tilted her head back and leveled him with those melting dark eyes. "Appears that way."

"In your PJs," he noted.

She looked down at herself. "It's my Man-Repellent. Guaranteed to deflect a guy's interest with a single glance."

The PJs were baggy, but there was a breeze plastering the material to her body, which was a complete showstopper. He laughed softly, and she narrowed her eyes. "What?" she asked.

"Let's just say they're not as bad as you think."

She blinked, then lowered her gaze, taking the time to carefully brush some sand from her feet.

It occurred to him that he was making her nervous by looming over her, so he shifted back a foot or so and crouched low to make himself nonthreatening. He added a smile.

She visibly relaxed. "You probably shouldn't flash that smile at me too often," she said.

"Why?"

"It's . . . attractive," she admitted. "You're attractive. Which you damn well know."

"But I'm wearing my woman-repellent gear," he said, and she laughed. It was a really great laugh.

He'd felt the pull of their chemistry from the very beginning, and had wondered if she did as well. No need to wonder now; it was all over her, however reluctantly she felt it. He needed to walk away now, before this got any more out of hand.

Instead, he spoke. "Is there a reason you want me to be repelled?" he asked.

"You mean am I crazy, or in a relationship?"

"Yeah," he said. "Either of those."

"Not in a relationship." She smiled a little thinly. "Jury's still out on the crazy thing, though. You?"

He gave a slow shake of his head. "Negative on both."

She dropped the eye contact first, instead taking in his body in a way that revved his engines. "Do you always run that hard?" she asked, her voice barely carrying over the sound of the surf hitting the sand.

He shrugged.

"I see you sometimes in the mornings," she said. "And you do. You always run that hard."

He smiled. "Peeper to the bone."

"Can't seem to help myself," she admitted.

He dropped to the sand beside her and didn't miss the fact that she stiffened up at his quick motion. To give her a minute, he stretched out his tired legs. "I worked at sea for seven years. I missed running. I promised myself when I got off the rig, I'd get back to it."

She took her gaze off his body to look into his eyes. "What was the job?"

"I worked for a consulting firm monitoring the deep drilling rigs. We'd go out for months at a time, no land in sight."

"We?"

"I had a crew," he said.

"You were out at sea with a bunch of guys for months at a time?"

"There were a few women too," he said. Three, to be exact, one of whom had neatly sliced Cole's heart in two.

"What was your job out there?" Becca asked.

"OIM. Offshore installation manager." He shrugged again. "Basically just a fancy title for babysitting the operation."

"All of it?"

"I handled the business side of things," he said, "the shifts, the tasks, everything."

"Sam knows everything," she said softly. "That's what people keep telling me."

He didn't know everything. He didn't know, for example, why he was so drawn to her. Or what made her so wary.

"Must have been a tough job," she said.

"The job was hard as hell," he agreed. He had few good memories of those years, working his way up from grunt worker to manager. After they'd lost Gil, he and Tanner had come back to Lucky Harbor with Cole, who'd wanted to be here to take care of his mom and three sisters. Tanner had needed recovery time. And it'd been as good a place as any to start their charter company.

"So you retired from the rigs and now you run, surf, take people out on charters, and handcraft boats," she said.

He slid her a look.

"Peeper, remember?" she said. She bit her lip but a sweet, low laugh escaped. "Plus, I looked you up."

Now it was his turn to narrow his eyes. "Why?"

She squirmed a little, which he found fascinating. Actually he found *her* fascinating. "I've spent the past three mornings at the diner for the free WiFi," she said. "I've been . . . researching."

"Me?"

"Not *just* you. But I was curious," she admitted.

"Yeah? You didn't get enough information from watching me out the window?"

"Hey," she said on another laugh. "I can't help it that you're pretty to look at."

At this, he went brows-up. "You said attractive. You didn't say pretty."

"Pretty," she repeated, still smiling.

He loved her smile. "I'm not pretty." But he was smiling now, too.

"Okay," she said. "You're right. *Pretty* is far too girlie a word for what you are."

They looked at each other. The air seemed to get all used up then, and his heart beat in tune to the pulsing waves. "What else did you learn about me, in your . . . *research?*" he asked softly.

Her gaze dropped to his mouth. "That you guys take people deep-sea fishing, scuba diving, that sort of thing. Also, your charter company's got four and a half stars on Yelp — although I'm pretty sure some of those reviews were written by women who want to date you because there's lots of mentions of the three hot guys who run the company."

He winced, making her laugh again.

"Might as well own it," she said. "Also, did you know that the town of Lucky Harbor has a Pinterest account? The woman who updates it has a board there for her favorite things."

"Lucille," he muttered.

"And one of her favorite things," Becca

90

said, "is *you.*"

He grimaced. "Lucille's a nut."

"She seems very sincere."

"Okay, so she's a *nice* nut," he said. "A nut's a nut."

"People around here seem to look to you as a leader, as someone to turn to," she said. "If there's a question, people say *Sam'll know,* but I've noticed something." She waited until he met her gaze. "No one seems to really know *you* except for maybe Cole and Tanner."

That was just close enough to the dead truth to make him uncomfortable.

"I think it's because you come off as a lone wolf," she said, head cocked as she studied him. "And then there's your approach-at-your-own-risk vibe."

Hard to deny the truth, so he didn't bother.

"I mean you're really good on the fly," she said quietly, as if talking to herself, trying to figure him out. "And you're good at helping people, but you're not readily available to get to know."

It was a shockingly accurate insight, but he went with humor. "Not seeing the problem," he said.

"Well, it's *interesting,* is all."

"Interesting?"

"Yeah." Again she looked at his mouth. "Because your distance is perversely making me curious to know more. And I haven't been . . . curious in a long time."

There was another surge of that something between them. Heat. Hunger. At least on his part. Testing, he shifted a little closer, moving slowly because he was learning that fast tripped a switch for her, and not in a good way. As he came in, she dragged her teeth over her lower lip and her eyes went heavy-lidded in invite. Their mouths nearly touched before she suddenly pulled back, jerking to her feet. "Sorry," she said breathlessly. "I thought I heard something."

They both listened. Nothing but the waves hitting the rocky sand, and her accelerated breathing.

She grimaced. "I guess not."

He stood as well and kept things light by giving her some space. "You didn't keep the waitressing job."

"Turns out I'm not much of a waitress."

"What are you?" he asked.

"Well, I'm supposed to be a jingle writer, but that's not working out so well, either."

"A jingle writer?"

"I write songs for commercials," she said. "Nothing nearly as difficult as risking limb and life at sea for seven years, I know, but it presents its own challenges."

"Would I recognize any of your jingles?" he asked.

"Maybe, but nothing recent. The one I just turned in was for Cushy toilet paper."

He grinned. "Nice. What are you working on now?"

She hesitated, nibbling on her lower lip again. "Diaxsis."

"Which is . . . ?"

She blew out a sigh. "An erectile dysfunction med."

He laughed. "And you're having a . . . *hard* time?"

"Funny," she said. "It's all fun and games — unless you have to write the jingle. At the moment, I'm wishing I had a job serving ranch-flavored popcorn on the pier instead. Or *anything.*"

"I used to want to be a rock star," he told her.

"Yeah?" she asked. "What stopped you?"

"I'm completely tone-deaf and can't sing worth shit."

She laughed, and he smiled at the sweet sound of it.

"Is that why your music's so loud that the windows rattle?" she asked. "You're in there pretending to be a rock star?"

"I work to it," he said. "Or I did. The past

few days I've been listening to whatever it is you're listening to."

She froze. "You can hear me messing around on my keyboard?" she asked, sounding horrified.

He paused. "That's you? You're fantastic."

She immediately shook her head. "No."

"Actually, yeah."

"No, I mean you can't listen." There was a new edge to her voice, and she took a step back. "I can't play if I have an audience."

"Why not?"

"Because I choke," she said, sounding genuinely upset.

"Okay," he said quietly, taking in the fact that she was now pale by moonlight. "I'll pretend not to listen. How's that?"

"No." She didn't relax or smile. "Because I'll know you're only *pretending* not to listen."

She wasn't being coy here, or searching for compliments the way women sometimes did. She was truly unable to bear the thought of him hearing her play. "I could wear earplugs," he said.

She stared at him, then looked away, to the water. "I sound crazy, I know. But I don't play for audiences anymore. I'm only playing for myself now, while trying to come up with my next jingle."

"You used to play for an audience?"

"Oh, God, Becca," she muttered, "just shut up." She pressed the heels of her hands to her eyes. "I really need a subject change."

"Is that why you left New Orleans?"

"How is that a subject change?" She dropped her hands and sighed. "I left New Orleans because I needed a break from . . . things. Family, to be honest. It's hard to explain."

"Maybe that's the problem," he said. "Maybe you're too focused on the past instead of the here and now."

She stared at him.

He stared back.

"Maybe," she finally said softly. "You don't ever do that? Get stuck in the past?"

Sam didn't like to think about the past at all, much less try to get back to it. "Hell no."

"So . . . you're a little broken, too?" she asked hopefully, her eyes locked on his with great interest.

"I'm not broken."

She sighed. "Of course not, since you have a penis."

"What does that mean?"

"Guys don't admit to being broken," she said.

He laughed, and she stared at him.

95

"Okay," she said, "you've really got to stop doing that, laugh all sexy-like, Mr. Broken Sexy Grumpy Surfer."

"I'm not broken," he said again. *Much.*

"Well, if you were, I should let you know, I've heard of this remedy . . ."

"Yeah?"

Again she dragged her teeth over her lower lip. "Maybe it's not a remedy so much as a . . . temporary fix. Like a Band-Aid," she said, tipping her face to his.

There was an intimacy that came with the dark night, and with it came an ache. An ache for a woman. This woman. It'd been a while since he'd held someone, gotten lost in someone. The truth was that no one had tempted him in a while.

Becca did. Becca with the dark, warm eyes, the sweet smile, and the pulse racing at the base of her throat. He wanted to put his mouth there. He wanted to put his mouth to every inch of her, and he reached for her hand, slowly pulling her in so they stood toe-to-toe. "What's the Band-Aid?"

"Seeing as you're not broken," she said, "it doesn't matter."

Sam ran a finger along her temple, tucked a stray strand of hair behind her ear, and took in the quick tremble that racked her body at his touch. "What matters to me is how *you* got broken," he said.

She closed her eyes, and his smile faded. "Someone hurt you," he said.

"No." She turned away. "It was a long time ago."

Yeah. Someone had hurt her. He turned her to face him and waited for her to open those soulful eyes. Whatever had happened to her had cut deep, but she wasn't down for the count.

He could relate to that.

"I don't talk about it," she said.

"Instead, you put a Band-Aid on it."

"Yes." She hesitated, and then set her hand on his chest, slowly, lightly dragging her fingers from one pec to the other as if testing herself out for a reaction. He hoped she was getting one because the simple touch stirred anything but simple reactions within him.

"It's been a while," she murmured, "but I remember this as a proven effective method for healing all."

He loved that she wasn't too shy to speak her mind. And frankly, he also loved that she'd made the first move, hesitant as it was. He'd make the second. And the third. Hell, he'd make whatever moves she was receptive to, and hopefully chase away her demons while he was at it. But when she leaned into him, he slid his hands down her arms, capturing her wrists to stop her. "I need to take care of something first," he said.

"Oh." Some of the light died from her. "I get it."

"No." He held on to her when she would have pulled away. "This isn't a rejection, Becca. I want you." He dipped down a little to look right into her eyes, wanting to make sure she really got him. "I want you bad, but I'm all sweaty from my run. I need a shower, a quick one, I promise. But my shop doesn't have one, and my house is ten minutes away, so I need you to be patient while I —"

"I've got a shower," she said. Her gaze dropped to his mouth, her tongue darting out to wet her lips. He groaned and gave in, kissing her.

Fucking perfect.

That was how she tasted. She made a little mewling sound and pressed closer, like she thought maybe he was going to vanish.

Fat chance.

He slanted his head and kissed her the way he liked it, open-mouthed, wet, and deep. He let go of her wrists and things got a whole lot hotter real fast. Their hands bumped into each other as they moved, grappling for purchase, hers running over his chest and arms, his gliding up her sides, inside the bulky sweatshirt she wore.

She moaned into his mouth.

He lost his head a little bit then. Or maybe he'd lost it the moment he'd first laid eyes on her, he didn't know. She made him so dizzy he couldn't think straight. "Becca," he said, and from somewhere, he had no idea where, he found the strength to pull her back.

Their gazes met, and at the heat — and uncertainty — in hers, he kissed her again, soft this time. When she let out a shaky breath and slid her arms around his neck, he held her off again. "Shower first," he said.

"And then?"

The hopefulness in her voice went straight through him, and he kissed her again, until she moaned into his mouth, her reaction taking away his ability to think clearly. "And then," he promised, "whatever you want."

CHAPTER 7

It wasn't often Becca acted recklessly, or with abandon. In fact, it was almost never.

But Sam of the beautiful eyes and sexy voice and surprisingly sharp wit was bringing it out in her. She deserved this, she reminded herself. A night of no strings, a night lost in a man's arms.

This man's arms.

She led the way to her front door. She had the very hot and sexy Sam Brody standing at her back, and she was wondering if she was really going to do this.

Could she?

Then Sam leaned in and kissed her neck, and she quivered in arousal.

Oh, God. Yes. Despite her trepidations and unease and the fact that her lady bits might have rusted up and withered from disuse, she was going to do this.

And she was not going to let anything intrude.

She was going to get naked, and she was going to have a good time while she was at it.

Olivia entered the building just then, walking fast, head down. When she looked up, she nearly tripped over her own feet at the sight of Becca and Sam standing there. "Oh," she said in clear surprise.

Sam nodded at her. "Olivia."

They knew each other, Becca realized, with an odd pang of something. Jealousy? Nah, that couldn't be.

Could it?

Olivia nodded back at Sam and started to walk past them, but then she stopped and turned back to Becca. "I know I owe you an apology for the other night."

"For what?" Becca asked.

Olivia was in another pair of jeans, very cute high-heeled wedges, and a gauzy top that showed off her enviable figure. She was beautiful and aloof, and her expression was hooded as it had been the other night, but she had the good grace to grimace. "Slamming my door on your nose," she said. "I'm not really a people person."

"Duly noted," Becca said drily.

Olivia grimaced again. "I know you were trying to be a nice neighbor, and I was a jerk. I'd like to make it up to you. Seriously," she said at Becca's look of surprise. "Food fixes all, right? I make the best homemade pizza out there. So dinner, on me." She slid Sam a glance. "When you're not busy."

Becca swiveled her gaze to Sam, wondering how he stacked up against homemade pizza.

He arched a brow at her.

Olivia shocked Becca by laughing. "Another night," she said, and vanished inside her place.

"You wanted to give me up for pizza," Sam said.

"*Homemade* pizza," Becca corrected, and put her key in the lock, jerking at the feel of his hot mouth on the back of her neck.

"I'm going to make you forget about the pizza," he whispered against her skin.

She shivered, having underestimated the power of a man's kiss on her neck. "Are you sure you want to make a promise you might not be able to keep?" she managed.

"I always keep my promises."

She hoped so. God, she hoped so.

Five minutes later, Becca stood outside her bathroom, hands and forehead on the door, body thrumming with emotions she almost didn't recognize.

Desire.

Need.

From the other side came the sound of her shower running.

She had a man in her shower.

Good Lord, she had a man in her shower. Picturing Sam in there all hot and naked, using her soap, rubbing his hands over his body, was making her good parts tingle. And she had a lot of good parts, many more than she remembered . . .

She smiled in relief, then shook her head at herself. Why was she fantasizing about the naked man in her shower instead of being *in* the shower with the naked man?

She chewed on her thumbnail another moment, giving brief thought to being shy, but then quickly discarded that as it hadn't gotten her anywhere all year.

Open the door, Becca.

She opened the door.

Steam rolled over her as the water beat against the tile floor. Taking a deep breath, she fixed her eyes on the sight before her. The glass door was fogged over but she could see the faint outline of Sam's body. She had a side view, and it was a good one. He had one hand braced on the wall in front of him, his head hanging low as he let the water pound between his shoulder blades.

Becca's gaze followed the trail of water down his sleek back, over the perfect, succulent curve of his ass, and down the backs of his legs to his feet.

He was gorgeous.

Sweating now, she had to strip off her bulky sweatshirt. At the movement, he glanced over. Seeing her there, his gaze went fiery and suggestive. Teeming with raw passion, he reached for the soap, running his hands with perfunctory speed and precision over himself.

Becca stared. She started to say something, but then he wrapped his hand around himself. Eyes locked on hers, he held on but didn't stroke, and she got all hot and bothered from wishing he would. "You didn't lock the door," she managed. "So I, um . . ."

He smiled a very dangerous, alluring smile.

She stood there, her entire body vibrating with need, but trying desperately to be cool, like having a man in her shower was no big deal. In truth, it was a big deal. A *huge* big deal. Her heart was just about racing right out of her chest.

Her terms, she reminded herself. This was on her terms and she was in control. She could stop this at any time.

But she already knew she wasn't going to want to stop.

Sam lifted his hands and shoved his hair back from his face.

Her body tingled. And though he was the one in the shower, she was the one getting damp. Reaching over to a drawer, she pulled out the sole condom she had. She'd gotten it as a party favor a few years back, and because it was blue, and blueberry-flavored to boot, *and* an "extra, extra" large, she'd kept it for laughs. It'd been a while since she'd had use for a condom, and she sort of wished it wasn't blue, but it was better than nothing.

Water and suds continued to sluice down Sam's body, and, even hotter now, Becca pulled off another item of clothing — her long-sleeved tee.

Sam swiped at the fogged-up glass on the shower, presumably to better see her, and smiled. "You've got a lot of layers on."

She flushed. "I was cold earlier."

"I'll keep you warm."

She utterly believed him. She pushed off her flannel PJ bottoms next, which left her in a thin cotton cami and an equally thin pair of cotton panties.

Given the fire in Sam's eyes, he approved, but she hesitated, because whatever came off next was going to reveal more of her than had been seen by another human being in a while.

"Keep going," he said, voice husky.

Erotic.

When she didn't move, he gave her a come-here finger crook.

Her legs took her the last few steps, and then she was in the shower, the water plastering her cami and panties to her body.

Sam groaned at the sight and hooked an arm around her, settling a hand low on her back, pulling her into him. He did this slowly, giving her plenty of time to stop him.

She didn't.

Not only didn't she stop him, she reached up and slid her fingers into his wet hair and pulled him down, hoping for a mindless kiss.

"You're shaking," he murmured. "Still cold?"

"No."

He met her gaze. "You're nervous."

"Aren't you?"

He gave her a heart-melting smile. "It's going to be good, Becca, I promise."

Another promise. She could have told him she didn't believe in them, but there was something so absolute about his voice, something so sure in his eyes. "Okay," she whispered.

He smiled against her lips, and then brought his other hand up, tilting her face to suit him as he kissed her. Soft at first, then serious and demanding, and though she'd hoped he'd take her out of her own head for a while. He did even better than that, and an utterly unexpected wave of desire washed over her. She sank her fingers into his thick, unruly hair and held on.

He was right so far. It was good.

So good she lost herself in the sensations of being held, the barrage of heat and need, and a hunger so strong it made her weak in the knees.

When was the last time a man had made her weak in the knees?

A long time.

Too long.

His tongue swept along hers, and she moaned into his mouth. At the sound, Sam pulled back and gave her a very hot look. She tugged him in again because he was a good kisser. The *best* kisser. In fact, he was the king of all kissers, so much so that when he ended the next kiss, she'd have slithered to the shower floor in a boneless heap of arousal if he wasn't holding her up with a strong arm around her back. The fingers of his other hand unpeeled hers to see what she still held fisted. When he caught sight of the extra-large blueberry condom, he smiled.

"I was planning ahead," she whispered.

"Love a woman who plans ahead." He set the condom on the soap rack, and then nudged a wet cami strap off her shoulder. Lowering his head, his lips grazed her jaw, her throat, across her collarbone. "Mmm," he murmured against her skin, then pulled back a fraction of an inch to meet her gaze, his own hot as fire and intense. "Tell me this is what you want, Becca."

She opened her mouth but nothing came out. Why was nothing coming out?

"If I stay," he said very gently but with utter steel, "I'm going to take you to your bed and make you feel so good that you forget whatever is putting that hollow look in your eyes. I promise you that."

Another promise, but this one seemed as irresistible as the last one, so in answer to his very alpha-man statement, she mustered up some courage and pressed up against him, running her hands over sleek, hot, wet, male skin. God. God, he felt good.

His hands went to her hair, releasing it from her ponytail so that his fingers could run through the wavy, wet mess. "Becca?"

He wanted the words. "Stay," she said.

He peeled her out of her cami and panties

and groaned at the sight of her bared before him, kissing her long and hard and wet and deep. He grabbed the soap, and with a dark, heavy-lidded smile, started with her arms. Her stomach and chest were next. Slowly and deliberately, his hands stroked upward, teasing the heavy undersides of her breasts until she sighed with pleasure, her head falling back to thunk against the tile. "Sam."

"Learning what you like," he said, and then kept teasing her until she said his name again, not so soft, and finally, oh God finally, his thumbs brushed over her nipples.

She sucked in a breath and trembled from head to toe. So long. So long since she'd felt this way.

He let his fingers come into play then, meeting up with his thumbs, gently rolling. "Well, you like that."

She couldn't talk, but if she could have, she'd have said she *loved* it. Luckily he didn't seem to need words because he dropped to his knees and soaped up her legs next, running his hands up the backs of them, cupping her ass, squeezing, before stroking back down. Then he began again with the front of her, up her shins, her thighs. And then between.

She gasped. "Sam —"

"Open, babe."

"Um —" she started, thinking she was in *way* over her head, but he took over, his hands urging her to spread her feet. She did, and found herself wide open in every possible way, but there wasn't any space in the shower or her head for self-consciousness, not with his hands on her.

And his mouth. And God, his mouth . . .

He took his sweet time about it, too, stroking, touching, kissing, licking every single inch of her so that she was breathing like a lunatic, worked up into a near frenzy. "Sam," she gasped again. "Sam, I'm going to —"

"Do it," he said, mouth still on her. "Come."

She flew apart, but he was right there to put her back together again, holding her, slowly bringing her back. When she could, she blinked her eyes open and caught his slow, sexy-as-hell smile.

He'd watched her lose it, and she realized she badly wanted to do the same for him. Pulling him upright, she admired his gorgeous, tough, hard-muscled body with her hands first, and that was so good that she had to taste, too. She slid to her knees to do just that.

Pressing her mouth low on a very sexy spot just beneath his hip, she watched in pleasure and fascination as the muscles in his abs jerked. She wasn't too sure of her skills in this arena, but he looked good enough to lick. So she did. And then again.

And then she took him into her mouth.

He made a low, rough noise, and she looked up at him through her lashes. His head was tipped back, eyes closed, the water flowing over his face and down his chest. His fingers slid in her hair and held on. She tensed, but his hold remained gentle, not guiding or pushing her. It was more like he needed the grip just to hold on, which actually made her feel powerful, and sexy. So sexy . . .

All good signs, she figured, and continued on, absorbing the groan that came from above her and echoed against the tiled walls when she experimented a little bit.

"Sweet Jesus," he muttered, his body as tense as a tightly coiled spring ready to snap. After a few moments, he swore and roughly hauled her up.

"What's wrong?" she asked.

Nuzzling his face in her neck, he shook his head. "Gotta slow down or I'm gonna come."

"Wouldn't that be only fair?"

He groaned again, kissed her, and then said against her lips as he hoisted her up, "I want to be inside you when I come, when we *both* come."

The words nearly sent her up in flames, but she needed to tell him —

"Hold on to me," he said. Leaning her into the tile wall, he slapped a hand out for the condom. "Magnum blueberry," he read with a lip twitch.

She'd had her hands around him. And her lips. So she was speaking on good authority. "At least the size is right."

He snorted and, holding her pinned against the wall, seared his mouth to hers. She parted her lips for him and garnered herself a low, sexy growl from the back of Sam's throat as their tongues touched. She'd been doing her best to stay lost in his gaze, in his kisses and touches, and not let Real Life intercede, but she still had to tell him. "Sam."

He sucked at the sweet spot right beneath her ear and her eyes nearly crossed in ecstasy. "Sam," she said again, but he wasn't listening. She tapped his chest. "Sam, I need to —"

"Anything," he murmured and kept kissing her, his hot mouth robbing her of cognitive thought.

"I —" She blinked. "Anything? You can't offer me anything."

"Why not?"

She paused and appeared to process this question very seriously. "Well . . . I could take advantage for one."

"Go for it," he said hotly, letting out a slow, absolutely wicked bad-boy smile. "Just remember, paybacks are a bitch."

She shivered, not in fear but in arousal. Good Lord, he was potent. "I'm trying to tell you something."

"Okay, babe," he murmured, and kissed his way along her jaw toward her mouth. "You tell me whatever you want while I —"

"Sam!"

At the seriousness in her voice, he again lifted his head, giving her his full attention. Which she'd totally and completely under-estimated, because Sam's full attention made it difficult if not impossible to think. "I don't want to disappoint you, but —"

"Becca." His features immediately softened. "You won't. You couldn't —"

"I won't come with you inside me," she blurted out.

He went still for a beat. "No?"

"I . . . can't." Oh, God, this was embar-rassing. Why had she thought this a good idea? She should have faked it. But she wasn't good at faking it. "I want to, I try to, but it just doesn't happen for me. And

113

sometimes that can be . . . upsetting for a guy, I know, and I just really don't want you to be upset."

Something passed across his eyes, and it wasn't pity or she'd have shriveled into a tiny ball and died. She couldn't put her finger on it because he kissed her, softly at first, then not so softly, and before she knew it she was panting for air and whimpering with need, gripping him like he was her lifeline.

"Becca."

"Huh?" she asked dimly.

"Open your eyes."

She did with difficulty and met his very intense gaze.

"You couldn't disappoint me if you tried," he said, and with that, he turned off the water, grabbed a towel, and dried her.

She was so lost in the pleasure of him running the towel over her body, and the way he then tossed aside the towel to use his hands — and mouth — deliciously rough, demanding, and thorough, that she didn't even realize they were moving until they fell together on her bed.

There he began all over again from the beginning, with long drugging kisses and teasing touches that had her rocking into him, desperate for release. He made her come twice like that, once with his fingers, and then again with his mouth, so that she was still thrumming with adrenaline and shuddering with it when he finally rolled on the blue condom and pushed inside her. His hands slid beneath her bottom and pulled her into him, grinding the two of them together with every stroke. Her eyes drifted shut but he nipped at her lower lip until she opened them again.

His gaze was intently fierce, so much so that she quivered. "Stay with me," he said. He had one arm wrapped around her; the other slid down the back of her thigh, further opening her up for him as he thrust long and hard and deep, holding her gaze captive in his the entire time. The muscles in his arms and shoulders strained with the effort of holding himself back, keeping the pace slow.

Heaven.

She was close, so shockingly, desperately close, her nerves were screaming. "Please," she gasped, unable to say more. Luckily for her Sam didn't need additional instruction. It took only a few more of those hard, masterful strokes for him to bring her to the very edge of sanity, and then his arms pulled her in even closer, so that they touched in every way possible, skin on skin, and the exquisite slow sliding of friction sending her flying. As the surprise orgasm rippled through her, she clenched tight around him, absorbing his low, rough groan. With one more thrust, he came right along with her.

It was a long few moments before she regained control of her limbs and could loosen the arms she had in a death grip around his neck. "Sorry," she murmured and tried to pull back.

But Sam was having none of it. "Stay with me," he said again, and then brushed a kiss over her damp temple. Lifting his head, he studied her. "You okay?"

"I — You —" Words failed.

He huffed a soft laugh and kissed her. "Yeah, you're okay," he said, and slid out of her. She made a sound of helpless regret at the loss, and he kissed her again. "Don't move," he commanded, and vanished into her bathroom.

He was back in less than two minutes, sliding beneath her covers and hauling her in tight against him. He'd made good on his promises, proving that when he warned her about something, it was best to listen. It'd been good, and he'd indeed made her forget about the pizza.

He held her for a while, certainly long beyond what she'd have deemed the polite amount of cuddle time, his cheek resting lightly on top of her head, his arms around her. She had her face plastered to his bare chest and was listening to his steady heartbeat beneath her, waiting for him to extract himself.

He never did.

Finally, exhausted, she fell into a coma-like sleep and woke with a smile on her face to the sun streaming in her windows.

And an empty bed.

CHAPTER 8

Sam might have left Becca's bed as surprisingly as he'd arrived in it, but the bigger surprise had been what had happened in it.

She smiled every time she thought about it, which was often enough to prompt Olivia to stop in the hallway the next day and ask Becca what was so damn wonderful.

Becca had laughed but shaken her head. She wasn't going to share, but it turned out that despite Sam's silent departure, having crazy hot sex was good for a person's frame of mind.

Real good.

Becca didn't come up with a jingle for Diaxsis over the next few days, but she felt infinitely relaxed about it. She felt infinitely relaxed about everything, including the fact that it was time to supplement her jingle income. The only thing that could have improved her mood was a Sexy Grumpy Surfer sighting.

But she didn't get that. Not from her window, not on the beach, not from his boat, not anywhere Sam I am . . .

She did get pizza with Olivia. And as promised, it was homemade, and out of this world. Becca learned that Olivia not only ran the vintage store but owned it, which explained her fabulous clothes. She also made a mean chocolate chip cookie, and if Sam hadn't already rocked her world, Becca might have said the cookies were better than orgasms. As it was, the cookies were a close second.

But though they'd spent several hours together, Olivia didn't open up much, and her eyes stayed hooded.

Olivia had secrets.

As Becca had her own, she hadn't pushed.

She spent a few days perusing the want ads and cleaning up her space, making it a home. She realized that said a lot about Lucky Harbor being more than a so-called pit stop, but she wasn't going to feel bad for loving it here.

Three days after her night with Sam, she'd unwrapped a new — to her — lamp and couch she'd bought from Olivia's shop and was lugging the paper the lamp had been wrapped in to the Dumpster when she realized Sam was there with his shop vac. He was emptying the bag when he caught her staring. He stared right back like maybe he liked what he saw. He did that, she'd noticed, showed his appreciation in nonverbal ways. With his eyes. His slow, sexy smile. The sound he made deep in his throat when he —

"Hey," he said.

Wherever he'd been, he'd gotten some sun and, as usual, looked good enough to eat. "Hey yourself." She turned to go.

"About the other night," he said to her back. "I didn't mean to vanish on you. I got called out on a job that took me away for a few days. And out of cell range."

She had to admit that she'd wondered if he'd disappeared to distance himself from what had proven to be an explosive chemistry between them. At the realization that this wasn't what had happened, something loosened in her chest. *Relief.* She hadn't scared him off. "You're covered in sawdust," she said inanely.

He looked down. "Got home late last night and went right to work on a boat I'm building for another client." He shifted closer and stroked a thumb over her jaw. "You okay?"

Something about his proximity made her a little speechless, so she nodded.

120

His eyes never left hers as he appeared to search for the truth in this statement. He sifted his fingers through her hair, gently gliding his thumb beneath her eye. "Your bruise is gone."

"Yes, and I've grounded myself from reading my e-reader at night."

He flashed that dangerous smile, which faded some when his cell buzzed. "Talk," he said into it, and then listened a moment. "Cole already left? Shit. Did you flush out the engine? Check the water pump? Yeah? It's got good water flow? The water hot or warm?" He listened some more. "Sounds like something's stuck in the out-flow tube. Shut it down, I'll be there in ten." He ended the call.

"Problem?" she asked.

"There always is."

"And you're the go-to guy?"

"At the moment," he said, master of short sentences. He looked at her then. Like really looked at her, in a way no one else ever seemed to. "How's the jingle writing going?"

She mimed hanging herself with a rope.

He smiled. "Need another Band-Aid?"

The words were like a hot caress, and she felt her nipples react hopefully. "You have an engine problem requiring your attention," she reminded him.

"There's always time for a break."

She laughed. Spoken like a man. "I'd have my mind on work," she said.

He flashed her a very bad-boy smile. "Becca, I can promise you, your mind wouldn't be on work."

Her pulse took a hard leap at yet another promise. "I suppose everyone's entitled to a little bit of a break now and again," she said softly. "Right?"

His eyes darkened, and he stepped closer, just as a car tore into the lot. A woman leapt out, slammed her door, and went hands on curvy hips as she tossed back her long blond hair. "So you *are* alive," she said, glaring at Sam.

"Selena." His voice was so carefully neutral that Becca took a second look at him. His expression, fun and sexy only a moment before, was now closed off.

The woman standing in front of them was tall, leggy, and built like Barbie. Beachy Barbie. She wore a red-and-white sundress that looked so good she might have walked right off the runway and gave Becca a hard, speculative look before turning to Sam. "That was fast."

Becca knew she should've been insulted, but actually she was secretly tickled pink if this beautiful creature was jealous of her.

"I've called you like twenty-five times and left you a bunch of texts," Selena said to Sam. "Your phone broken?"

"No," he said.

Becca waited for him to explain. He'd been gone for a few days, out of range, yet he didn't say a word in his defense.

Steam practically flew out Selena's ears. "So you're what," she asked in disbelief, going up in volume with each word, "*ignoring me?*"

"It's been a month," he said. "I thought there was nothing left to say."

"I've got plenty left to say!" Selena screeched. "And if you'd answered even a single call, you'd know it!"

Sam looked pained. "My office then."

"Oh, *hell* no," Selena said. "This shit's going public now. You took me to Cottonwoods. Cottonwoods is a *serious* place, Sam. It says we're in a relationship."

"We went to Cottonwoods because you *asked* to go there," Sam said. "It was our second date, and over appetizers you informed me you were researching sperm donors so you could get inseminated."

Selena's crazy eyes narrowed. "And?"

"*Sperm donors,*" he repeated, as if this explained all.

"You saying I scared you off?" Selena asked. "You're not afraid of anything, Sam, and you damn well know it."

Becca swiveled to get Sam's reaction. She might not have dated him twice, or gone to Cottonwoods — wherever that was — but even she already knew Sam Brody wouldn't admit to be scared off by a single thing.

When Sam didn't respond, Selena whirled to storm off, giving Becca a not-so-accidental shoulder shove. "He's dead inside, you know," she snapped. "He's magic in the sack, but trust me, he's not worth it."

Becca didn't respond, and Selena shook her head. "Don't say I didn't warn you."

A moment later, her tires squealed as she left the lot.

There was an awkward silence as Becca and Sam watched her go. Well, *Becca* was feeling awkward. Hard to say what Sam was feeling. He kept his own counsel. "Okay, yeah," she finally said, "I can see why you might not like to live in the past."

Two days later, Sam stood in the hut at the front counter. He had notes on three different napkins, one scratched in ink on his forearm, and another on a piece of wood from his shop in his back pocket.

And the phone was still ringing.

He was at the end of his rope, for lots of reasons. He hadn't managed to break away from work long enough to get any time alone with Becca. And he wanted to be alone with her. Not just to get her naked again, though he wanted that, badly. But he also wanted to get inside her head and learn more about her.

Cole came in from the boat. He and Tanner had taken out a group of twelve before the crack of dawn for a deep-sea fishing trip.

Sam had stayed behind to catch up on paperwork — which he hadn't gotten to thanks to the phones. "This place is insane," he said. "No one writes shit down."

"You're the one who won't use the schedule," Cole said.

Tanner trailed in behind Cole, dripping water everywhere as he limped in, carrying some of the gear. "He doesn't use the schedule to prove a point."

"Not true," Sam said.

Okay, it was totally true.

"I'm trying to work." He jabbed a thumb in the direction of the warehouse behind them. "But the fucking phones keep ringing, and no one's answering them. Why isn't anyone answering?"

"You know why," Cole said. "We haven't hired anyone yet. Were any of the calls from prospective applicants?"

"Yeah," Sam said. "Which is why I'm in here. I made appointments with three people. One didn't show."

"And the other two?"

"One was Lucille," Sam said. "Again. She showed up in a bikini to prove she was —" He used air quotes. "Beach-savvy."

They all shuddered.

"I reminded her that we'd discussed this, that there were age limitations to this job," Sam said. "And then she accused me of being a geriatric bigot. She said I should be expecting to hear from her lawyer."

Tanner grinned. "And the third?"

Sam looked at Cole. "Your sister."

"Aw, Christ," Cole muttered, scrubbing a hand over his face. "Which one?"

"Does it matter?" Tanner asked. "They're all crazy."

Cole held out a palm to Tanner. "Pay up."

"What?" Tanner said, still dripping water everywhere.

"You swore you wouldn't make fun of my family anymore, remember?" Cole asked. "And I said that you couldn't stop yourself, and you said you could, too, and then I said I bet you, and you said no sweat, and I said put your money where your mouth is, and you said fifty bucks. So . . ." He wriggled his fingers. "Fifty bucks, man. Right now."

Tanner shrugged. "Can't. I'm holding all this wet gear. I can't reach my wallet."

"Turn around, I'll get it."

This made Tanner grin and shake his head. "It's in my front pocket."

Cole yanked his hand back like he'd been bitten. "No way am I touching your front pocket. Sam, *you* do it."

"Why me?"

"You get me my money, and I'll hire someone today so you can stop bitching."

Sam sighed and shoved his hand down Tanner's front pocket.

The door opened behind them. Becca walked in and stopped short at the sight of Sam with his hand down the front of Tanner's pants.

"Am I interrupting something?" she asked.

Cole was grinning like a Cheshire cat. "Yes."

"No," Sam said, and pulled out Tanner's wallet. He flipped it open, pocketed all the cash, then shoved the wallet back at Tanner.

"Hey," Cole said.

"Hey," Tanner said.

Ignoring them both, Sam turned to Becca. She waved an ad that he recognized from

127

the local paper. *Their* ad. He met her gaze and saw the truth — she was going to apply for the job. "No," he said. He couldn't hire someone he'd slept with. No matter how good a time he'd had. And he'd had a *great* time.

"Too late," Becca said. "I already applied online as the ad suggested. And I don't want to toot my own horn or anything, but I'm pretty perfect for this job."

"Still no," Sam said.

She gave him a long look. "Afraid I'll scream at you about you being dead inside like your ex did?"

Cole and Tanner cackled at this like two annoying hens while Becca tapped the ad. "— It says right here that you need someone strong on phones and with good people skills." She lifted her gaze and looked at all three of them. "I'm both, by the way. I worked as an admin in a New Orleans ad agency all last year while I was writing jingles."

"Jingles?" Cole asked.

"I write jingles for commercials and stuff," she said. "It's all in the application. You'll see."

"No shit," Cole said, looking impressed. "You any good?"

"At jingles?" She shrugged. "I did a big

soup campaign. Oh, and you know the commercial for Indie Burgers?" She began to sing, ". . . tell me how you like it, tell me how you want it —"

Cole joined in for the finish, "I want it smokin', I wanna feel the heat . . ." He grinned. "That was a good one. What else did you do?"

Her smile went a little stiff. "Well, nothing for a while after that. But I just finished up one for Cushy toilet paper. Now I'm stuck on my latest project."

"What's it for?" Cole asked.

She paused. Sighed. "Diaxsis."

Cole shook his head, looking clueless. "What's that?"

Tanner grinned. "I know."

"Probably shouldn't be proud of that, man," Sam said, laughing when Tanner gave him a shove.

"What the hell is it?" Cole asked.

Tanner held up a limp finger and then straightened it. He accompanied this with a brow waggle.

Becca sighed. "Back to my application," she said. "The good news is that if I could keep a staff of twenty-five organized, most of them angry women, the three of you'll be a piece of cake."

"You think men are easier than women?"

129

Cole asked.

Becca laughed.

"Yeah," Cole said, smiling at her. "You're probably right."

Okay, Sam thought, so there was more to cute, sweet Becca than met the eye. She had brains, and she wasn't a pushover.

But neither was he. "You'd need references," he said.

"You can call mine," Becca said, but then her easy smile faded some. "But as I already noted on my app, I'd appreciate it if you wouldn't say exactly where your business is located, or where I am."

There was a beat of silence as this request was absorbed, and Sam felt something tighten in his chest. "You in any sort of trouble that we should know about?" he asked, just as serious now as she.

"Nope," Becca said quickly. *Too* quickly.

Damn.

Sam exchanged a look with Cole and Tanner. Not a one of them didn't recognize a problem when they saw one.

Becca lifted the ad again. "You need someone to start ASAP. Luckily, that happens to be exactly when I'm available." Her smile was back. "ASAP."

"I gotta ask," Tanner said. "You any better at phones than you are at waitressing?"

Cole gave him a dirty look, but Tanner shrugged.

"Yes," Becca said, not looking insulted in the least. "I'm much better at phones than waitressing."

As if on cue, the phone rang. Cole, Tanner, and Sam groaned in unison.

Becca gestured to it. "May I?"

Cole waved at her, like *Please.*

She leaned over Sam, teasing him with her scent and a brush of her arm against his as she grabbed the phone. "Lucky Harbor Charters," she answered. "How can I help you?" She paused, listened politely, and then said, "I'm sorry, Sam no longer works here. No, there's no forwarding address. Thank you for calling." She disconnected.

"What the hell?" Sam said.

"It was Selena."

Cole grinned. "You're hired."

Tanner nodded. "And keep that snooty tone in your voice. Sounds authoritative and sexy. I like it."

"No," Sam said.

"Two to one," Tanner said.

Sam gave him a look.

"What?" Tanner said. "She's prettier than you *and* friendlier than you."

"Plus, I just promised you I'd hire someone today," Cole said. "Voilà, *done.*"

Sam ushered Becca to one of the stools in front of the counter. "Give us a minute," he said.

Then he manhandled Cole and Tanner out the front. The three of them stood on the beach. "No," he said firmly, arms crossed.

"Give me one good reason," Cole said.

Sam searched his brain. He couldn't come up with one *good* reason. But he had lots of *bad* reasons, starting with the fact that he'd slept with her.

Except there'd been no sleeping.

And every night since, he'd dreamed of her. Really hot dreams about how she'd felt writhing beneath him. She had this way of helplessly whispering his name over and over again — Christ. He had to stop thinking about it. "This isn't a good idea," he repeated.

"She wants the job," Cole said. "And we need her." He paused. "Unless there's a reason working with her would be a problem? Like, say, she's an ex who's a nut job? But usually, that's Tanner's area of expertise."

"Hey," Tanner said.

Cole gave him a long look, and Tanner sighed. "Fine," he said. "That's definitely my area of expertise. But Sam doesn't go

132

for nut jobs. He keeps his entire life com-partmentalized. He wouldn't work with someone he likes."

Cole's face changed. "Shit, that's it." He turned back to Sam. "That's why you said she was off limits. You *like* her."

"What is this, high school?" Sam asked.

"No," Cole said. "Because you didn't like anyone in high school. You loved them and left them."

Definitely not going there, Sam decided. "We're not doing this, and before you whine about it, you both owe me. You," he said, pointing at Tanner.

"Me, what?"

"The night you went skinny-dipping with some chick. She stole your clothes and you had to walk home butt-ass naked."

Tanner winced. "That was a million years ago, man."

"You came knocking on my window for clothes," Sam said, "which I handed over without giving you shit. Well, not too much shit anyway. And you." He turned to Cole.

Cole opened his mouth, but Sam plowed ahead. "Remember the night you were grounded and not supposed to go out? Except you did, and you got drunk, and I had to drag your trashed ass home, and when your mom caught us at the door I let you pretend it was me who was plastered, that it was me who'd needed saving so that you didn't get grounded for the rest of your life."

"Why do you remember this shit?" Cole asked, mystified.

"For days just like this."

CHAPTER 9

Becca knelt on the stool beneath the open window, shamelessly eavesdropping on the guys. She'd spent several days now searching for a viable, short-term job that would fit her criteria. One, she wanted to stay in Lucky Harbor for at least the summer. Two, she didn't want anything too demanding, as after a day of work she'd then be putting in long hours writing her jingles. And three, it had to be something she was good at.

She was good at being in control, good at being in charge.

She could really see herself doing this job. What she hadn't seen was Sam's reticence, though she should have. Of course he didn't want to work with the woman he'd so spontaneously boinked almost a week ago.

Except it'd felt like a lot more than just a quickie.

And really, there'd been nothing "quick" about it, or Sam. He'd taken his time with her, touching, kissing . . . *everything*. And she'd responded to him. Fully. That'd been the most shocking. She'd more than merely responded to him. She'd gone up in flames for him.

But that didn't mean he wanted a repeat.

Or that he'd want to hire her to work for him.

Damn it. She leaned in toward the window, trying to see better. The three of them stood close, and though they looked like laid-back surfers, there was clearly a lot more to them than that. Cole was the most approachable of the bunch, but he wasn't a pushover. Tanner had a look to him that said he'd been around the block and it hadn't been an easy ride.

And then there was the tough, impenetrable, guarded, hard-to-crack Sam.

At the moment, they were talking, shades locked onto shades. She wasn't quite close enough to hear what they were saying, but their body language fascinated her. Damn, she wished she could catch their words. She got down, scooted the stool closer to the window, climbed back up, and pressed her ear to the screen.

"If you're having trouble hearing, maybe you should just stick your head out the door."

At the unbearably familiar voice behind her — *Sam's* — she squeaked in surprise and fell off the stool.

"A peeper to the end," he said, sounding not surprised at all. His arms easily lifted her up, straightened her out, and released her.

A little frazzled by the way his hands on her reminded her of their night together, she blinked him into focus and flashed a charming smile.

He didn't return it. "You need this job," he said flatly.

This wasn't worded as a question, but she knew he was asking nevertheless. "Yes," she said.

He didn't look happy. "You realize that you're totally overqualified. Why here?"

"I like the beach."

He stepped closer. "Why else?"

"I —" It was hard to think now, with him in her space. "I need the money to supplement the jingle income, at least until I get back onto a higher tier of products."

"You could play the piano," he said. "You're amazing. I bet you could get a job —"

"Not an option," she said flatly.

Sam studied her for a moment, during which she did her best to look like a woman with no secrets.

He clearly didn't buy it. "I've got a couple of problems," he said. "You lied to your brother about your job. And you don't want anyone from your reference list to know where you are." He stepped into her, his hands cupping her face, tilting it up to him. "Are you in some kind of trouble, Becca? Do you need help?"

Her throat tightened at the concern in his eyes, but she shook her head. "No."

"Then why?"

"I don't want to talk about it," she whispered.

His thumbs glided over her jaw. "I'm pretty sure I'm missing pieces to your puzzle," he finally said.

Yes, he was, but those pieces were for her only. Besides, *she* couldn't put herself back together again, so she didn't expect others to be able to do so. "Look, I'm no big mystery," she said. "Just a girl who could use a job."

When he spoke, his voice was surprisingly gentle, and nearly broke her. "If that's true, why not tell me what's going on? Maybe I can help."

She closed her eyes. He'd already helped and didn't even know it. "I just want to go back to being successful at something on my own."

He was quiet for a moment. "There's more to this story," he finally said.

Fed up, she tossed up her hands. "Well, of course there is. Isn't there more to you than being a sexy, grumpy surfer? Are you going to tell me why *you're* all tough and guarded?"

"No," he said. "But I'm not asking you for work, either."

She let out a breath. "I'm going to do a great job for you," she said, the one thing she was utterly confident about. "Isn't that enough?"

He just looked at her, and she sighed. "Look, if I suck," she said, "you can let me go. No hard feelings, I promise."

"And what about our other feelings?"

This stopped her. "Aren't we done with those feelings?"

He considered this, and then set her heart to racing when he slowly shook his head. He then stepped even closer and pulled her into him. Their thighs brushed. Other things touched, too, her soft abs to his deliciously concrete ones, for example, as he slowly lifted her to the counter. He splayed his big, callused hands on her thighs and spread them so he could step in close.

He was hard, deliciously so.

Her breath caught. Her heart kicked.

Lowering his head, he ran the tip of his nose along her jaw, and then his mouth was there, too, on the sweet spot beneath her ear.

Her entire body gave a hard tremble, and she tried to close her legs but he was still between them. His index finger lifted her chin, and their eyes held as he let his lips touch hers. Then he threaded his hand through her hair, tilted her head farther back, and kissed her again, parting her lips, slowly stroking her tongue with his own.

When he finally released her, she realized she was gripping him tight. She let go and blinked as she struggled to regulate her air intake. "Okay, so we're not done with those feelings," she admitted.

He just looked at her, all dangerous and alluring. "You wouldn't like working for me," he said.

He had no way of knowing that she could handle just about anything. "I can handle you," she said, "even if you can be a little bit badass and hard."

"Sometimes harder than other times," he said, and she blushed.

His eyes heated.

"You know what I think?" she asked. "I think you're all hard-crusted on the outside, but you don't scare me because I know the truth."

"And what's that?"

"That on the inside, you're soft and gooey," she said.

"You're wrong about the soft."

She gave a slow shake of her head. "It's a compliment. There's nothing wrong with soft. I'm soft."

"On the outside," he agreed. "And I love it. But you're pure steel on the inside. I love that, too."

"Are you going to hire me?" she asked.

"The girls are insisting."

"The girls?" she asked.

"Cole and Tanner."

She smiled.

A faint one curved his lips as well, but his eyes remained steady. Solemn. "There are conditions, Becca."

"Oh, boy," she said.

His smile met his eyes at that, but it faded and she got Serious Sam again. "If we work together," he said, "we're not sleeping together."

"Because you'll be my boss?"

"Because working with someone and sleeping with that same someone is a bad decision."

"And . . . you don't make bad decisions?"

she asked. "Ever?"

"I try very hard not to."

Well, good for him. But she didn't happen to have his self-restraint or discipline. She'd made a lot of bad decisions, and apparently that wasn't going to change anytime soon. "Are you saying I need to pick between the job and sleeping with you again?"

"*Again?*" Cole asked.

Becca turned to the door where, yep, Cole stood, looking fascinated by their conversation.

"Shit," Sam said. He strode to the door and shut it in Cole's face. Turning back to Becca, he went hands-on-hips, looking ticked off.

But Becca was annoyed, too. And a little insulted to boot. He thought she couldn't separate out their physical heat from the job. Or even worse, he was worried she'd get attached to him and yell at him about being dead inside . . . "You know there's a difference between having sex with someone and having a white picket fence with that someone, right?" she asked.

He just looked at her.

Okay, so it wasn't playtime. And she wasn't feeling playful anyway. "Seriously, Sam? You want me to choose?" Her lips were still tingling from the kiss he'd laid on her, and if she was being honest, so were other parts of her body — such as every erogenous zone she owned. This was because she now knew *exactly* what he could do to her. Which was more than any man in far too long. If ever.

And he, apparently, could take it or leave it.

Take or leave *her.*

"I pick the job," she said. Look at that, it was an easy decision after all.

He didn't react. He just studied her for a long beat. "The hours are five to two," he finally said, giving her no clue as to how he felt about her decision.

"Five . . . *a.m.?*" she asked in disbelief.

His lips twitched. "You want to change your mind?"

Oh, hell, no. Even if she loved to sleep.

"You could get better hours playing at the Love Shack for their dinner crowd," he said.

"I want *this* job."

"And your brother," he said. "Didn't he offer you a good-paying job?"

"Not interested."

Again she received a long look. And again she got a little tummy quiver. He was good at evoking that.

"The early start is because we're almost always booked for an asscrack-of-dawn deep-sea trek or a sunrise scuba tour. We need someone to open up shop, start the coffee, greet the customers, and answer the phones."

"What about the later part of the day?" she asked. "Don't you take people out for sunset or whatever?"

"Yeah, but it's the mornings and midday when we get the most traffic. We can handle the evening stuff ourselves for now."

Five. In the morning . . .

"Think about it," he said.

She looked out the window. Tanner and Cole were stripping off what looked like scuba gear. They'd both lost their shirts, leaving them in just board shorts.

Holy hotness, Batman.

"In New Orleans, my office view was the brick wall of the building right next to me," she said. "This view is better."

She didn't hear Sam move, but suddenly she felt him at her back, warm and strong and stoic as ever. Her eyes drifted shut as he stroked a finger down the side of her throat, making her body tremble yet again.

Yeah, he was real good at that.

He was good at a lot of things, she was discovering.

"Think about it," he said again softly.

And then he was gone.

144

CHAPTER 10

Becca knocked on Olivia's door and waited. After a moment, she felt movement behind the peephole and knew she was being studied. She hoisted the bag of sandwiches she'd just bought from the diner. "Hot pastrami on rye," she said, waving the bag enticingly. "And fries."

The door opened. Olivia's gorgeous dark hair was piled up on top of her head, held there with a fabulous silver-and-pearl clip that Becca knew had to be vintage. Olivia looked her usual beautiful and remote, but there was something new.

She was covered in paint.

"What are you doing?" Becca asked.

"You can't hear my paintbrush as I paint my bathroom?" Olivia asked. "Because the insulation is so nonexistent, I can hear you breathing when you're not playing your keyboard."

Well, crap. "How do you know it's not

my radio?"

"The radio doesn't have the musician swearing *Oh shit, that sucks* after each song."

Good point, Becca thought. She sighed. "I'll keep it down."

"I like it," Olivia said.

"You like my playing, but not necessarily me?"

Olivia shrugged. "I made you pizza," she said. "Which I don't do for anyone else. So I must like you a little. What's with the food?"

"Funny you should ask. I'm actually trying to bribe you into liking me more." She waved the food again. "Is it working?"

"Maybe." Olivia peered at the bag and inhaled deeply. "Did you say fries?"

"Yep. And brownies."

Olivia narrowed her eyes. "*Store*-bought brownies?"

"Yes," Becca said, "but give me a break here; I need a friend. And trust me, store-bought is way better than my homemade."

Olivia didn't look impressed.

"They're from the bakery," Becca said, which was a little piece of heaven and everyone in town knew it.

Including, it seemed, Olivia. "Yeah, okay," she relented, and let Becca in.

Olivia's place had been transformed. The

open, empty warehouse was now filled with warm, comfy furniture, floor lamps, and throw rugs. "Wow," Becca said. "It looks like a real home now."

"That's the idea." Olivia dug into the food like she hadn't eaten all day.

"What's behind there?" Becca asked, gesturing to an antique screen that blocked off a good third of the open space.

"Overflow stock for my store. Now you. You're doing the hot surfer."

Becca choked on a bite of her sandwich.

"Sam," Olivia clarified.

"I know who you mean," Becca said on a laugh. "I'm just not sure my question and your question are on equal measure."

Olivia smiled. "Yeah. You're totally doing him. You going to eat your brownie?"

Becca sighed and handed it over. "I want points for that."

"You get points for the hot surfer."

Sam punched in the phone number for Becca's first reference. He was leaning against their front counter. Tanner was sitting on it, absently rubbing his aching leg, watching him. They'd just come in from a scuba excursion with a bunch of college students, which had been a little bit like herding wild horses.

"You trust her," Tanner said, reading her application on his tablet. "Or you wouldn't have slept with her."

Jesus. "Cole has a big mouth," Sam said in disgust.

Tanner flashed a grin. "Cole didn't tell me shit. You just did."

Sam considered putting his fist through that grin.

"You won't," Tanner said, reading his mind.

"Only because I wouldn't want to mess up your pretty face."

Tanner couldn't be deterred. "So," he went on. "You trust Becca, which means you're calling those references for something else. It's about *her,* not you. You're wondering about her."

Wondering. Worrying . . .

"You could do this the old-fashioned way, you know," Tanner said, "and just ask her what you want to know."

"Calling her references is the smart thing to do," Sam pointed out. But Tanner was right, he *did* trust her. At least as much as he trusted anyone. What he didn't trust was the flashes of unease he sometimes saw in her pretty brown eyes, or her claims that she wasn't in trouble.

He wanted to know her story.

Her first reference was her boss at the ad agency.

"Excellent employee," the guy said when he came on the line. "Hard worker, loyal, compulsively organized. A great office manager, not so great at the jingles. We were sorry she had to leave town so suddenly. I'd hire her back in an instant as an admin, but she said she wouldn't be coming back to New Orleans for a while. Shame. Still, she's on contract for the jingles, and I'll take what I can get from her."

Next up was a co-worker. "Becca Thorpe?" the woman asked. "Loved her. Very hard to see her go. She struggled with jingle writing, I know, but she didn't struggle to keep us organized. Such a sweet thing, too. She'd give a stranger the very shirt off her back. Certainly gave much of her life over to her family. Her brother mostly. That was a rough situation, but she's resilient. You'd be lucky to have her."

Sam didn't believe in luck. Sam believed in good, old-fashioned determination and making one's own path. He knew what his path was.

But now he wanted to know about Becca's.

Not in the mood to put together a meal for

herself, Becca went back to the Eat Me diner for dinner. She was half-way through bacon and eggs — nothing said comfort food like a hot breakfast for dinner — when an old woman slid into the booth across from her and smiled.

"Hi," she said to Becca. "You don't know me, but I know you. And I just wanted to say that you play the piano like an angel."

"Um," Becca said. "Thanks."

The old woman just kept smiling at her.

Where Becca had come from, if a stranger slid into your booth, you had your cell phone in hand, your thumb hovering over 911. Especially if that stranger knew something about you, like, say, the fact that you played the piano — which you'd told no one.

But the thing was, this stranger was barely five feet tall, had blue-gray bristle for hair, matching blue-gray eyes gone filmy from age, and wore bright red lipstick. She also had more wrinkles than an uncooked chicken, and a harmless-looking smile that Becca didn't buy for a minute.

"I'm Lucille," she said. "I kinda run this place."

Becca looked around. "The diner?"

"No, Lucky Harbor."

"So you're the mayor or something?"

Becca asked.

Lucille smiled. "Not the mayor, but actually, that's a great idea. I'm more of a . . . social organizer."

"Oh," Becca said, having no idea what a social organizer might do for an entire town, but impressed that a woman of her age had a job at all.

"I was at the bar the other night, late," Lucille said. "I got my hormone meds mixed up and couldn't sleep. Jax makes a mean hot toddy."

Becca went still. Late the other night she'd walked to the Love Shack, and when the bar had emptied out, she'd played. "I didn't see you."

"I know," Lucile said, smiling. "I'm geriatric stealth. You're an amazing piano player, anyone ever tell you that?"

Becca felt nauseous. "Maybe once or twice."

"You playing tonight?"

"No." Maybe.

"I'd sure like to hear you again," Lucille said.

"Sorry, but I don't play for an audience." Anymore. "I write jingles now."

"Yeah? Like what?"

"Like for soup, and toilet paper." She grimaced, thinking of her latest assignment, which she still hadn't figured out. "I'm currently a little bit stuck."

"Really?" Lucille brightened. "I'm real good at making stuff up. What product?"

Crap. "Diaxsistheerectiledysfunctionmed."

"What's that?" Lucille cupped hand around her ear. "Speak up, hon, I'm old as dirt."

Becca sighed. "It's Diaxsis."

"Shut the front door," Lucille said on a wide grin.

"It's an erectile dysfunction med —"

"I know what it is." Lucille cackled and rubbed her hands together in delight. "And now you're speaking my language. What are you stuck on exactly? You oughta write a song that someone of an age could sing to her man! Like how he shouldn't be embarrassed to need the pill, 'cause us women need *it,* and by *it* I mean —"

"I know what you mean!"

"I'm just saying, those commercials all miss my age demographic. We're not dead yet, you know."

"I'll take that into consideration," Becca said. "Soon as my muse comes back."

"Maybe your muse needs a distraction. Something to fuel your creativity. You ever teach music?"

Becca actually found a laugh at that. She'd

played music, dreamed music, worked for and about music, ate and slept music, then run like hell from music, but she'd never taught. "No."

"Could you?"

"Well, probably," she said slowly. "But . . ."

"But it'd be better if it was, say, younger?" Lucille asked, reading her mind. "Like, young, eager-to-learn school-aged kids?"

"Well, maybe," Becca said, failing to see where this was going.

Lucille grinned. "I was hoping you'd say that. The rec center needs someone to teach kids for Music Hour on Monday, Wednesday, and Friday afternoons. I'm on the board, and you have no idea how happy everyone'll be that I found you."

"Wow," Becca said, impressed. "You tricked me."

"Only a little. We'd pay you."

Becca had already been shaking her head, but she stopped at the pay part. "You would?"

"You bet. We'll need references, of course, someone who could vouch for you not being a felon or anything of that nature." Lucille slid her a card. It said ORACLE OF LUCKY HARBOR and gave a cell number, website, and a physical address. "The website is my Pinterest," Lucille said.

Becca stared down at it. "I've been to your boards."

Lucille smiled. "Yeah, they're good, right? I used to be on Facebook, but got kicked off. The addy's for my art gallery. Email me your résumé and references today, okay? We can get you going by tomorrow. The kids'll be so excited."

By the time Becca got back home, she was excited, too. Maybe she couldn't play in front of people, but she could sure as hell teach kids to do so. She sat on her bed and played around on the keyboard, determined to come up with something for Diaxsis and get it off her plate. After a few hours, she had a jingle. She hadn't been able to give Lucille her wish about aiming the song at the eighty-ish crowd, but hopefully they'd appreciate it anyway. She sent it off and then crawled beneath her covers, her thoughts on the fact she now had *three* jobs.

She could only hope at least one of them worked out . . .

When Becca's alarm went off the next morning at the obscene hour of zero dark thirty, she spent a moment revisiting the pros of the charter job. Or, more accurately, the cons. But in the end, she rolled out of bed, showered, dressed, and made her commute into work, which was the short walk across the alley.

Cole was already there. "You look like you could use some coffee," he said. "Maybe the new girl could do it."

Becca laughed and headed to the coffeemaker. She went through the motions while yawning, and then realized nothing was happening. The coffeemaker was playing possum. She waited another moment, yawning again. Outside, the sky was dark. This was because the sun hadn't risen yet, since it was five oh five.

In the morning.

She actually wasn't even sure that she'd ever seen this time before.

And still no caffeine emerged from the coffeemaker. "I'm counting on you," she said to it. "I need you, bad."

"Sometimes you gotta give it a good whack," Cole said, looking more awake than anyone should ever look at this ungodly hour. He was in loose board shorts and a T-shirt advertising some dive shop in the Caicos.

Unlike her, who in deference to the early chill was in jeans, boots, a tank, a tee, *and* a sweatshirt, complete with hoodie, hat, scarf, and gloves. Yes, it was summer, but this was Washington State. At this time of morning, it was forty degrees, and she believed in comfort over style.

"Here," he said, nudging her over. "I've got it. If Sam shows up before there's coffee, he'll bitch like a little girl."

Becca had seen Sam grumpy, but he was more of a silent grump. She couldn't imagine him actually bitching about anything, and at her expression, Cole laughed. "You ever catch him early in the morning?" he asked.

"Nope." He'd been long gone from her bed by daylight.

"Well, he's a bear," Cole said. "We usually just toss him some caffeine and then stay out of arm's reach until it sinks in." Cole hit the side of the coffeemaker.

Nothing happened.

He went to hit it again, but the door opened and in came the bear himself. He was dressed almost identically to Cole, with the addition of a backward baseball cap, his mirrored aviator shades — even though the sun still wasn't up — and a scowl. He met her gaze, and despite that scowl, something shimmered between them.

Becca knew she wasn't going to survive this without caffeine, so she smacked the side of the coffeemaker like Cole had.

"What are you doing?" Sam asked.

156

"Working."

"No, I meant why are you beating the shit out of the coffeemaker?" he asked, his voice still morning-gruff, like he hadn't used it yet.

She had no idea why she found that so incredibly sexy. "Cole said I have to beat the thing up to get it to work."

Sam gave Cole a head shake and came up behind Becca, reaching an arm around her to stroke the machine. "Come on, baby," he murmured. "You know what I want."

Cole snorted.

Becca melted.

And the coffee machine purred to life.

"Show-off," Cole said, and headed to the door.

"Hey," Sam said. "Where are you going?"

"Tanner's on the boat. We've got a group of eight."

"Yeah, I know," Sam said. "Because *I'm* taking them out with him."

"Uh, no. I am," Cole said.

"Uh, no," Sam said, imitating Cole's voice. "*You're* training the new girl."

The "new girl" grimaced.

Cole shook his head. "*I'm* with Tanner today. It's on the schedule."

"No, it's not," Sam said.

Cole pulled out his phone and began to

thumb the screen furiously.

Becca raised her hand. "Yeah, hi. If one of you would just train me already, I'd be able to straighten out this very sort of thing."

Cole looked up from his phone. "No one can *ever* straighten this shit out."

"I can," she said, doing her best to look confident in that fact. Scheduling was a piece of cake. It was writing jingles that was killing her. "I'll bet you."

"Competitive little thing," Cole said to Sam. "I like her."

Sam looked at Becca. "You lost your last bet," he reminded her.

And the one before that, but who was counting. "I won't lose this one," she said, determined. *Desperate.* She had to get something right. This was it, she could feel it.

She felt Sam's gaze linger on her, felt the weight of his consideration. "Is everything a competition with you?" he asked.

She met his green eyes, and like it always seemed to between them, the air shimmered.

"Ha! It finally loaded." Cole waved his phone beneath Sam's nose. "See? I *am* the one scheduled for this morning."

"You changed it," Sam accused.

Cole's expression went innocent. Far too

158

innocent. "Why would I do that?"

"So I'd have to stay and train the newbie."

"Oh, for God's sake!" Becca exclaimed. "Standing right here!"

"He didn't mean it," Cole told her.

"Yes, he did," Sam said.

Cole rolled his eyes. "I'm heading out," he said to Becca. "We're on radio. Our Float Plan's behind the counter. We'll check in. Have fun." He paused and sent Sam a quick look. "And whatever you do, don't let him intimidate you. He's all bark, no bite."

"I'm not worried," Becca said. She was sure she could handle Sam. She took a peek at him. His expression was cool, irritated, and not in any way as friendly as he'd been while buried deep inside her body. She amended her earlier thought to *possibly* she could handle him.

"You'll be great," Cole said, patting her shoulder. He took one last look at Sam's face. Whatever he saw there made him smile. "But maybe you should go a little easy on him; he's had it rough."

She looked at Sam's face, too. "Rough as in dating gorgeous blondes named Selena who yell at you in the alley, or rough as in getting to go boating all day long for a living?"

Cole tossed back his head and laughed. "You get a raise for that. I'll tell our accountant." He turned to Sam again. "Give her a raise."

"Sam's the accountant?" Becca asked.

Cole was full-out grinning at Sam now. "Yeah."

Sam narrowed his eyes and Cole sidled to the door just as Tanner stuck his head inside. "Come on, man, paying customers waiting."

"We were just discussing who gets to train the new girl," Cole said.

"I'll do it," Tanner said, flashing a smile at Becca. "I'd be happy to."

Sam jabbed a finger in the direction of his partners. "You. And you. Outside," he said, shoving his glasses to the top of his head. "Now."

Once again, the three alphas moved outside.

Becca moved to the window and watched their shadows have a huddle in the predawn light. This time, unfortunately for her, the window was closed. Still, their body language was fascinating. They stood close — no avoiding eye contact. Clearly they knew each other well enough to get in each other's faces without worrying about the niceties.

Becca's inner circle consisted of family, her mom, dad, and brother, and they were pretty laid-back, go-with-the-flow kind of people. They'd rather pull their own teeth than have a confrontation or hurt anyone's feelings.

Especially Jase's. Her brother was the desperately yearned-for son, the prodigy, the wonder child. He had to be protected and coddled and taken care of, at any cost. Always and forever. Becca had been tasked with this, and she'd done her best, even through his stress and anxiety and ultimate pain pill addiction. She'd done everything she could for him, until it had cost her.

Big time.

She'd left to save herself, and there'd been no fight about it. No discussion at all, really.

Unbelievably, the silhouettes of the three big tough guys didn't fight, either. They stepped back from each other and . . . began a game of . . . rock paper scissors?

Less than a minute later Sam strode back in.

"You won," Becca said, surprised.

He gave her a long look. Nope, he hadn't won.

He'd lost.

CHAPTER 11

"I called your references," Sam said.

Becca sucked in a breath. She'd known he would, because no matter what their appearances, he and his partners were not just three fun-loving guys. They were also sharp businessmen and smart as hell. "And?" she asked.

"You were widely beloved at your last job, and everyone was sorry to see you go." He paused and gave her a long, speculative look. "In such a hurry."

Her heart skipped a beat.

"Care to explain the hurry?" he asked.

"No."

"There was a rough situation with your brother."

She felt herself go still. "What?"

"One of your references mentioned it. Said you were resilient, though, and that I'd be lucky to have you."

Becca closed her eyes.

"Is he the one who hurt you?"

She opened her eyes and met his, and the concern in them. "I never said anyone hurt me."

"But someone did."

"Jase wouldn't hurt a fly," she said.

Sam didn't point out that she'd just given him a non-answer, but it was in his gaze as he poured a mug of coffee, then surprised her by handing it over.

She took it, then began to add creamer and sugar. Sam poured another mug and leaned back to watch her add more sugar to hers. "So you take a little coffee with your sugar then?"

Grateful for the subject change, she shrugged. "I like it sweet."

He drank from his steaming mug. "I like it hot."

She got all tingly, damn it. No more tingling for him! Feeling very warm suddenly, she unwrapped the scarf from her neck.

Sam remained silent, but his lips tipped at the corners.

She tugged off her gloves as well.

"Déjà vu," he said.

At the mention of her striptease in her bathroom, she felt herself blush. "It's cold here in the mornings. Very cold."

163

"Bird bones," he said.

She opened her mouth and then shut it. "Okay, I'm trying to drum up some outrage at being compared to a bird," she finally said. "But I have to admit, it's better than some other things I've been told about myself."

"Such as?"

"I once had a date mention something about a Butterball turkey."

Sam went still. "Did you kill him?"

Becca knew she wasn't heavy, but she was curvy. She used it to her advantage when she dressed. It was only in her . . . undressed activities that sometimes her insecurities came out. "No."

"Want *me* to kill him?"

"No!" she said on a laugh. "It can be true, from certain angles."

"Bullshit." He didn't make a move toward her, didn't touch her with anything but his eyes, which were flashing temper now. "You're perfect."

She laughed again, and he smiled. "Your body," he clarified. "Your *body's* perfect."

"But the rest drives you crazy," she reminded him.

"*Everything* about you drives me crazy." He drank his coffee and set down the mug. "So. You've made a choice."

"Actually, that was you," she reminded him. "I'm not on board with the whole having-to-choose thing. At all." Deciding to let him digest that, she took a moment to look around.

The hut had a front counter, several stools in front of it, a love seat, and a small refrigerated drink display and snack shelf. One entire wall was taken up with a display: scuba gear, snorkel gear, a paddleboard, a kayak, paddles, and more. "So what's the routine?" she asked.

"No routine, every day's different." He walked with her behind the counter. "But this is where you'll be most of the time." He unlocked a drawer and pulled out a laptop. "The schedule's here, but there's a problem. It's never up to date because we end up just scratching stuff down whenever and wherever we answer the phones."

She looked at the stack of notes on napkins, scribbled on paper bits, and even on a piece of wood.

"Yeah," he said to her unspoken question. "Asinine, we get that. But the Internet is painfully slow — Cole's working on that — and in the meantime, this is our way of dealing with it."

"Because you're guys?"

He lifted a broad shoulder. "What can I

say, we're messy and unorganized."

"Which is how both you and Cole showed up for the same job this morning," she said, boggled at the chaos.

"Actually, no. Cole's a cheat, and can be bought by a pretty face."

"A pretty face?"

"The client's an LA print-ad model whose parents live here in Lucky Harbor. She's home for a short visit, and as she always does, she's taking her brothers and dad out fishing."

She narrowed her eyes. "Which is why you and Cole were fighting for the job."

"Actually," he said, "all three of us fought for it, but Tanner won."

"Fought?"

"We raced to the end of the harbor and back for it."

"Tanner's the fastest runner?"

"Swimmer."

Her eyes bugged out. "You guys *swam* from here to the end of the harbor and back?"

Sam shrugged. "Even with his bad leg, Tanner's a fish; no one can catch him. But then the client added four friends, so Tanner needed an assist."

"And you wouldn't have minded . . . *assisting.*"

He shrugged again, which translated — in guy speak — to no, he wouldn't have minded assisting.

"Men are annoying," she said.

He didn't look bothered by this blanket assessment of his species. "We don't do the clientele."

"Or the employees," she said.

"Or the employees." He pointed to the phone. "That's going to ring all day. People call for information. They ask questions or want to see about booking a trip. We've been trying to build a mailing list, so when the calls come in, we've been gathering contact info for a database."

He was standing close. He didn't have much of a choice; the space behind the counter was tight, and he was big. Normally, she really liked her own space bubble, and in fact got claustrophobic without one, but with his hair still damp and curling around his ears from a recent shower, and his warm, strong bod so close they kept brushing together, claustrophobia was the last thing she was feeling.

"The gist is this," he said, either ignoring their chemistry or no longer feeling it. "We have a fifty-foot Wright Sport boat. We're available for hire for just about anything. Cruises, deep-sea fishing, whale-watching, snorkeling, scuba diving — novice or expert. Tanner handles most of the planning and charting of the scuba, snorkeling, and fishing expeditions. He's lucky as hell and can always find the sweet spot. Cole's the captain of the boat, and our mechanic."

"And you?" she asked. "What is it you bring to the table?"

He met her gaze. "I'm the people person."

She laughed, and he actually flashed a smile at her. "Okay," he said. "That might be a little bit of a stretch."

"You do okay," she said softly.

Their gazes locked, and then his dropped to her mouth. "I have my moments."

His voice gave her a rush of warmth, but before she could say anything else, the phone rang. Sam gestured for her to sit at the stool and answer. As she picked up the receiver and said "Good morning, Lucky Harbor Charters," Sam pulled over the second stool. Their thighs brushed, his hard and muscled.

The space behind the counter seemed to shrink even farther.

"Hi," the caller said in her ear. "I heard you guys might have a big summer bash, complete with fireworks. Is that true?"

Becca looked at Sam.

Sam shook his head.

Becca put the call on hold.

"It's something we talked about," Sam said. "A sort of customer-appreciation thing. But no one has time to even think about it."

"I can do it for us," she said.

He went brows up at the *us,* but he shook his head again. "It's too much work, the organization of the party, and fireworks and —"

"What do you have against fireworks?"

His look said he realized she wasn't referring to actual pyrotechnics, but the hot sparks between the two of them. "*No* fireworks," he said. "Besides, none of us is certified to do a fireworks show."

"I thought all males knew how to blow stuff up."

"I didn't say we don't know how. I said we're not certified."

"So we hire someone." She tapped the computer. "Show me your schedule for August."

Sam leaned in, and his fingers worked the keyboard. Their thighs were still touching, and so were their upper arms. He was big and toasty warm, and he smelled good enough to lick, but she controlled herself.

He'd chosen.

And then she'd chosen.

Sam showed her the screen and then didn't move back, which she found interesting.

And arousing.

Their August schedule was indeed already busy. Plus, she had to take into account all the trips that hadn't made it onto the calendar yet because they were still floating around as scribbled notes, but there was still room. "You have the beachfront, right?" she asked.

"Yeah."

"So let's throw that customer-appreciation bash," she said.

He just looked at her.

"You have me now," she said, and felt herself blush again. Why was everything sounding sexual? "I can help with the planning and the work."

He just looked at her some more.

"Okay, I'll plan *all* of it," she said. "Your clients will love it."

"Are you always this relentless?"

"Yep. Stubborn as hell, too. Sorry, I forgot to put that on my job application." And then, sensing his acquiescence, she leaned in and kissed his firm, hard mouth. She'd meant it to be just a quick peck to soften him up, but that's not what happened. In fact, it was the opposite of what happened,

170

because he hauled her off her stool and onto his lap.

One of his warm, hard arms banded around her hips, the other hand cupping the back of her head, tilting it to the angle he wanted. And then he claimed her mouth like he meant it. In less than two heartbeats, he'd made her forget her own name, that she had a caller on hold, and what day of the week it was. When he was done — and he took his sweet-ass time about it, too — he lifted his head and surveyed her expression, his own a lot more mellow, his eyes heavy-lidded and sexy.

Clue one that she wasn't the only one affected. Clue two was currently poking her in the butt. She had one arm tight around his neck and the other hand fisted in his hair, holding on. That was all she could ever do when he got up in her space like this — hold on for dear life.

With one last indiscernible look, he dropped her back into her chair.

"We having fireworks or what?" she managed.

"Shit," he said, and scrubbed a hand over his face. "Yeah. We're having fireworks. More than I realized, apparently."

With a smile, she picked up the phone. "Yes," she said to the waiting customer.

"We're having a bash complete with fire-works. If you leave your information, I can make sure you're in our system, and that way you'll get our invite."

Sam shook his head when she'd hung up. "Hope you can pull this off," he said.

"I can." With her eyes closed. She was good at organizing and planning. Really good. "What else do I do?" she asked.

Sam showed her a list of services and prices so that the next time someone called, she'd be prepared to book a trip. "Stick to what we've got listed here," he said. "Don't add anything new unless you check with one of us. If anyone needs something you can't answer, Cole or Tanner are on radio."

"But not you?"

"I don't typically spend a lot of time in here," he said.

"Because using your people skills is really hard on you?"

"Yeah," he said drily, "and because if I'm not out on the water, then I'm in the shop working on the financials, or building a boat." He stood up. "Another thing you'll do is check out our rental equipment. Snorkel gear, paddleboards, kayaks . . ." He moved to a door behind her and opened it up to a back room.

Sam led her in there and flicked on the

light. There were no windows here. The place was tight quarters and filled to the gills with gear and equipment on racks that looked well taken care of and perfectly organized. One wall was lined with a huge industrial sink.

"The cleaning tank," he said. "We bleach the rental gear between uses to hotel standard code."

She nodded but took in the dark, closed-in feel of the room. The claustrophobia was relatively new, as far as her neuroses went, and even as she thought it and remembered what had caused it, the air was sucked from her lungs. "You need a bigger hut," she whispered.

"Undoubtedly," he said, his back to her as he eyed the shelves. "You ever snorkel? Paddleboard? Kayak?"

She swallowed hard. "Not a lot of that where I came from."

He laughed quietly, and she might have reveled in the deep, masculine sound, but she was starting to sweat. The walls were closing in on her; she could feel them. "Um, I need to . . ." She gestured to the door, and practically leapt back to the front room.

She thought she'd covered her tracks pretty well as she leaned casually against the front counter and managed to stay still while sucking in big gulps of air, but when she looked up, Sam was standing close watching her.

He didn't try to touch her, for which she was grateful. Touching her in the midst of a burgeoning anxiety attack only made it worse. "Whew," she said with a fake smile. "It's hot back there, right?"

He walked to the glass-fronted fridge and pulled out a bottle of water, which he uncapped and then handed to her.

She gulped it down, grateful he was going to let her have her little freak-out. "I'll learn all this stuff real fast," she promised.

He met her gaze. "You have nothing to prove here, you know that, right?"

Uncomfortable with the straightforward, brutally honest words that conflicted with his oddly gentle voice, she just nodded. "I know."

"But if the guys and I are out on the boat and you get a customer, you've got to be able to go in there," he said quietly.

"I know. I get it. I'll be fine." She held her breath, thinking he was either going to fire her on the spot, or push for details.

He did neither. "All right," he said, apparently trusting her. He could have no idea how much that meant to her, and it took her a moment to swallow the lump in her throat.

He didn't miss that, either. He simply gave her the moment she needed, watching her closely but not interfering as she got her shit together. "Hang on a second," he said, and vanished into the equipment room for a moment. He came back with a tote slung over one broad shoulder.

He held out a hand, which she took without even thinking, and let him lead her down to the dock. The boat was gone, but he opened the tote and spread out some gear. "Consider this lesson number one," he said.

"For what?"

"Life."

She laughed. "What does snorkeling have to do with real life?"

"Teaches you how to live in the here and now, for one thing." He looked up at her in the early dawn light to see if she got him.

She got him.

"Plus you need to know how this stuff works," he said. "If you stick, we'll have more lessons."

"I'm sticking."

He didn't respond to this. Instead, he stripped out of his ball cap and T-shirt, rendering her mute.

He slid into the water and showed her how to work the snorkel gear.

She nodded a lot, and said "uh-huh" a lot, and tried not to drool. When he was done, he effortlessly hoisted himself out of the water and back onto the dock. He shook like a big, shaggy dog, spraying her with water.

"Hey," she said.

He surprised her with a quick grin that short-circuited a few brain cells. Then he gathered the gear and carried it back to the hut and into the equipment room, dumping it into the sink to be cleaned. She watched from the doorway while he returned everything to its place and then moved aside for him to pass.

Instead, he stopped with her in the small space. "You okay?"

"Yes." Even with him near, she was okay. Actually, she was more okay than usual — and she had no idea what to make of that.

His mouth smiled, but his eyes remained serious. And possibly a little bit sympathetic, which she didn't want to see, so she moved into the front room. And because her knees were a little weak, she sank to the couch.

"Is it tight spaces?" he asked quietly, "or being in tight spaces with a man?"

She stilled, hating that she'd been so

transparent. She studied her feet, and then picked at a nonexistent piece of lint on her sweatshirt.

"I see," he said.

But he didn't see. He couldn't possibly see . . .

He pulled on his shirt again, and then his hat, and crouched in front of her, balancing with ease on the balls of his feet. "Customers aren't allowed back there, period," he said. "Now that you're on board, none of the three of us needs to get into it, either. It's all your domain during the hours you're here. Got me?"

He was saying that she had no reason to feel anxious here. A warm feeling filled her stomach and started to spread. She smiled, and this time it was real again. "Got you."

He studied her for a moment, and his mouth quirked. "You're going to be good for us," he said. "You smile like that at any of our customers, and they'll be lining up for our services. Ready for more training?"

"Ready."

Once again he moved behind the counter with her. They stood close and remained that way while he showed her how to check the equipment in and out. In doing so, they kept brushing against each other, and she began to heat up again. She pulled off yet another of her layers, leaving her in just the tank top that was now sticking to her like a second skin.

Sam closed his eyes, took off his baseball cap, shoved his fingers through his hair, and then replaced the cap. Everything about him said big, bad, frustrated testosterone overload. She met his gaze.

"You're right," he said. "We need a bigger hut."

CHAPTER 12

That day Becca went to the rec center after work. Lucille had called and said they'd be waiting for her. Assuming she was going in for an interview, she changed into a cute sundress from Olivia's store, added a denim jacket and wedge sandals, and made her way over there.

She was met by a really great-looking guy in navy-blue cargoes and a polo shirt with a firehouse insignia on the pec.

"Jack Harper," he said, offering her a hand. "Fire marshal. How you doing?"

"Great." She pulled her résumé from her bag. She'd doctored it up some. Okay, a lot. "I know I don't have teaching experience, Mr. Harper, but I do have a four-year degree in music and —"

"Jack," he said, and took her résumé, which he promptly scanned and then rolled up and shoved in his back pocket. "And you're hired." He gently nudged her down the hall and to a classroom, filled with at least twenty kids, all in the neighborhood of . . . young. "You've got an hour and a half with them. Good luck."

"Wait." She grabbed his arm. "Are you telling me I start now?"

"Actually," he said, looking at his watch. "Five minutes ago. And between you and me, I wouldn't dally. They're good kids — until they get bored."

Indeed, the natives were restless. She could see two girls, twins by the look of their matching wild red hair and toothless grins, climbing up on their desks to do God knew what. A couple of boys were throwing balled-up paper at each other. Two more were crawling beneath the desks on some mysterious errand.

Jack swore beneath his breath, leaned into the classroom, and gave a sharp whistle.

Everyone froze.

"Good," Jack told them. "More of that. Pink and Kendra, get down. Alex, Tray, Jose, and Carlos, don't make me come in there." He paused while everyone got into their seats like little angels. "Now stay just like that," he commanded, "until Ms. Thorpe says otherwise. She's the boss, and what the boss says goes."

"Impressive," Becca muttered to him.

"Trust me, that'll only work for a minute tops," Jack said. "If all else fails, there's a bag of candy in the teacher's desk. Use sparingly. Sugar's their crack."

"But . . ." She stared at the kids. "I didn't realize I'd be starting today. I don't have a curriculum. Or instruments. Or —"

"We have some stuff that was donated." He fished a key out of his pocket and set it in her palm. "In the storage closet." He gave her a quick heart-fluttering smile. "Good luck."

He'd handled the kids with a few quiet, authoritative words, no problem, and she hoped to do the same. Heart pounding, she walked into the room. "Hey, kids. So who likes music?"

Everyone's hands shot straight up into the air like rockets.

Becca smiled in relief, walked over to the storage closet, and unlocked it. There was a pile of flutes and a string bass that had seen better days. There was also some percussion — and by that she meant two beat-up snare drums, a set of crash cymbals, and a xylophone. It all gave her a bad flashback to middle school band practice.

Turning from the closet, she pulled her iPad mini from her purse and brought up her keyboard app.

Immediately six of the twenty kids were able to do the same on their phones. "Look at that," she said. "We're halfway to a band already."

The kids cheered. Laughing, Becca pushed her desk back, sat on the floor, gathered everyone around her, and did the only thing she knew how to do.

Plowed her way through.

The next day, Sam was at work in his warehouse. He'd sheathed the wood hull with a layer of fiberglass cloth for durability, both topsides and bottom. Now he was applying resin, making the weave of the cloth virtually transparent, bringing out the wood's natural tone. The result was a stiff, strong, stable, watertight composite wood/epoxy/fiberglass hull that was virtually impervious to the effects of moisture. He was concentrating, his every muscle aching from the strain, so that he almost didn't hear the door open and close.

Almost. Because here, in his shop, he heard and saw everything. He never invited anyone in here. Even Cole and Tanner rarely ventured in.

It was his place, his zone.

He didn't turn to look at the door; he didn't have to. He recognized the footsteps as Becca's. Soft but not hesitant, her spontaneity and easy joy showing in every step despite whatever life had handed her — which clearly hadn't been all rainbows and kittens. Boggling, and a little bit scary.

"Hey," she said, coming up behind him. "Is it okay for me to enter the Man Cave or do I need to perform the secret handshake or something?"

He laughed. "Smart-ass."

"Sorry," she said, not looking sorry at all. "My mouth's always been a problem."

Yeah, a *big* problem. He remembered that mouth, and exactly what it felt like traveling the length of his body. Even now, in the light of day, her lips were full and shiny with gloss, and he had a hard time looking away from them. And then there was the fact that she smelled like peaches and cream.

He wanted to eat her alive.

"I've got a few messages for you." She stepped to his side, taking in his work. "Pretty," she said. "Is there a good profit in making boats?"

"Not really."

She ran a hand over the sleek wood. "So you do it because . . . you're good at it?"

"No."

She looked up at him. "Okay, man of mystery. If not for the profit, or to show it

183

off, then why do you build boats?"

"For myself."

"For yourself?"

"Yeah," he said, and because a slight frown had formed between her brows, he reached out and stroked a finger there to ease the tension. "You should try it sometime," he suggested. "Doing something for yourself."

"I moved across the country for myself."

"That's not why you moved," he said.

Something flashed in her eyes and was gone. "You think you know why I moved?" she asked.

"You needed to get away from something," he said.

She made a noncommittal kind of noise, not giving a thing away. Then she paused. "So what do you think I should do for myself then?"

"Whatever feels right."

She stared at him for the longest beat, and then she surprised him. She stepped close, so close they were toe-to-toe and everything in between, and his only thought was Oh, Christ, *this* feels right. He let his hands go to her hips.

"Something for myself," she murmured.

"Yeah."

"Hmm." Her hands rested on his chest,

her fingers gripping the material of his shirt over his pecs. He wasn't sure if she was holding on for courage or because she wanted to touch him.

"I haven't been able to think of something to do for myself for a long time," she said.

"And now?"

She stared at her hands on him. "I still might need help in that area."

He tipped her face up to his and looked into her eyes, and he saw that she had courage in spades. "Several things come to mind," he said.

"Are these things . . . good for me?" she asked.

"Not a single one."

She both laughed and trembled against him, and damn but that shouldn't send lust rocketing through his veins, and yet it totally did.

"Good's overrated anyway," she whispered.

He couldn't believe how much he wanted her. Wanted to press her up against the boat. Or bend her over it. Both ways, he decided. All ways. "We said we weren't doing this anymore," he said, more than a little shocked at how gruff his own voice was and at the need coursing through him. "Not while you work for me." And he'd meant it.

He fucking one hundred percent had.

"No, *you* said that," she reminded him. "*I* didn't sign on for the not-doing-it program. And besides —" She made a big show of looking at the time on her phone. "I'm off the clock." She smiled at him guilelessly. "Lunch break. And last I checked, it wasn't an employer's business what his or her employee does on their lunch break."

Closing his eyes, Sam let out a long, admittedly shaky breath. He was in trouble here. Big trouble. "Becca —"

"Shh," she said. "Or the boss'll fire me. We have to be really quiet. Really, *really* quiet." And then she rocked her hips into him.

And rocked his world. Because just like that, he was a dead man. He tightened his grip and groaned at the feel of her, and she murmured "Shh" again, softly, sexily.

Using the hand he had tangled in her hair, he drew her in closer. Meeting him halfway, she went up on her tiptoes and snagged an arm around his neck. He already knew she kissed like she appeared to do everything else: with her entire heart and soul.

In other words, amazing.

He was halfway to heaven, his tongue buried in her mouth, his hands full of warm, soft, curvy Becca, when a throat clearing had her jerking away from him.

Sam was much slower to lift his head, to let go of her sweet, hot body and register that Amelia stood there, smile in place, brows arched in that way mothers the planet over had nailed down.

"I brought you cookies," she said, "but you look like you're already having your dessert."

Sam bit back his sigh. "Amelia —"

Amelia arched her brow further.

Years ago, maybe the second or third time he'd landed in her house, she'd tried bossing him into a curfew. He'd been a smart-ass and had called her Mom. He'd been joking, but she'd liked it, preferred it, and to this day she made him call her that. *"Mom,"* he corrected.

"Better. Now, don't mind me," she said, coming into his shop the way no one else ever did.

Well, except the woman who'd been in his arms only a few seconds ago, the woman now staring at Amelia, gaze confused, probably wondering at the "Mom" thing.

Amelia smiled a warm welcome at Becca as if she was the hostess at a tea party. "And you are . . . ?"

"Becca."

"Ah," Amelia said, offering a hand. "The

new hire." She sent Sam a long, hard glare that wasn't all that hard to interpret. It said: *Why are you tangling tonsils with the new girl?*

Sam scrubbed a hand over his face and took the container of cookies from Amelia. "Becca, Amelia is Cole's mom and —"

"Just Cole's mom?" Amelia interrupted, eyes flashing.

Well, shit, here we go, Sam thought. "And okay," he said. "Also a sort-of mom to me."

Amelia snatched the container of cookies back, making Sam grimace.

"You know what I mean," he said.

"No," she said. "You'd best clarify. Immediately, if you want these cookies. And let me just tell you right now, they're your favorite — double fudge with chocolate chips — and they're my best batch yet. And also, keep in mind that what I just saw going on in here is blackmail material, so make it good, sweetheart. *Real* good. *Sort-of* mom?"

There were few people who'd ever gone out on a limb for Sam, and he didn't even need the fingers of one hand to count them. Amelia was one. "How about you were the only mom I ever had?" he asked.

"Oh." Her beautiful blue eyes filled, and she sniffed as she stepped toward him, her arms outstretched. "Oh, Sam, you're so sweet."

Sam endured her hug and a kiss to each of his cheeks, and then she was gone. "Sorry about that," he said to Becca, who was nibbling her lower lip, her thoughts seemingly far away. "You okay?"

"She was like a mama bear with you," she said, sounding a little bit awed. "She'd probably fight to the end for you."

"Would, and has."

When she just looked at him, he let out a breath. "My mom died when I was five. My dad was never real great at being a dad. I landed in foster care. A lot."

Her eyes softened. "Oh, Sam."

"Amelia used to take in the occasional foster kid, and the minute I ended up at her place, she . . . claimed me." He gave a small smile. "She's protective."

"That's where you met Cole."

"Yeah."

"He claimed you, too," she said.

"The apple didn't fall far from the tree there," he agreed. "But we claimed each other."

"That's incredibly sweet." Her eyes were suspiciously shiny, but before he could get a good look, she turned to the door. "I gotta get back to work."

And then she was gone, too, leaving him to wonder at the sadness he'd seen in her gaze. Had no one ever been willing to fight for *her*?

CHAPTER 13

Becca tossed and turned, one odd and uncomfortable dream chasing another. Her parents were there, only they weren't her parents. They were her employers, asking her to take care of Jase.

"I already do," she said.

"You left him. You walked away," they accused.

And then Jase was standing there with him. "You did," he said. "You left me."

"No, I —" But she broke off when Jase turned into Sam.

She reached for Sam but he took a step back and was flanked on either side by Cole and Amelia.

"We've got him," they said.

She stared at them, seeing the bond, and turned back to her family.

Her parents and Jase had vanished.

She was alone. Feeling an odd sensation in her chest, she looked down and saw her heart crack in half. With a gasp, she sat straight up in bed.

She looked down at her heart. Still in her chest. That was good. As to whether or not it was cracked in half, that was another question entirely.

It was four-thirty. Since there would be no more sleep, she checked email and saw that she had one from the ad agency.

Her Diaxsis jingle had been accepted, and she'd been sent her next assignment. Eagerly, she'd loaded the doc and read.

The assignment was for a line of personal hygiene products.

She flopped on her back and stared at the ceiling, allowing a few moments of self-pity. When she was over herself, she sat up and stared at the email for another moment. Then she hit REPLY, responding with what she thought was calm grace, explaining that she realized she had to earn her way back into good graces after her year-long slow spell, but that she felt she'd come through twice in a row now and wanted a better product to write about.

Like, say, something, anything, that wasn't mortifying to put on her résumé.

It was hours later before she got a reply.

This is what we have. Take it or leave it.

She took it.

The day was a hot one. Sam went for a predawn run with Ben and then found himself trapped in his warehouse office hunched over the books for hours, sweat running down his back.

Or maybe he was hot because he'd headed to the hut earlier to check on Becca and had found her running his world with an ease and charm he'd never managed, wearing a snug white tee and bubblegum-pink shorts, looking heart-stoppingly amazing.

At the memory, he reached into his fridge to grab a badly needed soda and discovered it empty. Tanner, of course. The guy would walk all the way over here to steal Sam's last soda rather than hit the store.

Sam rose to go himself, when someone knocked on the open doorjamb.

His dad.

And behind him, Becca.

"Hey, son." Mark said this tentatively, and he had good reason. He rarely made an in-person visit, preferring the telephone to suck Sam dry.

"Dad," Sam said. "What're you doing here?"

Mark set a lopsided-looking snowman on Sam's desk.

"Found this in your mom's storage," Mark said. "You made it for me, remember?"

Sam remembered. He'd been seven and looking forward to a promised fishing trip. Sam had made the clay snowman with the lady who babysat him while waiting for his dad.

And waiting.

Mark had never shown.

"I know you don't like company in here," Mark said, "but your cutie-pie admin here told me where to find you. She said it'd be okay."

Sam gave his "cutie-pie" admin a long look.

Becca met his gaze, her eyes filled with sympathy.

Which, for the record, Sam hated.

"He wanted to see you," she said apologetically. "I know you don't like unannounced company in the Man Cave, but it's your dad, right? So I locked the hut and put up a sign saying I'd be right back."

Mark beamed at her. "You're great. Isn't she great, son?"

Sam thought about bashing his head against his desk. "Yeah. Great. What's up, Dad?"

Mark shrugged. "Nothing. Just came to see you."

"You never come to see me," Sam said.

Instead of responding, Mark turned his head and looked out into the open area of the warehouse, eyeing the boat Sam was building. "Impressive."

"I already put money into your account," Sam said, crossing his arms.

"Yeah." Mark didn't meet Sam's eyes, but kept them on the boat. "Thanks."

"Christ," Sam said. "It wasn't enough."

"No, it was enough," Mark said. "It was great. It's just that . . ." He trailed off.

"What?" Sam said. "It's just that what?"

"She kicked me out. Changed the locks and everything."

Sam stared at him. "Let me guess. She also wiped out your account."

Mark lifted a shoulder.

"Are you fucking kidding me?" Sam asked.

No longer smiling, Becca stirred. "Sam —"

"*Again?*" Sam asked Mark. "Seriously?"

Mark sighed with clear misery.

Sam wasn't moved. At all. They'd done this dance too many times. Hell, all Sam's life. His dad never learned. Nor, apparently, did Sam. "Why can't you do what you did last time and grovel?" he asked. "Or whatever it is you do that reels them in."

"Sam, he's got nowhere to go," Becca said

softly. "And —"

"Already told her your sob story, I take it," Sam said over her head to his dad.

Mark looked guilty as hell and Sam shook his head, working on not grinding his back teeth into powder.

"I thought maybe I could stay here," Mark said. "I'll stay out of your way."

Sam's gut tightened. Having his dad here would kill him. Or drive him to kill his dad.

One or the other.

"Mark," Becca said softly. "Can you give us a minute?"

"Sure, darlin'," Mark said, and with one last look at Sam he stepped out of the office.

"He said he's had some problems," Becca said quietly.

"Yeah," Sam said. "Lots of them. He gambles, he drinks, he lies. Pick one. You shouldn't have brought him here, Becca."

"Not her fault," Mark said firmly, back in the doorway. "She tried to tell me that no one comes in here without permission, so don't you blame her."

"And yet you came anyway," Sam said. "You took advantage of her sweetness and pushed your way through with one of your bullshit emergencies."

"It *is* an emergency," Mark said.

"Sam," Becca said with soft reproach. "He's —"

"No, darlin'," Mark said. "Don't defend me. It's okay. I deserve his mistrust, believe me." He met Sam's gaze. "I'm sick."

Sam felt this news reverberate through him. He searched his dad's expression. The truth was there, and his gut tightened painfully. "How sick?"

Mark grimaced.

"Cancer?" Sam asked. "Your heart?"

"No." Mark paused. "Liver stuff."

Sam drew in a long, unsteady breath, unable to reconcile all the years-old resentments with the new and terrifying fear for his dad's health. "I've got a spare bedroom at the house," he said. He spent the majority of his time here. This was his *real* home, his *first* real home that he'd gotten for himself, and he wasn't sure he could share it with his dad.

"Thank you," Mark said, with genuine humility. "I won't be a bother."

Feeling like a first-class dick, Sam reached into the desk, pulled out a key, and tossed it to his dad.

Mark pocketed it with a nod of his head. "See you later then. Love ya, son."

Sam closed his eyes, and when he opened them Mark was gone. Not quite trusting

197

himself to speak, he stayed still. After a moment, he felt a gentle hand slide up his back.

"You okay?" Becca asked.

He was a lot of things. Gut sick. Angry. Furious, even. And afraid. One thing he was not was okay. Shoving free of the desk, he dislodged her hand, picked up the snowman on his desk, and chucked it across the room.

It shattered on the far wall.

Becca leapt back, inadvertently slamming herself into his desk. At the impact, she jumped away and then tripped over his trash can, hitting the floor on all fours.

"Jesus." Sam crouched down and reached for her. "You okay?"

It was her turn to shove free of him, and he discovered he didn't like the feeling very much as she got to her feet on her own.

He got slowly to his as well. "I'm sorry. I didn't mean to scare you."

She shook her head. "You didn't. I . . . saw a spider. It's gone now."

Shit. He really was an asshole. "Becca —"

"I'm . . . fine. Totally fine."

"You said it twice."

"So?" she asked.

"Saying it twice implies that you're not fine at all."

"No. Saying it twice makes it true," she said.

Sam let it go because she was desperately trying to calm her breathing while not meeting his gaze. He watched her hand shake as she lifted it to push her hair from her face.

"Becca," he said softly.

"I'm sorry, I shouldn't have brought him back here without asking —"

"It's not your fault. Becca —"

"Is he really sick?" she asked, clearly not wanting to discuss her reaction.

"I have no idea, but I'm going to find out."

She stared at him. "And if he is?"

"I'll take care of him."

She eyed the snowman on the floor in a thousand pieces. "My break's over," she said, moving to the door.

As gently as he could, he caught her by the wrist and slowly reeled her back in. Her breathing was still a little off, and her eyes were far too bright, but she met his gaze. "What?" she asked.

There were lots of *whats* going through his mind, but he settled on one. "You're safe here," he said. "You know that, right?"

"Of course I know it."

"I was just pissed off because —"

"He drives you crazy. But he's your dad. I get it."

He could see that she did, but they were going to have to circle back to that fascinating subject because it wasn't what he wanted to cover right now. "You thought I was going to hurt you."

"No," she said. "Of course not."

Chest tight, he bent his knees to look into her eyes as he slowly slid his hands up her arms to cup her face.

"My break's over," she said again.

He shook his head and pulled her into him.

She remained frozen for one beat, then relaxed against his chest, pressing her face into his throat. They stood like that for a long moment. "I didn't think you were going to hurt me," she said. "I just . . . you surprised me."

"I lost my temper." He pulled back and met her gaze. "It doesn't happen very often, but I can lose my temper and not hurt you."

She nodded. "I know."

He wanted to believe that. He pulled her in again but the phone started ringing, accompanied by that stupid red light Cole had put in to be funny, and Becca backed away. "Later," she said.

Sam tried to go back to the books, but after an hour he gave up. He pulled out his cell and called his dad. "Define liver problem."

There was a long pause. "I don't know medical shit."

"Dad." Sam rubbed his temple. "Be straight with me. For once."

"It's a liver problem," he repeated.

Sam drew in a deep breath and let it out slowly. "What's the plan?"

"My insurance's crap."

Of course it was. "What's the plan," Sam repeated.

"I don't know yet. I'll fill you in when I do." Mark paused. "Your woman's a real catch, you know. You should hold on to her."

"She's not my woman, dad. She's my employee."

"Son, if that's true, then you're not as smart as I've always thought. She gave me a sandwich."

"Becca gave you a sandwich."

"Yeah, and she put chips on it. The girl's brilliant, I tell you."

"When did she feed you?"

"After I left your shop, I sat on the beach for a while, then wandered back to the hut. Becca asked if I needed anything, and I said not unless she had a sandwich, and she said she *did* have a sandwich, and yeah. It was amazing."

"You realize that you probably ate *her* lunch."

"She said she didn't want it."

Sam rubbed his temples again but it didn't help. The headache was upon him. "She was just being nice," he said. "Next time, if you're hungry, come to me. Got it? Not her, never her."

"Why not?"

"Because she'd give you the shirt off her back, Dad." *And you'd take it . . .*

"She said it was okay," Mark said stubbornly. "She said I could go see her any time I wanted."

Sam could actually feel his blood pressure rising. Before he had a stroke, he said, "I've got to go."

"You coming home soon?"

The thought of going home to his dad didn't help the blood pressure levels one little bit. "I don't know."

"Can't work the remote."

Sam closed his eyes. "I'll text you directions." He disconnected and considered throwing his phone, but then he spotted the pieces of the snowman still on the floor. *Shit.* He headed out and down to the hut, telling himself it was to get a soda.

He found his newest employee working the phones, the computer — hell, everything around her — with quick order.

When she saw him watching her, she tossed him the key to the back room. "Need two kayaks for these gents," she said, nudging her chin in the direction of two college kids waiting off to the side.

Sam caught the key but kept walking toward her until she was forced to tip her head up to meet his gaze. "You gave my dad your lunch?" he asked quietly.

Something flickered in her gaze. "Working here, Sam."

"You gave my dad your lunch."

"He was hungry."

"He's a fucking mooch, Becca."

"He's still your dad, Sam."

He dropped his head and studied his feet for a moment, then lifted his head. "Are you hungry?"

"No."

She wouldn't tell him if she was. He knew that damn well. Her picture was in the dictionary under Stubborn.

"The kayaks," she said, clearly not wanting to discuss this. Or anything. Not that he blamed her. He hadn't wanted to talk to her earlier, and she'd been right the other day when she'd told him she was a quick learner. She'd learned from him how to be emotionally unavailable.

■ ■ ■ ■

Sam watched the clock and tried to catch
Becca after work, but he got caught handling the boat with Cole because Tanner
had a previous commitment. By the time
they finished mooring it, the hut was closed
up and Becca was gone.

No strains of a haunting piano came from
her windows, and she didn't answer her
door. With no reason to stand there in the
hallway and wait for her like a stalker, he
went back to his shop to work. He had the
table saw on when a sound penetrated.

A piano?

He snapped off the saw and the music,
and lifted his head.

Nothing.

He was losing it. He went back to work,
but five minutes later he hit the switch again
when he was sure he heard a piano.

It stopped immediately.

And then he got it. She was only playing
when she thought he couldn't, or wouldn't,
hear her. Goddamn it. Dropping everything,
he strode out the door. Night had long ago
fallen. He had no idea what time it was.
Late.

Becca's place was dark, but he was on to

her now. He moved across the alley and knocked. She didn't answer, but he'd expected that. He pulled out his phone and called her.

No answer.

He texted: *Open your door.*

Her response was immediate: *Not home.*

Bullshit. He could *feel* her. He didn't care how crazy that made him, it was true. He knocked again, just once, softly. "Not going away, Becca."

There was a huge hesitation from the other side of that door; he could feel that, too.

Then it slowly swung open.

CHAPTER 14

Becca had answered the door against her better judgment, and at the sight of Sam standing there, a little bit edgy and a whole lot hot, she cursed herself for being weak. "You should be at home with your dad," she said, and started to close the door.

He caught it and held it open. "I have questions," he said.

"I'm busy."

He looked around at the apartment. "Doing . . . ?"

"Writing a jingle. A very important one." She crossed her arms. She'd admit she was writing for a line of feminine products . . . never.

"I'll start with an easy one," he said, apparently not caring. "Ben told me he saw a Snapchat of you teaching at the rec center."

"Snapchat?"

"It's an app where you send a picture, but whoever you sent it to can only see it for a few seconds —"

"I know what Snapchat is," she said. "What was I doing on it?"

"That's what I'm asking."

She stared at him. "One of the kids," she muttered. "My money's on Pink."

"So it's true?" he asked. "You're teaching music to kids?"

"Apparently."

He took that in for a moment and nodded. "It suits you. Moving on to the next question."

She leaned on the doorjamb, all casual-like, as if she wasn't aching at the sight of him so at ease in his own skin — which, by the way, was dusted with wood shavings. "You miss the I'm-busy part?" she asked.

His eyes softened. Warmed. "I'll make it worth your while."

Her knees wobbled. Stupid knees. "No, you won't," she said. "You've gone all prim and proper and stodgy on me."

"Stodgy?"

She shrugged.

He stared at her, then let out a sound that might have been a laugh as he hauled her in close and personal, and kissed her right there in the doorway. It was a really great kiss, too, all slow and long and deep and hot.

Finally, when she was good and speech-less, he pulled back and looked into her eyes. "Why do you play the piano when you think I can't hear you?" he asked.

Still not the question she expected, but not exactly one she wanted to answer, either, so she dropped her gaze from his beautiful, piercing eyes and looked at his throat. But this only reminded her that she liked to press her face there and inhale him because he always smelled amazing, like the ocean, like the beach, like one hundred percent *yummy* man. "That's ridiculous," she finally said.

He put a hand on her stomach and nudged her clear of the doorway, then stepped inside her apartment.

"Hey," she said.

He eyed the portable piano keyboard on her bed and the blankets wrinkled like she'd just been sitting right there playing — which, of course, she had.

He turned back to her, brow raised.

She crossed her arms. "I —" But she broke off because he got right in her pre-cious space bubble. Like he'd forgotten he'd made her choose between him and the job. She'd been trying to maintain some dis-tance, but it wasn't easy because . . . well, because she still wanted him, damn it. And she especially couldn't maintain any distance with the taste of him still on her tongue.

Then he cupped her face and made her look at him, and she couldn't remember her name much less why she didn't want him to cup her face like she was the most precious thing in his life.

As if.

"Why do you play the piano only when you think I'm not listening?" he asked again, his eyes unwavering, telling her that her answer really meant something to him.

She closed her eyes.

He merely shifted closer. "And why," he whispered against her lips, "are you giving me attitude when you used to give me sweet, like maybe you *want* to piss me off so I'll go away and leave you alone."

"Because I want you to go away and leave me alone," she whispered back.

"Because you don't want to talk about things," he said, calling her on it. Didn't he know that wasn't the polite thing to do? The polite thing to do was let her hide, damn it.

"You prefer to live in your head instead of the here and now," he said.

"Correct," she said back, and gave him a long look from beneath her lashes. "And anyway, you've asked your questions.

Where's my *worthwhile*?"

His gaze heated about a gazillion degrees as he leaned in and kissed first one corner of her mouth, and then the other.

She tightened her grip on him, closed her eyes, then moaned and dropped her head to his shoulder when he stopped.

"You still work for me?" he asked, voice gruff.

Great. They were back to that. "Unless I'm fired."

"If I fired you, would you go get a job that better suits your abilities?" he asked.

"Like?"

"Like . . . being a full-time music teacher. Or writing more jingles."

"Because I just love writing about feminine products." Damn it, she hadn't meant to let that slip. "If you laugh," she warned, "our friendship — or whatever this is — is over."

He paused, as if doing his best to bite back his amusement. "How about doing whatever floats your boat?"

"Why do you care about what floats my boat?" she asked.

He didn't have an answer for that, apparently, since he said nothing, just looked at her with those eyes that seemed to see far more than she wanted him to.

"Stop worrying about me," she finally said. "It's not your problem. *I'm* not your problem."

"I don't know what kind of men you've had in your life, Becca, but that's not how I work."

"What are you saying? You're in my life?"

"Yes."

She didn't know what to make of that, so it was her turn to say nothing, but she couldn't help but stay a little too close. It was his warmth, she told herself. In any case, she wasn't the only one feeling . . . things. She could feel him still hard against her. "Your body doesn't agree with the not-sleeping-with-your-employee decree."

"You know I still want you," he said. "That's not exactly a secret. But I want to know what happened today in my office more."

She pulled back, but he caught her. "It was nothing," she said.

"Becca." His eyes were still on hers, his voice low but oddly gentle, as if he knew she'd just told a big, fat whopper.

And then, oh God and then, he cupped her face yet again and lowered his head, brushing his lips across hers. "It was a lot more than nothing," he said with another soft, devastatingly gentle kiss.

She sighed and pressed her face into his neck.

"I get that you don't know this about me yet," he said. "But you can trust me."

She lifted her head. "I do trust you."

"Not yet, you don't." He let his thumb glide over her lower lip, the one tingling for more of his mouth. "But you can," he repeated.

"Sam —"

"You'll tell me when. I won't push, Becca." And then with one last soul-warming kiss, he was gone.

Over the next few days, the guys were busy nonstop and nearly always gone. During that time, Becca had plenty to keep her occupied. Her mind was something else entirely. She wondered what Sam would do if she said *When*.

She wondered if she even could say *When*.

Lucille stopped by to visit.

"Thought I'd see about trying paddle-boarding," the older woman said.

Becca tried to picture Lucille on a paddle-board in the harbor, but mostly all she could see was the Coast Guard trying to rescue her. "Um . . ."

"You don't think I'm too old, right?" Lucille asked.

"Well . . ."

"Because I keep in great shape." Lucille pointed to a biceps. "I've been hauling cans of prunes to the senior center all morning —"

"It's just that the guys are out of town," Becca said. "And first-timers need instruction."

"Oh." Lucille sighed. "Damn. That's a shame."

"A big shame," Becca agreed.

"I'll just come back another time." But she didn't leave. Instead, she made herself comfy on a stool. "So how's the jingles going? What are you working on?"

Becca sighed. "Feminine products."

Lucille grinned. "Sorry, honey, can't help you with that one. I don't need 'em anymore. Why don't you get something good to write about, like denture glue? I need a new brand and could use a suggestion."

Once Lucille finally left, Becca took a lunch break and went to work on a curriculum for the kids at music hour. She needed to keep them busy, she discovered, or tiffs broke out among their ranks over who got to play what. So in addition to teaching them basic chords, they were working on how to respect other people's space bubble. The latter was a far more difficult lesson, but it would come along.

Everything would come along.

Or so she told herself in the deep, dark of the night when her insecurities beat the crap out of her.

After another homemade meal with Olivia — to-die-for lasagna this time — Becca finally wrote a passable jingle for the feminine products and sent it off.

And late at night, when she couldn't sleep, she played. Afterwards she'd walk home from the Love Shack at two-thirty in the morning, alone with the salty ocean breeze and the moonbeams and her own troubled thoughts. A few nights back, on her first night playing, she'd heard something, someone, and she'd run the half mile to the warehouse, slammed into her loft, and with the lights still off plastered herself to the side of one of her windows.

Just in time to watch Sam vanish into the shadows.

The second night, she'd felt him as well, but when she'd stopped in the middle of the street and spun a circle to confront him, she'd been alone.

The next morning, when he'd come in for coffee, she'd searched his calm, even, handsome features for some sign that he was walking her home every night, but he gave her nothing.

So she kept it to herself. Because she knew what he was doing. He was just trying to give her back something he thought she was missing — her music. She appreciated that, even as she resented the fact that she was also missing something else.

Him in her bed.

You'll tell me when.

The man confused the hell out of her. But denial had always been her friend, and that hadn't changed. Early one morning, she unlocked and opened up the hut. She might have been hired to answer phones and greet customers, but she'd taken over handling their website, too. And then there was the ongoing planning for the upcoming Summer Bash, which had taken on a life of its own.

She started the coffee, brought up the schedule, handled all the charter's online email and site correspondence, and then got to the Summer Bash stuff. Sam had reluctantly signed off on the pyrotechnics contract, the band, and the promos on Facebook and Twitter.

Becca was still planning out the logistics, hiring high school kids from the rec center for the setup on that day, renting tables and chairs and awnings. She was figuring out the decorations, too, some of which she'd found in the back storage room. She'd hauled out a big duffel bag filled with strings of white lights, wanting to use them along the dock and to decorate the boat. Problem was, the lights were literally in a huge ball, a tangled mess.

She'd been working on that here and there, and was at it again, sitting cross-legged on the floor, when Sam came in. He strode straight for the coffee. Saying nothing, he brought his mug up to his delectable mouth and eyed her over the rim as he drank. When the caffeine sank in about two minutes later, he finally spoke. "Mornin'."

"Morning." She paused, wondering which direction to take this conversation. Were they mad at each other? Still circling each other? Ignoring each other?

She gestured to the stack of paper, napkins, and whatever else they'd been writing email addresses on for months. "I realize you all had a system going here with this lovely pile, but I have good news — my system's better. I've got you all caught up."

He smiled. "Glad to hear that. You've been busy."

"More than you know. Right now I'm working on the decorations." She gestured to the big mess of lights in front of her.

Stuck on yet another knot, she swore beneath her breath. "And by the way, this is a really stupid way to store your lights."

"Yeah, and if Tanner sees that mess, he'll kill Cole. Tanner's pretty fanatical about the equipment." Sam hunkered in front of her, took the ball, shoved it back into the duffel, and rose, slinging it over his shoulder.

"What are you doing?" she asked.

"Taking care of it."

"You're going to untangle that mess?" she asked.

"I'm going to take care of it," he repeated.

Okay then. So she rose, too. "How's your dad?"

"Sprawled out on my couch watching movies and eating me out of house and home."

"So he's . . . okay?"

"I don't know," he said. "I'm seeing his doctor later today."

Sam didn't give off a whole lot of "tells," but neither did he hide much. If he was feeling something — anger, amusement, arousal, whatever — he didn't seem to have much of a problem showing it. When his gaze met hers, she saw hints of worry mixed with irritation.

He didn't yet know what to think, and he was withholding judgment until he knew.

Which made him a whole lot smarter than her.

She tended to react first and think later. Hence the dreaming about him. The yearning for him. The kissing him the other night . . . In order to not repeat that mistake, she tore her eyes off his fine-ass self and instead looked at the walls.

There were a bunch of pictures, and she'd had a lot of time to study them. Most were of clients, some holding up large fish, others in scuba gear or just mugging for the camera on the boat and dock. There was one of a younger Sam, along with Cole and Tanner and another guy, the four of them on what appeared to be an oil rig, looking pretty badass. The next picture was in the same locale, but just Sam, Cole, and Tanner, with Tanner on crutches. "Seems like it must have been a real rough job," she said. "And dangerous."

Sam nodded, though to which she couldn't say. Maybe both.

"Did Tanner get hurt out there?" she asked.

"Yeah." He came to stand next to her, his gaze on the picture. "We nearly lost him along with Gil in a rig fire."

"Oh, my God." She turned back to the pic of the four men. She looked at Gil, so

218

young, so full of life, and felt a pang for what they'd been through. "I can't imagine how awful it must have been."

"It sucked."

Sam didn't use a lot of words. He didn't need to. The few he chose were effective. She imagined *It sucked* covered it all. She took in the rest of the pictures, one with the three of them on a smaller boat than the one currently moored outside. "You've upgraded," she said. She turned to face him. He was wearing black board shorts today and a plain gray T-shirt. No ball cap this morning, but his sunglasses were in place. "You've given yourself a great life here," she said, realizing she was more than a little envious. "Working with your closest friends. All the adventures . . ."

A customer walked in. Actually, four customers, college buddies who wanted to rent surfboards along with Sam's expertise to tutor them. Becca logged the equipment rental, and Sam headed out with them.

On the beach, all of them stripped out of their shirts, but Becca had eyes for only Sam. She tried not to look but she honestly couldn't help herself.

Then he turned back, and caught her staring.

She considered dropping to the floor like

she'd done when she'd gotten caught staring at him before, from her apartment, but it was far too late for that.

"Hey, Peeper," he called, and crooked his finger at her.

Damn. She met him halfway on the dock.

"You got a suit?" he asked.

She tore her gaze off his chest. "Suit?"

"A bathing suit," he said, looking amused. "Are you wearing a bathing suit under all those layers you're so fond of?"

"Yes," she said. "But I don't know how to surf."

"Lesson number two, in five minutes."

Oh, my God. "I don't —"

"You're still living in your head," he said. "Can't live in your head when you're surfing. On the water, you live for the here and now. Log yourself out a wet suit so you don't get cold. Five minutes," he repeated. "Give yourself an adventure." And, as it turned out, he gave her the adventure. She wasn't ever going to become a pro surfer, but she'd had the time of her life.

Late that afternoon Sam walked into the town medical building for a meeting with his dad's doctor.

Dr. Josh Scott had been ahead of Sam in school by about five years, but they'd gone rock climbing together a bunch of times, so Sam expected to spend a few minutes bullshitting before getting to the nitty-gritty of his dad's health problems.

What he didn't expect was to find his dad in the waiting room.

With Becca.

"Hey," she said, coming to him. "Your dad asked for a ride."

Mark nodded but didn't rise. It was hard to tell if his small smile was the usual *I'm up to shenanigans,* or an apology. "Next time," Sam said, looking into Becca's eyes. "Call me. You don't need to spend your time driving him around."

"I don't mind."

"I do," he said.

Her eyes narrowed a little bit, but she said nothing. She turned to his dad. "You take care of yourself," she said. "And if you need another ride, or anything, you know how to get me."

Mark gave her a real smile. She leaned in and kissed his cheek, and then, without another look at Sam, headed to the exit.

"Becca," he said.

Her response was to shut the door, with her on the other side of it. Great. Sam turned his head and met his dad's gaze.

"Son, seriously," Mark said. "I really

believed you had all the brains in the family."

A nurse brought them to an exam room, and Josh came in wearing a white doctor jacket with a stethoscope around his neck and a ready smile. "Mark. Sam," he said. "Good to see you both. Sorry about the circumstances."

"And what exactly are the circumstances?" Sam asked.

Josh looked at Mark.

Mark looked guilty.

"You didn't tell him?" Josh asked.

"You do it so well," Mark said.

Josh gave him a pained look and turned to Sam. "Liver's failing. Slow, long deterioration, most likely caused by alcohol abuse. It's not acute. I've put him on meds and requested a diet that includes no alcohol and a moderate exercise plan. A lot of the time, the meds work and slow the deterioration down, but sometimes they don't."

Sam sat heavily. "And if they don't?"

"We'll see. Maybe a transplant if there's a serious lifestyle change," Josh said, and paused. He didn't say it, but Sam heard it — *if he's lucky.* Sam looked at his dad.

Mark met his gaze, the usual flash of guilt in his eyes.

Shit. "It's going to be okay," Sam said.

Mark nodded.

"It is," he reiterated, because like Becca said, saying it twice would make it so.

CHAPTER 15

"Sweet baby Jesus," Olivia whispered.

Becca hummed her agreement but didn't take her eyes off front and center, which was a pack of three surfers out in the water. Cole, lean and rangy. Tanner, with more bulk to his muscle.

Sam, of the broad shoulders and ripped abs.

Becca stared at them and took a lick of her ice cream.

Olivia stared at them, too, and took a lick of her ice cream.

It was Sunday afternoon, and they were both off work. They'd made a pit stop at Lance's ice cream stand on the pier, where Becca had also bought a bag of ranch-flavored popcorn for herself for later, and then they'd planted themselves on the sand to watch the show.

"I'd have paid money for this," Olivia

said. "Who's the deliciously mocha-skinned one?"

"Tanner," Becca said.

"Tanner's pretty damn fine," Olivia said.

"They're *all* fine."

Olivia snorted. "Like you're looking at anyone besides Sam."

This was true. Still, Becca tore her gaze off the guys to look at her cohort. "How do you know Sam but not Cole or Tanner?"

"Sam stopped one night on the highway when I had a flat tire and helped me fix it. Until I moved into the warehouse, I'd never seen the other two; they're not exactly my shop's usual clientele."

Becca smiled at the thought of any of the three guys shopping at the very lovely but very feminine store Olivia had created. "You could probably easily go out with either of them, if you're interested."

"I'm not," Olivia said. "At all." But she kept looking.

So did Becca.

That night, Becca FaceTimed with Jase, who was at her parents' house. He asked her again to come to Seattle for his upcoming concert.

And though Seattle was only two hours

from Lucky Harbor, she once again declined.

Her mom and dad tried to pressure her into saying yes. They were worried about Jase, and for good reason. But Becca couldn't carry that burden alone again, not even for Jase.

"He can't continue without your support," her mom said.

Becca wanted to say, *And what about me? Who's giving me support?* But it was far too late for that question.

Jase had nudged their mom out of the way and rolled his eyes at Becca. A we're-in-this-together gesture that was so familiar, Becca *ached.* He looked good, she thought. Great actually. Rested. He'd gained some of his weight back, but the telltale signs were there, and she knew why her mom and dad were worried. He talked too fast, too scattered, and his eyes were way too bright.

He didn't ask her about herself. He didn't dare, because he knew. And when Becca came right out and asked him if he was using, their connection was suddenly lost.

She tried calling him back but he'd gone radio silent.

And a radio-silent Jase was never a good thing. Anxiety kept her up all night, watching the moonbeams dance across her walls.

At dawn, she forced her concerns out of her head and went to work. Since she was early, she started the coffee and used her phone to search for cheap sheet music for the kids.

A minute later, Sam walked in. As he did every morning, he went straight for the coffeepot. He was in his usual uniform of loose, low-slung board shorts and a tight rash-guard T-shirt that clung to his mouth-watering body, complete with the cool sunglasses that made him look like the perfect combination of delicious and trouble. "Good weekend?" she asked.

"I worked on a boat."

"You did?" she asked. "I never saw you."

He eyed her over the rim of his mug. "Yes, you did. You and Olivia watched us surf."

"Oh." She felt the blush creep up her face. "Saw that, did you?"

"Little bit," he said, obviously amused. "So did Lucille, by the way. She posted a pic of you on Pinterest, and you both look like you might be drooling."

"It was really good ice cream," she said weakly, and desperately sought a subject change. "So, how's your dad?"

"He's facing liver failure, but there's meds, and his doctor is hopeful."

"And you?"

"I'm going to kick his ass if he screws this

up," Sam said simply. "He's not acting like a guy who got some really bad news. He's acting like he was awarded a trip to Disney World."

"That's because he's living with you. It's a dream come true for him."

Sam didn't say anything to this. Instead, he gestured to her phone screen. "What's that?"

Clearly, he'd made his own subject change. "I'm trying to find music for the kids."

"You get a budget, or you spending your own dough?" he asked.

"No budget." She shrugged. "It's not too expensive, and I want to do this right with them. What's going on with the lights?" she asked, pointing to the duffel bag on his shoulder.

He set it at her feet.

She bent down and unzipped it, and then stared at the neatly stacked lights, still in their packaging. "You bought new ones," she accused.

"Yeah, so?"

"So that's cheating."

"You had a problem, it's solved," he said simply.

She stared at him. Wasn't that just like a guy. "I could have untangled them," she said. "Eventually. I'd have saved you money."

"Now you don't have to."

Maybe she should have been annoyed. Instead, she felt that frisson of awareness skitter up her spine. His gaze met hers, his heated, and she had to remind herself to breathe. Not just awareness, she admitted, but hunger.

Need.

Damn. He was potent.

Luckily the phone rang, and she shook off the lust and answered, "Lucky Harbor Charters, how can I help you?"

Unluckily, she sounded breathless and . . . aroused.

Sam drank more coffee, but he had a definite smugness to him, cocky bastard.

"The grouch in yet?" Mark asked in her ear.

Becca watched Sam mainline the coffee and wondered if he was ready to face his dad this early. "Uh . . ." Sam's laser beam eyes were still on her. She smiled reassuringly.

He didn't return it.

"Darlin', I know he's there. If you're there, he's always nearby somewhere."

Was that true?

"How about you just hand him the phone."

Her gaze was still locked on Sam's. "Maybe I should take a message."

"Darlin', you're sweet. Way too sweet for the likes of him. And if I wasn't dying of liver failure, I'd prove it to you myself."

Sam took the phone from Becca's hand. "Stop trying to protect me," he told her. "And stop flirting with my employee," he said into the phone.

"Just showing you how it's done," came Mark's tinny voice, loud and clear, making Becca realize that Sam had heard everything his dad had said.

"You okay?" Sam asked.

"Never better. Except for the fact that I'm on my deathbed. But you, you're not okay."

"What are you talking about?" Sam asked.

"You've got a good couple of decades left before you've got old-man problems and need a blue pill to get it up, and you're ignoring that pretty young thing right in front of you."

Sam looked at Becca.

Becca busied herself by racing her fingers over the keyboard of the computer.

Sam leaned over her and booted up the dark screen.

Becca bit her lip and met Sam's amused

gaze. With a blush, she turned away.

"What do you need, Dad?" Sam asked. "I left you breakfast on the stove."

"Oatmeal's disgusting," came Mark's answer.

"Oatmeal's good for you."

"Sheila called," Mark said. "She wanted to remind me I promised to pay for the crib."

"Didn't she already steal all your money?" Sam asked.

Mark sighed.

"You ask for that paternity test yet?"

"Only an asshole would do that right now," Mark said.

"A *smart* asshole," Sam countered.

"It's not an expensive crib," Mark said. "I told her to go cheap with all this shit."

Sam rubbed the spot between his eyes. "You can't go cheap, Dad. Not with a baby."

"It's just a loan," Mark said.

"Uh-huh," Sam said.

"So . . . you've got enough to cover it?"

"Yeah, Dad," Sam said. "I've got enough."

"You're not going to have to steal it, are ya?"

"Dad —"

"Kiddin'," Mark said. "Sheesh. This kinda reminds me of when we needed rent money,

231

and you nearly got the shit beat out of you for —"

"Yeah, great times," Sam interrupted. "Gotta go. Check your account later on today."

"Love ya, Sam."

Instead of responding, Sam reached past Becca and hung up the phone.

"That was nice of you," Becca said into the heavy silence. "To loan him money."

"It won't be a loan."

She figured. "It's sweet he always says he loves you," she said. "Really sweet."

Sam looked like maybe he wanted to say something, but he didn't.

"What?" she asked.

"They're just words."

"Well, yes," she agreed. "But it'd be nice to hear them."

He looked at her for a moment. "So your parents, they never —"

"They're not . . . demonstrative." How the hell did they get on this? Oh, yeah. Her own big mouth. "I want to hear how you nearly got beat up."

"The rent was past due, and there was no food. We needed money." He shrugged. "So I found some."

"Found?"

"The apartment next door was a grow

house," he said. "The lady who ran the place liked me. She used to feed me sandwiches sometimes. I was in her kitchen when she was called to another part of the house. I went to her utensil drawer — which was where she kept her cash hidden — and borrowed some. Then I went to a house down the street where there was always a pool game. I doubled my start-up money in an hour. Where I got caught was trying to return the original amount to the utensil drawer."

She stared at him. "How old were you?"

"Thirteen."

"Holy crap."

He shrugged. "I was an old thirteen."

She imagined that to be true.

"My dad took a lot of shit from the neighborhood for it," he said. "We eventually had to move. It was really stupid of me."

"How was any of that your fault?" she asked indignantly.

He laughed. "I stole the money, Becca."

"You had no choice!"

"There's always a choice," he said.

She shook her head. "You were a kid. Practically a baby. You were stuck in a bad spot and didn't know better."

"The pool house where I played, those guys weren't exactly Boy Scouts. I brought some real trouble down on my dad's head."

She wondered if he always did that, took everything on his shoulders, but she already knew that he did. She rose out of her chair and moved toward him. And then, as he so often did to her, she got in his space and cupped his face. "Not your fault," she said.

He flashed a small smile that shifted his stubbled jaw against her palms and gave her a shiver of pure lust.

This seemed inappropriate given the conversation, so she let him go and stepped back. "So how many times did that happen, you nearly getting killed trying to keep you and your dad together?"

He made a noncommittal sound and turned to the counter to set down his empty mug, rolling his shoulders like his neck hurt. "You ask a lot of questions."

It occurred to her that he'd probably watered down the story, and hadn't even told her the worst of it. She moved close and set her hands on his shoulders.

His muscles were vibrating with tension.

"Shh a sec," she said, and dug into him, pressing her thumbs into the strained muscles.

He held himself still for a long moment under her ministrations, but finally she felt his shoulders drop and relax, and he let out a low, very male sound that seemed to have a direct line to her nipples.

"Seems like you do have a weakness," she murmured.

Reaching back, he grabbed her hand, bringing it to his mouth and kissing her palm. "More than one."

Her stomach fluttered. "So, tell me. Did you stay out of trouble after that?"

"Oh, hell no. There was the time I threw the football through the window of a different neighbor —"

"Ha," she said, laughing. "I did that, too. Only it was a softball. I had to work for a month on the yard, and my brother still teases me about it." She met his gaze and saw that he was smiling, but there was something else there. "Did you have to work on the yard to make up for the cost of the glass, too?" she asked.

"Not exactly. The ball sailed through the window and beaned the neighbor on the head, and gave him a concussion. Which wouldn't have been a problem, except he happened to be having sex with the woman who lived on the other side of him. While her husband was at work."

She gaped. "Serious?"

"Serious as the heart attack she claimed to have. The guy came after my dad with a tire iron."

"Oh, my God."

"Luckily my dad's tire iron was bigger," he said.

She blinked. "Holy cow. What happened?"

"My dad got arrested, and child services got involved."

"Oh, Sam," she breathed. "I'm so sorry."

He shook his head. "Don't be. That, and a whole host of other shit, landed me here, in Lucky Harbor. With Cole's family."

"And you don't blame yourself for any of it, right?"

He laughed, but the sound was mirthless.

She reached for his hand and entangled their fingers. "Okay, so you do blame yourself. I know you must feel pretty stupid about that, seeing as what I said before is still true — none of what happened was your fault."

He choked out another low laugh, but she could see how uncomfortable he was that he'd told her the story. She wasn't uncomfortable; she was the opposite. She was getting a real peek inside the tough, impenetrable Sam Brody, and she liked that peek. She liked the man. But she knew saying so wouldn't be welcome at the moment, just as she knew she had to lighten the mood or he'd leave. "You probably get a different reaction when you tell a woman that story, right?" she asked in a teasing tone. "You probably get all hugged up on and then taken to bed to be mothered."

His green eyes gave her a look that said he was on to her but that he'd play. "You want to take me to bed and mother me?"

"Well, mothering you isn't the *first* thing that comes to mind . . ."

He smiled. His arm slid around her waist, and he brought her up against his hard body. "That's good to hear," he said, "but I've never told a woman that story before."

"Why not?"

"You really do ask a *lot* of questions."

This was true. "It's the writer in me," she said. "Even if I'm just a jingle writer."

He laughed. "It's not the writer in you. It's the *nosy* in you."

"Maybe," she admitted.

"Once a peeper . . . ," he said, and kissed her neck.

She shivered. "It's hereditary," she claimed. "My parents, they're nosy about everything. Where's Jase's itinerary, what's Jase doing right now, why isn't he answering his cell, who's he seeing? Blah blah." She caught the look on his face and shut up.

"Does everything they're nosy about have

to do with Jase?" he asked.

From day one . . . "They don't really have to be nosy about me," she said. "I'm usually the together one. Terrifying as that is to imagine." She flashed a smile.

He didn't return it. Instead, he was looking at her like she was starting to make sense for him, and she didn't like the way that felt. "Jase has some . . . issues," she said. "He was born premature and almost died a bunch of times. He was small and weak, and played the piano like an angel. He wasn't exactly a popular kid. It didn't matter when we were traveling and playing together, but after I stopped, it was hard for him. I still protected him the best I could, but as it turns out, out I wasn't all that good at it." She paused. "He says he's been sober for a few months now, and I have high hopes he's being honest about it." Hope, but not a lot of faith.

"He's an addict?"

"Yes, but he's not a bad guy." And damn it, there she went defending him again. That was a hard habit to break.

"If he's a good guy, then why weren't you honest with him on the phone at the Love Shack?" Sam asked.

"Wow." She gave a little laugh, uncomfortable at the direction the conversation had

238

taken. Clearly, he believed Jase was a threat to her, but that wasn't the case. At all. "You have a long memory. I just don't want him worrying about me, that's all," she said. "He's got a lot on his plate with his upcoming tour. There's so much pressure there. He's got this huge musical gift, but he's not good at concentrating."

Sam looked into her eyes. Something intense there made her feel both good and just a little bit off her axis. "And what about you?" he asked quietly.

"What about me? I walked away from that life."

"Why?"

"I screwed it up. And *now* who's asking too many questions?" she asked. "Anyway, I went into jingle writing, and that's that."

"Everyone screws up, Becca," he said. "Some more than others." He raised his own hand in the air and waved it.

She laughed despite herself. "I'm not cut out of the same cloth as my family," she said. "I'm not nearly as talented. Jase is amazing. He's just not all that good about harnessing it. We're a dysfunctional family, I know, but I'm pretty sure that's the definition of family."

He nodded, clearly knowing all about dysfunction. "It's time."

"Time?"

"For lesson number three," he said.

The quick subject change threw her. As did how fast her body tightened at the thought of what that lesson might entail. At what she *wanted* it to entail.

"Boating," he said.

She sighed.

He laughed.

She gave him a little shove, or she went to, but he caught her up and surprised her by pulling her in for a hug that made her blow out another breath. "You know what you are, Sam Brody?" she whispered, wrapping her arms around his neck. "A big, fat tease."

They both knew there wasn't an ounce of fat on him. They also both knew exactly what she meant. She wanted him again. Still. And she knew she wasn't alone in that wanting. But she found she was alone in the falling. And she *was* falling, for him. She was falling for a guy who didn't intend to fall back. She got it, she really did. In Sam's head, love meant people relying heavily on you, and you couldn't necessarily rely on them back.

If she pursued a relationship with him, it'd be an uphill battle all the way, but that wasn't what held her back from saying

When. It was far simpler than that.

Just the one night with him had nearly ruined her for all other men. Another night would do her in for sure. "Boating sounds good," she said.

CHAPTER 16

Much later that night, Becca was sitting on her bed with her keyboard, staring down at her notebook where she'd scrawled some lyrics. She was playing her fingers over the keys, looking for a melody, when a knock came at the door.

She knew Olivia was working in her shop late tonight, so it couldn't be her. The third apartment was still vacant. Becca hadn't ordered a pizza, and she knew Sam was avoiding her at night because he was smarter than she was. Especially after he'd taught her how to operate their boat today, a venture that had ended up being more a lesson on self-control and restraint.

She'd never been good at either.

But now she could at least passably assist on any excursion if needed, and that ability, along with all the other new skills she'd picked up this summer, made her feel good.

Really good.

Setting the keyboard aside, she rose and made her way to the door. "Who's there?"

No one answered.

Going up on tiptoe, she peeked through the peephole.

No one. Odd. She backed away and sat back on her bed, but didn't reach for the keyboard. She glanced out the windows. Night had fallen, and she hadn't pulled the sheets over them. Which meant she was basically sitting in a fishbowl.

She heard a sound from the hallway.

Her stomach clenched as fear slid into it. She'd read somewhere that a brain recognized fear in less than one second and prepared itself by flooding the body with adrenaline. Turned out that was absolutely true.

You left the fear behind, she reminded herself. Long behind. Gone were the days of jumping at every noise outside her New Orleans apartment.

Besides, she was in Lucky Harbor. Nothing to be afraid of here. But she reached out and turned off her lamp. This made her slightly less visible, but it also put her in the dark. She moved to the windows and yanked the sheets across them. Halfway back to the lamp, she heard another sound from the hallway.

Fear stole her breath, and she backed up until she ran herself into the countertop of the kitchen. She could hear her own breathing, harsh and panicked, and it brought her back to last year. Angry at herself, she grabbed her purse and rifled through it for her phone. She stared at the dark screen. She didn't have a lot of options here. Calling her first choice was going to make her look weak and vulnerable, and oh, she hated both with a passion.

She called anyway.

Sam had closed up the warehouse and was halfway home when his cell vibrated from an incoming call. Not his dad telling him yet again why his crook of a girlfriend thought she needed a five-hundred-dollar stroller, though the name that flashed on his screen didn't ease his tension any.

Becca.

There was only one reason for a woman to call this late at night. And though he'd never been adverse to a booty call, he hesitated. A booty call was light. Casual.

But nothing was ever casual with Becca. They'd gone there once, and he now knew that she had the potential of getting to him, *really* getting to him, in a very big way.

The biggest.

And still, he answered. "Hey," he said. "What's up?"

"I don't know." Her voice was a soft whisper. A scared soft whisper. "You're not by any chance outside my door, are you?"

"No, but I can be." In the middle of the deserted highway, he whipped a U-turn.

In his ear, Becca let out a breath. "No. It's fine. I'm sure it's nothing. Never mind." And she disconnected.

Sam pounded out her number again and waited through three tense rings before she picked up.

"I'm sorry," she said. "I'm being ridiculous. Ignore me."

"Not gonna happen, babe. Tell me what's wrong."

"I heard a sound." She was still whispering and still sounding terrified, which just about killed him. "Thought I heard footsteps outside my door, and then a knock. But no one was there."

"Cole's still on the boat," he said. "I'm going to hang up and call him. Keep your phone in your hand. Ten seconds, Becca. I'll call you right back —"

"I don't want to bother —"

"Ten seconds." He disconnected and called Cole, waiting with impatience for him to answer, hating that Becca was scared and alone.

Cole finally answered with a "Yo, Grandma."

"You on the boat?" Sam asked.

"Yeah, I'm calibrating the —"

"Run over to Becca's. She heard someone outside her door and is terrified."

"On it," Cole said, good humor gone.

Sam disconnected and called Becca back.

"Are you here?" she asked breathlessly.

"Not yet, but Cole is," he said. "Any second now. I'm going to stay on the phone with you until he's got you."

"You don't have to —"

"I'm staying on the phone," he said firmly, grinding his teeth when he got caught at the train tracks just outside of town and had to wait for a train. "Is Olivia home?"

"No, she's working late," Becca said.

"You expecting anyone?"

"No." She blew out a breath. "God, it sounds so dumb now. I shouldn't have watched *Criminal Minds* earlier. I'm okay. I'm okay."

Hearing it twice, knowing she was trying to make it true, almost had him smiling as he downshifted for a light. "You locked in?"

"Yes, but seriously, I'm sure it's nothing. Someone was lost, probably . . ."

"Make sure you're back from the windows so you're not highlighted to anyone outside," he said. "Sit tight, I'll be there in five."

"You don't have to —"

"Becca. I'm already almost there. And Cole should be there any second."

Even as he said it, through the line he could hear three short knocks on the door, and then Cole's voice. "Becca. Honey, it's me."

"He's here," Becca said to Sam, her voice filled with relief.

"Peek first, Becca."

"I see him."

"Okay, babe. I'll be right there."

It took him three more very long moments to get back to the harbor. He ran up to Becca's door, and Cole answered.

"She's spooked," he said in a low-pitched voice. "But she won't let me get close enough to touch her. I don't know what's up. I don't think it's good, bro."

Sam's gaze searched out the loft and found Becca in the club chair by her bed. She had her arms wrapped around her legs, her forehead to her knees, looking like a ball of misery. He strode directly to her and crouched beside the chair. "Hey," he said softly.

"I'm sorry," she said to her knees. "I

totally overreacted. I'm fine, really."

Anyone could see plain as day she was just about as far from fine as she could get. He set a hand on her bare foot, and she nearly leapt out of her skin. "Just me," he said softly, keeping his hand on her.

Her skin was icy, but she curled her foot trustingly into his big hand.

Sam glanced back at Cole, who gave him a small shake of his head as he filled a glass of water and brought it over.

Sam took it from Cole and handed it to Becca. "Drink this."

While she did, Cole quietly said, "I ran the exterior to get here. Didn't see anyone. The door to the building was closed but not locked. Her door was locked. No cars in the lot but mine." Cole squatted beside Sam and looked into Becca's pale face. "How you doing, honey?"

"I'm sorry," she said. "I really appreciate —"

"Never be sorry for wanting to be safe," Cole told her. He glanced at the hand she'd allowed Sam to set on her and gave her a small but warm smile. "Anytime. Okay?"

"Okay," she whispered.

He nodded. "You're safe with Sam. You know that, right?"

She met Sam's gaze and gave her own

small but warm smile, if a bit wobbly. "I do know it."

Cole nodded once more and left. Two minutes later, he called Sam. "There's a UPS package on her neighbor's doorstep. That's probably what she heard."

Sam hung up and told Becca.

Becca grimaced. "Way to overreact, right?"

"No worries," he said.

She nodded. "Thanks for coming, but you don't have to stay —"

"You're shaking." He pulled off his sweatshirt and tugged it over her head.

"I'm cold."

"I'm thinking shock," he said. "This, tonight, was a flashback for you, wasn't it?"

She busied herself getting wrapped up in his sweatshirt and didn't speak.

"Come home with me tonight, Becca."

She stared at him for a long beat. "You don't like people in your space."

"I don't," he said. "But you're not people."

For the first time since he'd arrived, her eyes lost their guard, and she laughed softly. "I'm fine here."

"Yeah. And you'll be even more fine at my house."

"I'm not sleeping at your house, I'm sleeping here."

"Who says there'll be sleeping?" he asked,

attempting to lighten her mood.

She rolled her eyes. "You don't mean it," she said so glumly that he laughed. "You're just being suggestive because you want me to get over being freaked out."

He rose and scooped her up out of the chair, smiling when she squeaked and threw her arms around his neck to catch her balance. "Maybe I just wanted an excuse to kiss you."

"But —"

He stopped her protests with his mouth and then selfishly kept kissing her because the taste of her was like a drug. When he finally pulled back, he set his forehead to hers.

She took a long, unsteady breath. "Thanks for being here for me," she whispered.

He started to answer flippantly, but stopped when he realized how much it meant to him as well, that he could be there for her. "Anytime, babe."

And for the first time in his life, he actually meant it.

CHAPTER 17

Becca strained to get a look at Sam's neighborhood as he drove. She knew enough about Lucky Harbor to know this was a very nice part of town, with big houses on bigger lots, overlooking the bluffs where a hundred feet below the Pacific Ocean churned against the rocky shore.

Sam's house was a beautiful older Craftsman style, white with blue trim, and too many windows to count.

Every light was blazing.

Sam swore beneath his breath as he opened his front door to a blast of Marvin Gaye wailing "Let's Get It On." "I'm going to have to kill him," he said.

Becca had wondered what Sam's place would look like, whether it'd be neat or messy, filled with guy crap or empty and sterile.

It was none of the above. The living room was large and airy and had windows facing the bluffs. There were big, comfy couches in the living room and an even bigger TV, in front of which were a few stacks of CDs and DVDs. There were various things strewn about, athletic shoes, a sweatshirt, a kayak leaning against a wall. No personal pictures, though, and nothing that said *hot single guy,* either. Definitely lived in, but not necessarily claimed.

Sam moved to the coffee table, grabbed a remote, and hit a button.

The music stopped.

Then he strode out of the room. Not ready to be left alone, Becca followed. The kitchen was gorgeous. Granite countertops, wood floors, high beamed ceilings. It was also a mess. The island was littered with the remains of what looked to have been a pizza-and-beer dinner. Clothing was haphazardly dropped across every surface; a man's pair of jeans, a woman's bra. A red lace thong . . .

"Definitely going to kill him," Sam muttered. The double French doors were cracked and led to a deck.

There was a hot tub there, from which came the whoosh of the jets and the unmistakable sounds of a man's voice and a woman giggling.

Sam stepped out the French doors, and

252

again Becca followed, figuring that by the steam coming out his ears, father and son might need a referee.

"You've got to be fuckin' kidding me," Sam said.

Mark was indeed in the hot tub with a woman, and as the undies had indicated, they were buck naked.

Becca immediately whirled back to the doors, but unfortunately she'd let them shut behind her when she'd come out, and naturally they'd locked. "Crap," she said, rattling the doors for good measure.

Behind her, Mark and the woman were making noises over the sound of the jet bubbles that were going to haunt her for the rest of her life. Sam, too, if the growl from deep in his throat meant anything. *"Dad,"* he clipped out, sounding like he was forcing the word past cut glass.

There was the sound of water sloshing, and she imagined the couple breaking apart. "Oh, hey," Mark called, and against her better judgment, Becca took a peek.

Thankfully, both the nudists were now in the water up to their necks.

"Didn't expect you so early, son," Mark said. "Next time I'll hang a tie on the door or something for notice, yeah?"

Sam shoved his hand into his pocket and

came up with his keys, which he handed to Becca so she could unlock the doors and get inside, but, working on sheer nerves now, she promptly dropped them.

"Hi, Sam!" the female called cheerfully, her hands over her ample breasts. "It's lovely to meet you. I've heard a lot about you." She grinned. "I'd shake your hand, but . . ."

Sam let out an inarticulate sound, and she peeked at him as he squeezed his eyes shut and pressed the heels of his hands to them.

"Sorry, son," Mark said. "After the stroller fight, I asked Sheila for a paternity test like you've been suggesting. She came clean — I'm not the daddy." He smiled at the naked woman. "So then I went out to celebrate, and met Brandy here at that bar out on Highway Forty-two."

Brandy giggled and waved, like there could be any guessing about which one of them was Brandy.

"You're not supposed to be drinking," Sam said. "And pizza's out, too. I took you to the dietitian, and she gave you the recommended list."

"I don't like salad or fish."

Sam's mouth tightened grimly. "Do you like living?"

"I was liking it a whole hell of a lot more

254

about four minutes ago," Mark said.

"You're supposed to be taking it easy," Sam said tightly.

"Oh, he was," Brandy piped up. "I was doing all the work."

Mark beamed at her. "And you're good at it, honey."

Sam let out a breath. "Gonna have to empty the tub and bleach it."

Becca had picked up the keys and was trying to find the right one.

"You two want to join us?" Mark asked. "The water's great."

"Fuck it," Sam muttered. "I'm gonna sell it. The whole house." He snatched the keys from Becca's hands and unlocked the door. He gave her a little shove inside, followed her in, and slammed the door behind them hard enough that the glass rattled.

"Sam —"

He leveled her with a dark look that for some inexplicable reason didn't scare her anymore. He evoked a lot of feelings within her, but fear wasn't one of them. "He's trying to be something to you," she said.

"Well, he succeeded. He's a pain in my ass." He hustled her out the front door and back to his truck, where he whipped away from the curb with a squeal of tires. Not all four. Just two.

Becca grabbed the dash. "If you'd just give him some of your attention, your time —"

"We're over this conversation," he said firmly.

She waited until they were on the highway. "Listen," she said gently. "I know he screwed up a lot while you were growing up, but I think he genuinely regrets —"

"*Over it,* Becca."

"Really?" she asked, feeling her own temper rise. Whenever *she* was over a conversation, he still pushed.

He must have heard the annoyance in her tone because he slid her a look that had male bafflement all over it, like she'd just asked him if she looked fat in these jeans or what he liked about her.

Somehow that was worse, that he truly didn't get it, the clueless man. "Why do you get to push me to talk, and I can't push you?"

"That's different," he said immediately.

"How?" she asked. "How's it different?"

He downshifted into a turn and said nothing.

"Yeah," she said, crossing her arms. "Thought so."

"Get off your soapbox, Becca," he said, apparently just as annoyed with her as he was with his dad. "It's not like you've ever really told me shit about you."

Okay, that was possibly true.

Five tense minutes later, he slid into a parking spot outside of the Love Shack and turned to her.

She made a point of looking out the passenger window.

Sam sighed, the sound filled with frustration and regret. "Look," he said, "he drives me crazy, okay? And I'm a total ass. I'm sorry."

So foreign was the notion of a guy apologizing to her for something that she jerked around to stare at him.

"You look confused," he said.

"One of us is supposed to be pissed off," she said softly. "Maybe both of us. But you're not mad at me. And I don't feel mad at you." She shook her head. "I don't know what to do with that. Or you, for that matter."

He slid his fingers along her jaw and into her hair, then pulled her close enough to press his mouth to hers. "If you weren't my employee, I'd show you what to do with me." He kissed her again and then whispered against her lips, suggestions on exactly what she might do with him, each hotter than the last.

She felt herself quiver and then get wet,

and she stared at his mouth, having some trouble with her thought process.

"We straight?" he asked.

"Um . . ."

His eyes were heated, but they lit with a little humor now as he ran the pad of his thumb over her lower lip. "Yeah," he said. "We're straight." He pulled back. "I could use a drink. You?"

"Yes."

He pulled her from the truck and into him, giving her a really tight, really hard, really great hug. "You're so damn sweet," he said into her hair.

She tipped her face up. "Because I interfere?"

He smiled. "Because you care enough to interfere."

"Yeah? You have your sweet moments, too, you know," she said. "Not a lot, mind you, but a few here and there."

He tossed his head back and laughed.

"What?"

"That's the first time anyone's ever said I was sweet," he said, still grinning.

"You apologized to me. And that was sweet."

"I apologized because I was an ass. That's what you do when you've been an ass."

"Not everyone who acts like an ass apologizes," she said.

His smile faded, and he hooked an arm around her neck, drawing her into him again, pressing his mouth to her temple. "They should," he said against her skin.

Cole and Tanner were at a table inside, and Sam and Becca joined them.

Cole smiled at Becca. "How you doing?"

"Better," she said. "Thanks again. I'm so sorry —"

"No apologies for that," Cole said. "Ever." He gestured to Jax behind the bar, who brought two more longnecks, one each for Sam and Becca.

Cole lifted his in a toast. "To Gil."

"To Gil," they all said, and Becca was moved by their low, serious voices that rang out together. They ordered sliders and fries and another round.

Sam made the next toast. "To my dad's health," he said.

This surprised and pleased Becca. "See?" she said to him. "*Sweet.* But your dad looked fine to me."

"Yeah," Sam said, "but I plan to kill him later, so —"

"Sam," she said on a surprised laugh. "You're not."

"Okay, maybe not kill him," he said. "Not all the way."

"What'd he do now?" Cole wanted to know.

"Doesn't matter," Tanner said. "You're not going to kill him because I'm not using our boat fund to bail you out again, not when we're getting so close to another boat."

"Again?" Becca asked Sam.

Sam gave Tanner a long look.

Tanner took a long pull on his beer and didn't look concerned. "Did we forget to tell you that you work for an international felon?" he asked Becca.

Her mouth fell open, and she stared at Sam, who flipped Tanner the bird.

Tanner flashed a grin.

"Yeah, it's true," Cole told her. "The last time we had to bail him out, I almost had to try and sell Tanner here for a night just to have enough."

"You *did* try and sell me for a night," Tanner said.

Becca choked out a laugh, and Sam rolled his eyes. "Why does that story change the more you drink?" he asked Tanner.

Tanner pointed his beer at Sam. "*You* weren't there. You were cooling off in a Mexican prison. We could've just left you there, you know. But did we? No."

"Instead you got yourself arrested as well,"

260

Sam reminded him.

"Hey, that was Cole's fault," Tanner said. "He told me to kiss the wrong woman."

"Okay," Becca said, setting down her beer. "I'm going to need to hear this story. The real story."

Cole grinned. "I'll tell it."

Tanner groaned but Cole ignored him. "We'd just left the rig job," he told her. "We'd bought our first boat, a real piece of shit to be honest, but she was all ours. Well, ours and the bank's. We were on the water, and our GPS went down. Tanner here insisted he could navigate without it. We were in the southwest Gulf, and he turned us a little too far south, where we came across some Mexican pirates —"

Becca gasped. "Oh, my God, pirates? Really?"

"Oh, yeah," Cole said. "They boarded us, too. Said they were the . . ." He used air quotes here. "Authorities. And genius here" — he jabbed a thumb at Sam — "decided that they were full of shit and told them so."

"Okay, yes, I did that," Sam said. "But in my defense, they were wearing a combo of outdated U.S. and British military gear. They looked suspicious."

"They hauled his big mouth off to the

261

clink," Tanner said.

"Which left me," Cole said, gesturing to himself, "the brains of the operation, to figure out how to spring him."

"Hey," Tanner said. "I did my part. You told me to sleep with the town mayor's daughter." He smiled at Becca. "She was in the bar we stumbled into to come up with a plan." He grimaced. "Except —"

"Except it turns out that she was the *wife,* not the daughter," Cole said. "Which left me bailing out the *two* of them."

"Did you have enough to bail them both out?" she asked.

"He sure as hell didn't," Sam said. "Because he'd used his month's pay on being stupid."

Becca looked at Cole, who shook his head. "That's another story altogether."

"So how did you bail them out?" Becca asked.

"He sold our fuckin' boat," Tanner said on a huge, sad sigh. "The *Sweet Sally,* gone forever."

"It was that," Sam said, "or leave you to become Big Bubba's jail-mate bitch. And afterward, we bought a better boat."

"He didn't care then," Cole said, and turned to Tanner. "You were still recovering and supposed to be taking it easy, but instead you were on this walk on the stupid and wild side, remember? Gil had just —"

"Hey," Tanner said, no longer smiling. "Don't go there."

"— died," Cole said.

"I mean it," Tanner said. "Shut up."

"What, we just toasted to his memory," Cole said, "but we can't toast to your trip to Crazy-Town?"

Tanner shoved free of the table. "I'm out."

"Aw, come on," Cole said. "Don't get like that —"

But Tanner was gone, striding out the door and into the night.

Sam set down his beer. "Really?" he asked Cole.

Cole sighed and got to his feet. "I suppose I should go after Mr. Sensitive."

"Maybe you want to give him a few minutes first," Sam suggested. "So he doesn't rearrange your face again."

"Yeah." Cole straightened his shoulders like he was bracing for battle. "Hey, if I don't show up for work tomorrow, call out a search party, okay? I'll be the one in concrete shoes at the bottom of the harbor, waiting on a rescue." He paused, and when Sam only shrugged, he sighed. "Nice knowing ya," he said to Becca, and headed out after Tanner.

"Is he really in danger?" Becca asked, worried.

"From his own big, fat mouth, maybe." Sam stood up and pulled her with him. "Want to play?" he asked, gesturing to the piano.

Her heart gave a little kick, and she looked around. The bar was still full. "No, but thank you for asking."

The night was dark and quiet. Becca looked up at her big, silent, gorgeous escort. "At least this time I can thank you for walking me."

He arched a brow.

"You usually vanish into the night," she said. "Like Batman."

He looked at her but didn't say anything, neither confirming nor denying.

At Becca's apartment building, Olivia came out of her door with a duffel bag. "Hey," she said. "There was a spider in my bathroom. I need to sleep on your couch." Without waiting for a response, she walked into Becca's apartment and left Sam and Becca alone in the doorway.

Becca looked at Sam. "You got in touch with her somehow."

He kissed her. "Night. Sleep tight."

"See?" she said. "Sweet." Then she caught

his hand, went up on tiptoe, and gave him a good-night kiss.

CHAPTER 18

After work the next day, Becca was walking across the alley toward her apartment when someone called her name. Turning, she came face-to-face with Mark.

"Hey there," he said with a smile. "I was just heading in, looking for Sam."

"The guys are gone," she said. "Out on the water with clients."

"Ah, gotcha." His smile was still in place, but he looked worried. Really worried.

"You okay?" she asked.

"Well . . . I had a little car mishap."

"An accident?" She put her hand on his arm, looking him over.

He took her hand in his and squeezed it. "I see why he's into you, darlin'; you're really something special. But no, I didn't have an accident. I'm fine."

"Oh. Good," she said relieved. "And Sam and I aren't —"

"Because he's an idiot. I know," Mark

said. He rubbed his jaw ruefully. "He might've gotten that from me."

"Actually," she said, "*I* might be the idiot."

Mark smiled. "See? Special. Because now you're protecting the idiot."

Becca laughed. "Tell me about your car mishap."

He went back to looking rueful. "I got my ride repo'd."

"Oh, Mark."

"I know, I know. I need to grow up. But right now, I need to get to the doctor, I have an appointment."

"You can borrow my car, if you'd like," she said. "Fair warning, though, it's a piece of shit."

"Pieces of shit are my specialty," Mark said. "You wouldn't by any chance have another of those amazing sandwiches with chips on it lying around, would you?" He flashed her a smile that was so similar to Sam's, she smiled back helplessly.

"No," she said, "but I can make you one."

"Yeah," he said with a smile. "Definitely special."

That night Becca sat in Olivia's apartment sharing Chinese takeout and some wine.

And woes.

They started with work woes. Olivia's

were physical. She'd been in Lucky Harbor for a year now and was outgrowing her store. It was why she'd moved into the warehouse apartment. She'd been living above the store, but that space was now needed for stock storage.

Becca's work woes were mental. She was trying to teach music to a group of kids who'd never played an instrument in their lives, and it didn't take a shrink to know that she needed this more than they did.

And then there was the fact that she was falling for her stoic, sexy boss. But as Olivia pointed out while refilling their glasses for the second or third or maybe fourth time, "If you put those two things aside, things are good for you."

This was actually true, of sorts. Work was going pretty well. She had the Summer Bash plans under control, and she'd finished updating the charter website. The guys had been doing double the work, taking calls for reservations and then having to enter everything into the system. But now the site was fully operational, and people could book themselves.

"I bet you're worth your weight in gold," Olivia said. "Come work for me; it'll be better for you."

"How's that?" Becca asked. "You have

three hot guys in board shorts, shirts optional, working at your shop to look at all day?"

Olivia snorted. "No, but if you work for me, then you can sleep with Sam."

Which brought them to the next subject — man woes.

"I'm not sure we're going there," Becca said. "And anyway, I'm not in a hurry to have him as an ex."

"Yeah," Olivia said. "Exes suck."

She looked at Olivia with interest. "Tell me an ex story."

"I once had a boyfriend who was an FBI agent."

"Wow."

"Wait for it," Olivia said, not nearly as impressed as Becca.

"Uh-oh."

"Yeah," Olivia said. "He said being an agent was why he had to come and go without warning, and why he didn't have to call."

"Well, that sucks," Becca said.

"Gets worse. One night I had a break-in, and he happened to be with me. He ran out the front door screaming into the night like a little girl, without so much as looking back for me." Olivia shook her head. "FBI agent my ass."

They both laughed. Some of the hilarity had to be attributed to the wine, but mostly it was Olivia's delivery. She knew how to spin a tale, and she knew how to be kick-ass, and not just the pretend, fake-it-till-you-make-it kind.

Becca needed to learn that particular skill.

"So . . . ," Olivia said, making the word about fifty syllables.

"So what?"

"So now it's your turn to regale *me* with an ex story," Olivia said.

Becca became suddenly extremely engrossed with finishing her wine. "I don't really have all that many," she finally said.

"Come on. Be serious."

"I am serious," Becca said.

Olivia had been lying flat on the couch, her head hanging over the side, while Becca — sitting on the floor — braided the long mass. But at this statement, Olivia lifted her head, pulling her hair from Becca's hands.

"Unlikely from a woman who looks like you," Olivia said slowly, taking Becca in, "with that gorgeous hair and those big, warm eyes, not to mention your amazing skin, which probably came from a rosy-cheeked baby with unicorn wings who poops golden fairy dust."

Becca laughed. "You should be the writer."

Olivia's smile reminded Becca that her new friend still had lots of secrets. "So no ex at *all*?" Olivia said, heavy on the disbelief.

"Well, sure," Becca said, busying herself with picking out a fortune cookie. "A few here and there."

"Name 'em," Olivia said.

"Taylor Bennett," Becca said. "He dumped me because I couldn't name the jazz songs he played."

"Uh-huh," Olivia said. "And how old were you?"

"Seventeen."

"That's the best you got?" Olivia asked.

She racked her brain. The problem was, during those years, she'd been traveling with Jase, and it hadn't exactly been a normal coming-of-age situation. She'd dated, but hadn't really sunk her teeth into any real relationships other than with Nathan. "There were others, just no one memorable."

"Come on, there's got to be a story to tell."

"Maybe." Becca nudged the fortune cookies around with her fingers. "But I don't like to revisit the only other one I've got."

Olivia was quiet a moment. "This have anything to do with our impromptu sleepover?"

Becca shrugged. She didn't want to go there sober, much less half-baked.

"Men are bastards," Olivia said with feeling.

Becca made a noncommittal response to this and opened her fortune cookie. *Your future is your own,* it said.

"Damn it," Becca said. "This one's defective."

Olivia peered over the edge of the couch and read it. "Hey, it sounds good to me. I like making my own future."

Becca shook her head. "I'd rather hear something like: *Your future is prosperity-filled,* or *You'll spin money from your ass,* or . . ."

"Or," Olivia said, *"There's a hot guy waiting for you if you only open your eyes?"*

"Yeah. That's a good one."

Olivia rolled her eyes. "It's a *true* one."

"That's ridiculous. My eyes are open."

Olivia laughed and came up on an elbow, eyes slowly going serious. "How do you not realize that you actually, really do have a hot guy waiting for you?"

"I don't."

"You *do.*"

"Don't."

Olivia sighed. "You're an annoying drunk."

This was undoubtedly true. "I chose the

job, remember?" she asked.

"Sam doesn't care about the job. That's not what's holding him back."

"How do you know?" Becca asked. "You've holed up in here, laid so low no one even hardly knows you're here."

Olivia shrugged. "I've got windows, don't I? And I've been around longer than you. I know that he looks amazeballs on a surfboard, that he looks amazeballs on a boat, that he looks amazeballs —"

"Okay, okay," Becca said, and she did laugh then. "I get it. He looks amazing *all* the damn time."

"Yes, but it's more than that. It's how he looks at you."

Becca sighed. "Listen, I pretty much forced him into giving me the job."

"Honey, no one forces Sam Brody to do anything."

Also true . . . But he'd known she needed the money, and that had been that. He cared about her. He cared about all the people in his life. Cole and Tanner, for example. He'd do anything for them, and had. The same went for his dad, and Cole's mom. Sam was a man who was careful with his emotions, he'd been brought up to be, and yet he could still give and care with every ounce of his body.

273

Unlike her.

Oh, she cared, but not deep. Going deep hurt. She'd learned that once and had never looked back. She loved her parents because they were her parents, but she couldn't count on them.

And then there was Jase. When that situation had gotten to be too much for her to handle, she hadn't just backed off. She'd backed off and moved thousands of miles away, leaving him alone to deal with his issues.

She couldn't imagine Sam doing that to someone in his life, ever.

They both jumped at the knock on the door.

"That's not my door," Olivia said. "It's yours." She got up and looked out her peephole. "Well, well, speaking of the devil."

"Oh, my God," Becca whispered. "Back away from the door!"

Olivia kept her eye glued to the peephole. "You know, he's got a really fantastic ass. And I'm only looking at the profile —"

"Shhh! He'll hear you."

Olivia turned to her in surprise. "You're not going out there?"

Earlier, that'd been all she'd wanted. A late-night visit from her sexy surfer. Now . . . now she didn't know what the hell she thought *that* would accomplish.

"It'll accomplish plenty," Olivia said, making Becca realize she'd spoken out loud. "You'd probably get boinked, for one. And nothing personal, but you're wound pretty tight. You could use it."

Becca came up on her knees, waving wildly for Olivia to shut up. "The walls," she whispered. "Thin. You can hear me breathing. I can hear you swearing. Which means *he can hear you.*"

"No, he can't."

"Yes, I can," Sam said.

Becca and Olivia went stock-still at the sound of his voice, right on the other side of her front door now.

Shit! "Don't let him in!" Becca hissed.

"I have a tin of ranch-flavored popcorn," Sam said through the wood.

"From the pier?" she asked, unable to help herself.

"Yep." The sound of the tin being shaken came through the door. "And it's good," he said, mouth sounding full.

"Hey," she called out, straightening up. "Are you eating my popcorn?"

"You bet your sweet ass. Lance warned me it was damn good, but I had no idea. You'd best hurry before I eat it all."

He'd bought her popcorn. Oh, God. She

was a dead woman.

"He's funny, hot, *and* he likes you enough to buy you popcorn," Olivia whispered.

"Don't let him in!" she whispered back.

"Don't listen to her, Olivia, let me in."

Just his voice, calm but steely, made Becca's nipples hard. Damn it. And Olivia was looking at her like Santa Claus had just shown up. Knowing she was too weak to be trusted, Becca leapt to her feet and looked for somewhere to hide. Unfortunately she tripped over the coffee table and went down with a thud.

That's when she realized she was maybe more than half-baked. She might be fully baked. Disoriented, she stayed there on her hands and knees a moment — until suddenly two hands slid beneath her armpits and lifted her to her feet.

"You gave my dad your car?" Sam asked.

She blinked. "Um."

"You gave my dad your car."

"A little bit, yeah." When Sam shook his head, she hurried on, "He's bringing it back tomorrow."

"Do you give anyone anything they ask for?" he asked.

"Not anymore," she said. "I'm on a break from doing that. Your dad just really needed the ride, and I'm not driving tonight anyway, so —" She hiccuped and covered her mouth. "Excuse me."

Still holding on to her, Sam peered down at her, a very small smile on his lips now. "You're shit-faced."

"Nope." Although there did seem to be two of him . . . Which was nice since both of him were smiling all sexy-like. "I'm not shit-faced. I don't get shit-faced. I don't drink."

Olivia lifted the two bottles of wine they'd decimated. Both empty.

"Who drank those?" Becca asked her.

"That would be us," Olivia said, and laughed. "Sexy Surfer's right, babe. We're shit-faced. We've gotta hit the sack, we both have to work early tomorrow."

"Huh," Becca said. She went to jab a finger at one of the two Sams in front of her, but missed. "Huh," she said again.

Sam was still grinning. "Need help getting home and to bed?"

"No!" she said at the exact same time that Olivia said "Yes!"

Becca whirled on Olivia to give her a very dirty look, but her world began to spin, and didn't stop. "Uh-oh," she whispered, and would've slithered to the floor again except that Sam hooked an arm around her waist. It was a really great forearm, too, all tanned and corded with strength. But it was the big, warm hand that landed just beneath her breast that really grabbed her attention.

"Here's her key," she heard Olivia say, and then her world was upside down because Sam had hoisted her up and over his shoulder in a fireman's hold, his arm wrapped around the backs of her thighs.

"Hey," she said to his ass. His very fine ass.

"Hay's for horses," Olivia said cheerfully, whacked Becca's ass, and opened the front door.

"Hey," Becca said again.

But she was talking to no one. Well, other than Sam's ass, of course.

"So romantic," Olivia said on a sigh.

Still upside down, Becca tried to imagine Sam being romantic. But she couldn't picture him giving a woman roses. "Do you?" she asked.

"Do I what?"

"Do you ever bring your women roses?"

"I'm not exactly a flowers type," he said. "But I do have the popcorn." He rattled the tin with his free hand.

The truth was, Becca would rather have popcorn any day of the week over roses. She might even have said so, but her world was spinning even more now, so she squeaked, slammed her eyes shut, and held on for dear life. And what she held on to was his butt — with both hands — earning her a chuckle from the guy who owned the butt. He balanced her and the popcorn with ease while unlocking her front door. Kicking the door closed, he strode across the open space, bypassing her bathroom, and dumped her on the bed.

She sat up, blew the hair out of her eyes, and focused on him standing there, hands on hips, looking sexy as all hell. "Come here," she said.

"You feeling sick?"

"No." She tugged him down over the top of her and pressed her face into that male throat she loved so much and inhaled him deep.

"Becca, I need a shower."

"Oh, boy," she said. "I've heard this story before."

He snorted, then rolled off the bed. She blinked as he leaned over her and pulled off her sandals. "Whatcha doing?"

"Putting you to bed," he said.

"But I thought you were going to shower and then do me."

He went still a moment, then tipped back his head and laughed. The sight was so beautiful she just stared at him for a long moment. "Wow," she breathed. "You're so damn pretty. Does Lucille know? She should pin pics of you in your board shorts, the blue ones that have the white stripe down the side, the ones that show off your butt, all over her Pinterest."

"If you suggest that to her, I'll . . ." He paused.

"What?" she asked.

"I don't know. I can't think of anything that wouldn't leave you scarred for life." He reached for the hem on her sweatshirt. "Lift up."

"Please," she said. "You mean lift up *please.*"

He gave her an alpha look and she lifted up, and then the sweatshirt vanished, leaving her in a cami top and a gauzy skirt.

He stared down at her, scrubbed a hand over his jaw, muttering something to himself about "being a fucking saint," and then he tugged down the blankets. "Get in," he said.

"Okay." She scrambled in, then waited for him to climb in as well. He didn't. "Hey," she said when he tugged the blankets up to her chin. "What are you doing?"

"Putting you to bed," he repeated, not quite as patiently now.

In fact, he was sounding downright strained.

"Without you?" she asked, confused.

"Without me. Becca, you're not paying attention to me."

Yes, she was. That was always the problem. She looked down at herself. "I'm still dressed."

"Yeah," he said, and again ran a hand over his rough jaw, which made a very male sound that turned her on even more. "I don't trust myself with you undressed."

"I do," she said.

At that, his eyes softened and he placed a hand on either side of her hips. Leaning in, he kissed her softly. "So fucking sweet," he murmured against her lips. "So damn sweet."

"But you still aren't doing me, are you?"

He actually lowered his head, closed his eyes, and groaned from deep in his throat. "I'm trying to be a good guy here, Becca."

"I don't want you to be good. Well, I do. The *good* kind of good, you know?"

He kissed her again. "Go to sleep."

"But I do trust you."

"Not all the way, you don't," he said. "Not yet." Then he kissed her again, and this time he gave her what she wanted, which was heat and lots of tongue. Then he tore himself away, breathing unsteadily. "Stop me," he said.

"No."

Sam groaned. "If I have to be the strong one here, we're in trouble."

"So don't be the strong one." She paused, and remembered. "When!" she yelled. "When, when, *when*!"

"You," he said, backing away, "are a menace to my self-control."

"Why the self-control at all? Forget the self-control! I just said *When.* That was our code word."

He looked pained. And strained. "You're under the influence. It doesn't count."

"Why?" she asked.

"You know why."

She gave him her I'm-not-impressed-with-that-excuse look, and he let out a laugh. "Look, we both know that intimacy between us is . . . inappropriate," he said.

"Hey, we crossed the intimacy barrier a long time ago."

"Yeah. Shit," he muttered, his voice a low, incredibly sexy growl that wasn't helping the situation one little bit.

"Tell me the truth," she said. "Is it because you're no longer attracted to me?"

"No. Christ, no." He dropped his head back and stared up at the ceiling for a beat, then came back to her. He let his weight cover her and rocked his hips, proving that he wasn't lying. He was absolutely attracted to her, in a big way if the erection he was sporting was any indication.

"I don't get it," she said, clinging to him. "I'm not asking for a marriage proposal. I mean, I'm not exactly relationship material, either."

He went still, then lifted his head. "You don't think I'm relationship material?"

She stared up into his beautiful green eyes, surprised by the fact he seemed insulted by this. "Are you?" she asked.

He didn't take his gaze from her. "Well, no."

"Are you a commitment-phobe?"

"No, definitely not," he said.

She slid her fingers into his silky hair. "So why are you complicating things by holding back?"

"It doesn't matter why," he said. "I said no. And as your boss, whatever I say goes."

She shivered at that, and laughed as she nudged her good spot to his. "Maybe I like that, you being all bossy."

He tightened his grasp on her hips to hold her still, but his eyes were so heated she was near melting point. "You need to stop playing with me."

She stared up at him. "Just tell me this — are you holding back because of me?"

"What?"

"Olivia said maybe it wasn't just the job, that maybe it was me, you were holding back for me." She was worried about this. "That's it, isn't it? You've got some misguided notion that I'm not ready for the likes of you, or something equally macho and alpha and stupid."

The truth was in his eyes.

He *was* holding back for her. Damn it. She hated that. "I hate that, Sam."

He kissed her again. Becca tried to remain unmoved but he was such a good kisser, and in two seconds she was kissing him back. Just when things started to get deliciously out of hand, he pulled back. "You're going to be the death of me," he whispered against her lips.

And then he was gone.

"Ditto," she said into the silent room.

The next morning, Becca staggered out of bed. Moving slowly so her throbbing head didn't fall off, she showered, dressed, and made her way to work.

The hut was open, lights on, coffee made, computer booted up. On her counter sat a mug of steaming coffee, three aspirin, and a whole tin of ranch-flavored popcorn.

Damn, he *was* romantic after all.

284

CHAPTER 19

Sam stayed in his warehouse most of the day, figuring that both he and Becca could use a little space.

At least he could.

So why he found himself watching the big, open doorway of his warehouse as if that was his job, he had no idea. But he was still watching when his dad pulled up in the alley with Becca's car. Mark got out and walked toward the beach hut, undoubtedly to return her keys.

Sam rolled his eyes, thinking Becca should consider herself lucky his dad hadn't sold the thing and pocketed the money.

A few minutes later, Mark was back in the alley, and when he caught sight of Sam, he waved. "Son, hey."

"Hey."

Mark came to the doorway. "So . . . what's your policy on letting houseguests drive your spare car?"

Sam's spare car had been Gil's and was a '68 Camaro. "My policy is fuck no."

Mark sighed. "Yeah. I get it. It's not like I deserve to borrow shit, especially since you've been letting me stay with you and eat your food and everything I should have done for you all those years ago, right?"

It was Sam's turn to sigh as he fished out his truck keys.

Mark grinned. "Thanks. Love ya."

And then he was gone.

Much later, Sam looked up from the boat he was working on and blinked, realizing hours had gone by and he hadn't been interrupted by a single thing. It had to be a record.

The phones had rung, but they'd been picked up. Apparently Becca was doing fine since she knew to call him if she needed anything.

She hadn't.

Which was great. After all, the whole point of hiring her had been so that he could be left alone.

His favorite state.

But Cole and Tanner were still out, and she'd been on her own all day.

Maybe something was wrong. Maybe she'd fallen and hit her head.

Maybe he was an idiot.

"Shit." He gave up wondering and headed toward the hut.

He heard her before he saw her, that bubbly, infectious laugh. When he turned the corner and saw the open hut, Becca was sitting behind the counter. She'd kicked off her sneakers and rolled her jeans into capris. She wore a red tank and a straw hat, which Sam recognized as the one Tanner occasionally wore in the bright afternoon sun, and a welcoming smile.

"That's perfect, Yvonne," she was saying to a customer. "You'll have such a wonderful time. The guys are all so great, you'll want to book another trip right away, I'm sure." She pointed to a spot on the iPad screen in front of her — onto which she'd loaded all their forms. "And don't forget to leave your email addy. You don't want to miss any specials we have going on."

She'd been right — she was a fast learner. She had a gift, a different one from anyone he'd ever met. She had the gift of curiosity and empathy, and of bringing people out of themselves, charming them, getting them to open up.

He knew that firsthand. He hated that she seemed to think her self-worth was wrapped up in her past, because that was bullshit.

The smart, determined, resourceful Becca Thorpe could do anything she set her mind to.

He wished she knew that.

Yvonne was beaming when she walked away, and Becca immediately turned her attention to the next person waiting.

It was Anderson, the guy who ran the local hardware store. He was in his mid-thirties, and had been in Lucky Harbor since he was a kid. He was an okay guy, Sam supposed, but he was a known dog when it came to women. And sure enough, he leaned on the counter and flashed Becca his on-the-prowl smile like he was God's gift. "Hey," he said smoothly. "I know you. I sold you some stuff a few weeks back."

"You most definitely did, thank you," Becca said. "What can I sign you up for today? A snorkel? A deep-sea fishing expedition?"

"Which one of those do *you* do?"

"I take your money," she said.

Anderson laughed. "How about I take you instead."

"Um, what?" she asked.

"Out to dinner." Anderson clarified this with a smile, leaning in closer.

"Like . . . on a date?" Becca asked.

"Yes," Anderson said. "A date. What are

you doing later?"

"She's busy," Sam said, stepping inside the hut and coming up behind Becca, laying a hand on her shoulder.

Anderson stopped drooling over Becca and straightened. "Hey there. I like your new front person. She's a whole lot cuter than any of you three. No offense," he said, and smiled.

Sam did not.

Anderson's smile faded. "Right, well, okay then. I'll just be on my way."

When he was gone, Becca very slowly, very purposefully turned to Sam. "What was that?"

Sam shrugged. "He thinks you're cute."

"No, I meant what was that, as in what were you doing just now?"

"Stopped him from harassing you. I came up to see how you were feeling after last night. And to see . . ." What, genius? "How you're working out."

He knew his mistake immediately, even before she narrowed her eyes. "I'm working out just fine," she said. "But *you* not so much."

"Excuse me?"

She moved closer and lowered her voice without lowering her annoyance level, which was blasting from her eyes. "You just acted

289

like . . . a caveman."

"A caveman," he repeated.

"Yes! You chased him away from asking me out. You might as well have dragged me back to your cave by the hair."

He stared at her and then turned and tugged down the hut's rolling door for privacy, intending to show her his inner caveman.

But though Becca's eyes were still fiery, she took an immediate step back.

Sam swore beneath his breath and shoved the door back up again, giving her the space she clearly needed.

Becca held her own. She'd crossed her arms, but looked more pissed than anxious. Which was infinitely better, but not ideal. He still had no idea what made her tick. All he knew was that she made *him* tick.

And that was a first for him.

Also, he wanted a few minutes alone with whoever had made her anxious in small spaces. He wanted that badly. "Okay," he said slowly. "You're going to have to make a lot more sense for me here. Are you saying you actually *wanted* to go out with Anderson?"

"You're missing my point on purpose."

"Maybe because you're not speaking English." He dipped his head so that they were eye-to-eye. "Tell me in English, Becca."

"All right," she said, nose-to-nose with him, toe-to-toe. "I want to date *you,* you big, stubborn lug. But you don't want to date me back. You have all these . . ." She waved a hand. "Stupid rules."

"No, just the one," he said. "And it's not stupid. It's to protect you."

"From what?" she demanded, then blew out a breath when he just looked at her. "Whatever," she said, unimpressed as she tossed up her hands. Then she drew in a deep breath, like she was searching for patience, which was a new one for him. Normally *he* was the one searching for patience. And here she was looking at him like *he* drove *her* crazy. Which made no sense since he was being perfectly reasonable and she was not.

"I'm new to town," she finally said. "You know this."

"Yeah," he said. "So?"

"So maybe I'm lonely."

He stared at her, and he could admit, that hadn't occurred to him. He liked to be alone.

But this sweet, tough, beautiful woman in front of him wasn't wired the same as he was, and he should have gotten that.

"Becca."

"Oh, no." She waggled a finger in his face. "Don't you dare feel sorry for me. I'm a big girl, and I take care of myself. You don't want to be with me that way, I get it. We did it once, and maybe it was so awful for you that you can't bear to repeat it, maybe —"

"You *know* that's not the case."

"Fine. But it doesn't matter. You won't *let* yourself be with me, for whatever secret reason —"

"It's not a secret, Becca."

"Yes, it is. I mean, you *say* it's because I work for you, and also because you think I'm not ready, but you know what I think? I think that's just an excuse. Which leaves me to believe you're afraid of me and what we had during our one night together."

He let out a low laugh. "I'm not afraid of shit."

"No?" she challenged, hands on hips. "Then prove it."

He stared at her and then drew in a deep breath and tried again. "I don't feel sorry for you."

"Great. But if you could not put on your scary alpha-man face and shoo away the next person who might want to be my friend, that would be great, too."

She couldn't be that naive. Could she? "Becca, Anderson didn't want to be your *friend*. He wanted to be in your pants."

She lost some of her bluster at that. "Well . . . that was for *me* to decide."

"So you *do* want to go out with him."

"Nooooo," she said slowly and clearly, as if he was a huge idiot. "As already established, I want to go out with *you*. But you're turning out to be an ass, and I try very hard not to date asses anymore."

"Anymore?" he asked.

And just like that, her expression closed. This got to him, in a bad way. "I think it's time we talk about you," he said quietly.

She turned away.

Reaching out, he gently snagged her hand and pulled her back around.

"I'm on the clock," she said. "We're not talking about this now."

"Becca —"

"Or ever."

He disagreed, vehemently, and began to reel her in, but her cell phone rang. It was sitting on the counter, which is how he saw it was a FaceTime call from Jase.

Becca stared at the thing as if it were a snake poised to strike.

"You going to answer?" he asked.

"Yeah. Sure." Taking a deep breath, she

slid her thumb across the screen to answer. "Hey, Jase," she said, back to her friendly smile. It was the one she gave out to his clients, Sam realized, which was different from the smiles she gave him. The smiles for him were . . . real.

"Becca." A guy's face filled the screen. He looked like Becca, with the same big, soulful brown eyes and easy smile. He also looked incredibly relieved. "You're hard to get ahold of."

"Yes," she said. "I know."

"Too busy to call me back?"

Becca didn't look at Sam. "I'm sorry." Her cheeks were red. Her ears were red, too. Her eyes weren't. They were just plain unhappy.

Jase's smile faded as he took in this fact as well. "Bex," he said, until he caught sight of Sam. "Who's that?"

"He's my boss," Becca said before Sam could answer. "I . . . got a job."

Jase's gaze came back to Becca. "A job?"

"Yes."

"But you have a job in New Orleans, close to home."

"I lied when I told you I'd taken a leave of absence," she said. "The truth is, I quit. And now I . . . answer phones."

"I'd have given you money," Jase said. "Bex, you should be playing, going for your dream of music. Not . . . answering some-one's phones. Jesus."

"It's more than phones," Sam said. "She's running a charter company."

Jase didn't look impressed, nor did he take his eyes off Becca. "Let me help you —"

"No. *No,*" she repeated, more gently, reaching behind her to give Sam a shove. "I told you when I left. I'll worry about me. You worry about you."

"There was a time when we worried about each other," he said sadly.

Becca shook her head. "I can't do that anymore, Jase. You know that."

"Yeah," he said softly. "I know that. I miss you, Bex."

"Jase —"

"No, I get it." Jase's face closed up, much as his sister's had. "You have to worry about you."

"Jase," she said again, more softly now.

But the connection had ended. Becca went still for a minute, then pulled her heels up to her chair, hugging her bent legs and dropping her forehead to her knees.

Sam slid a hand down her back.

"I'm okay," she said.

"Yeah. That's why you're curled in a protective ball."

Closing her eyes, she shivered at his touch,

and hoping that meant he was doing the right thing, Sam curved his palm around the nape of her neck and crouched at her side. "Talk to me."

"I'm fine."

Amelia had long ago schooled him in the fine art of *fine*. He knew that if a woman used the word *fine*, it actually meant the polar opposite of *fine*.

"You made it sound like I was running the free universe, rather than basically being a gofer," she said.

"You're more than a gofer, Becca. But Jase is right. You should be doing something with your talent, your dream —"

She lifted her head and leveled him — slayed him — with her big, luminous eyes. "You firing me?"

"No, of course not."

She drew in a deep breath and let it out again, purposefully, like she was releasing some tension. "You should know that, while I find your whole caveman thing really annoying, I realize you were just trying to protect me. For some reason, that's . . . arousing, but I don't need protecting. I can take care of myself."

"I know." Sam paused. "Arousing?"

She snorted and turned her head to look at him. "Is that all you heard?"

"I'm a guy."

"Yeah," she said. "I've noticed."

Before Sam could even begin to interpret that statement, Cole strode in.

Looking like she'd been given a reprieve from her own execution, Becca jumped up. Sam snagged her wrist before she could move off and put his mouth to her ear. "We're not done."

"Tell me something I don't know," she muttered, giving him a shoulder nudge that didn't need translation — she wanted space.

Cole, one of the most intuitive people Sam knew, took in both Sam and Becca and stopped short. "What did I interrupt?"

"Just a little show of Neanderthalism, that's all," Becca said.

Cole grinned. "He dragging his knuckles again?"

Becca slid Sam a look. "Just a little."

Cole nodded. "Runs in the family, along with our good looks."

"She knows we're not real brothers," Sam said.

"Hell if we're not," Cole said, losing his good humor. "When you first came to stay at my house — what were we, thirteen? You were a stick, half-starved and always sick, but you still beat the shit out of those ass-holes who kept jumping me after school.

297

You said we were brothers, and no one messed with your brother."

Damn. Cole was even touchier than Amelia about this family shit. "Listen, I just meant —"

"You said it, man." Cole turned to Becca, who was probably soaking up this new information like a dry sponge. "And then our first year on the Gulf," Cole went on, "that massive storm hit, remember?"

"I remember," Sam said. "You don't need to —"

"We huddled in that fucking tiny room the size of a postage stamp, the four of us," Cole said. "And when that lantern fell and hit Gil on the head and sliced Tanner's leg, I got cut trying to clear the glass. We were bleeding like stuck pigs. Tanner decided we were all going to die, and we were trying to keep him from bleeding out —"

"Jesus," Sam said. "Dramatic much?"

"You kept your head," Cole said. "Even when the blood was everywhere, even when you slashed open your hand trying to get the glass out of Gil. You got us through that night, and the next morning when we got outta that shithole, we all had each other's blood on us and you" — He jabbed a finger at Sam like there might be any question of who he was talking to — "you said again

298

that we were blood brothers. So go ahead, say we're not."

Cole had the patience of a saint, and a very long fuse to a nearly nonexistent temper. But one thing that pissed him off was whenever Sam brought up that they weren't really family. Cole was Amelia's son through and through. Sam shook his head and gave up. He met Becca's gaze.

Hers had softened, and there was something new there. Like maybe she'd let him in just a little bit more than she had in the past.

Tanner came in and sank to the couch. As he always did after a trip, he immediately began stripping off his wet suit.

"What the hell are you doing?" Sam asked him.

Tanner had gotten the suit shoved down low on his waist. Bare-chested, he stared up at Sam. "Stripping," he said. "What does it look like?" He went to shove the suit off the rest of him, and since Sam couldn't be sure Tanner was actually wearing board shorts beneath — sometimes he went commando — Sam gave him a nudge with his foot. Actually, it was more of a kick. When Tanner looked up with a fight in his eyes, Sam jerked his head toward Becca.

Becca was watching every single movement with avid interest.

Tanner stopped stripping and grinned at her. "Hey, sweetness, how did your day go?"

"Good," she said. "We made a killing today when a group of twenty stopped to kayak. Oh, and as for the Summer Bash, I've looked into some advertising, both online and print for your web presence. You could do better there. I've emailed each of you a suggested plan to up your visibility. I'm not as familiar with Lucky Harbor as I'd like to be, yet, but I'm pretty confident you could also do much better in print ads as well."

Cole smiled. "Are we paying you enough?"

"For now," she said sweetly.

Sam thought about how many different ways she could have answered that, and had to admit it impressed him. She impressed him. She was nosy and curious and frustrating. She was sweet and warm, and sometimes, when he was very lucky, she looked at him like he was the only man on her radar.

And thanks to the intriguing phone call with her brother, he knew she protected her secrets well.

Which only made him want to know all the more what they were.

CHAPTER 20

Becca found herself enjoying Lucky Harbor more every single day. Twice she'd realized she'd missed another call from Jase, and twice she'd tried to call him back but he'd ignored her return calls.

Not a good sign.

But she couldn't try to live his life for him anymore. Instead, she immersed herself in life here. Lucky Harbor was different from any other place she'd ever lived. She was used to people keeping to themselves. She was used to passing someone on the street and, if accidental eye contact was made, you nodded or smiled briefly and kept moving.

That's not how things worked in Lucky Harbor. People stopped her, wanted to know how her day was, how the jobs were going — and they really, genuinely wanted to know. They also wanted to know how she handled working for the three hottest single men in town.

And yes, that actually happened. But it'd been Lucille asking, so maybe it didn't count.

She spent lots of hours at the rec center with the kids. Just yesterday they'd graduated to putting their five newly learned chords together to make a song.

Of sorts.

They were working on "God Bless America," *working* being the key word. But the hours spent in that classroom were some of her favorite hours ever.

"Think we can have a concert?" Pink asked one afternoon. Her front teeth were starting to grow in, while her twin Kendra's were not, which made it easy to tell them apart. Well, that and the fact that Pink wore only pink.

The truth was, they were about as far from being able to handle a concert as Becca herself was, but who was she to dim their enthusiasm? "Who would we play for?" she asked instead.

"The whole town!" Pink yelled. She yelled almost everything; she couldn't seem to contain her own energy.

"You want to play in front of everyone?" Becca asked, surprised.

Pink nodded vigorously.

Becca looked at Kendra. Kendra nodded

vigorously.

Becca looked at the rest of the gang. They all nodded equally as vigorously.

They couldn't play one line of "God Bless America" without breaking up into giggles or a fight, not to mention they had no real skills, and yet they wanted to play in front of the entire town. It was the most awesome show of confidence Becca had ever seen, and suddenly she wished she were a kid again. "Well, I —"

Someone cleared his throat behind her. She turned and caught Sam, Jack, and Jack's cousin Ben standing in the doorway, each wearing a badass smile. Becca knew that Ben taught "craft hour." He'd been the one to bring in Jack and Sam. The kids raved about them all the time.

Becca didn't know much about Jack or Ben, but the sight of Sam standing there all sexy-cool in jeans and a T-shirt advertising Lance's ice cream shop altered her heart rate. She decided she had to just *not* look at him anymore. Mature, she knew, but this was not a time to visit Lustville.

"How about us?" Jack asked. "Maybe you guys can play for us."

"Oh," Becca said. "I don't think —"

But the kids had all burst out with hopeful "Yays!" and "Yes!" and "Oh, please, Ms.

Teacher!"

Becca sneaked a peek at Sam, who gave her a two-hundred-watt grin, damn him.

"Let's hear a few songs," Jack said.

"We only know one," Pink said, and flung herself at the big, bad, silent Ben, wrapping her arms around his waist, giving him a bear hug. Kendra did the same. Ben surprised her by gathering them in and hoisting them up so that their feet dangled above the ground — much to their squealed delight.

Jack ran his fingers along the classroom's xylophone, making a racket that had the rest of the kids giggling.

"Can they play with us, Ms. Teacher?" Pink asked, still hanging from Ben's arm.

"If they want," Becca said, unable to imagine that they did.

But the guys made themselves at home. Pink divvied up the instruments, thrusting a marching drum at Sam.

Shocking her, Sam sat down with the drum. The seats were made for kids, and as a big guy, he should've looked ridiculous stuffed into one. But he didn't look anything close to ridiculous. Actually, he looked pretty damn fine, not to mention sexy-adorable, and she wanted to gobble him up.

He caught her staring at him. "I don't know what I'm doing," he said, not looking

bothered by that fact one little bit. It probably never occurred to him to worry about
feeling ridiculous or making a fool of himself.

"That's okay," Pink told him. "Ms.
Teacher will teach you."

"Yeah?" Sam turned to Becca with mock
seriousness, his eyes laughing.

"Can you keep a beat?" she asked with as
much teacher-like seriousness as she could
muster.

"I don't know," her newest student said
softly. "You tell me."

Oh, boy. The kids had given both Ben and
Jack cymbals. Everyone was in place and
ready, so Becca gave the count. They began
playing — out of sync, of course, and off
key. Nowhere even close to a beat.

But at the end of the song, when they all
burst into applause, Becca took in the sea
of happy faces and had to laugh. "Good,"
she said.

"It was *great,*" Pink corrected.

When the class was over, Becca looked for
Sam, and found him standing with Jack and
Ben. Her heart skipped a beat at all the male
gorgeousness in such close range.

"Holy crap," said a female voice from
behind Becca. It was Mitzy Gale, the woman
who ran the kids' programs at the rec

center, and also the principal of the elementary school. She visibly shook herself. "Those three really shouldn't stand together; they're going to blow all the female brain circuits in the building." She looked at Becca. "That was great, by the way."

"It was?" Becca asked.

"Yes. You do so well with the kids. I'd love to hire you to run the after-school music program, both here at the rec center and also at the elementary school."

"You don't have a music program," Becca said.

Mitzy laughed. "Exactly. *You're* going to create one."

"Me?"

"Yes, please."

Becca's heart started beating faster in excitement. Hope. Thrill.

"Now, I should warn you, don't quit your day job yet. The hours are only part-time until our budget kicks in, which might happen for fall, and it might not. It's not a great offer. Frankly, it's a terrible offer, but you're so desperately needed and wanted, Becca, if that counts for anything."

"That counts for everything," Becca said.

She marveled over it for a few days.

Only a few weeks ago, she'd have described herself as an introvert. But here, in

Lucky Harbor, working at the charter company, she'd come to realize that she was actually an extrovert. The job demanded it, really, and so did Music Hour with the kids, but . . . she liked it.

She liked the kids. She liked the guys, too. She liked all of it. Everything. Here, she didn't obsess so much over her career — or lack thereof. Here she got out and met new people every day.

Lived for the moment.

She had Sam to thank for that.

One afternoon, he showed up just as she was closing up the hut. The pattern was that one of the guys was always there at closing. They were there anyway, cleaning up the boat, the gear, whatever, but one of them would grab their cash from the day and get it to Sam. Or Sam would come get it himself.

Today he stuck his head in the door. His hair was wind-blown, his face tanned, his eyes crinkled to go along with the rare smile on his face as he crooked his finger at her.

She looked behind her.

No one.

"Me?" she asked.

"You."

"Is this going to be lesson number four?" she asked, unable to keep from sounding hopeful.

He met her gaze. He hadn't shaved that morning, and maybe not the morning before, either. His unruly hair had been finger-combed at best. He looked like maybe he had questionable motives. He looked like he didn't care what anyone thought of him. He looked hot.

"Becca, when I give you lesson number four, you'll know it."

Her entire body reacted. But she was beginning to think that he talked the talk of a badass, and walked the walk, but he didn't have the true heart of a badass or he'd have taken advantage of her by now.

Damn it.

Against her better judgment, she followed him outside and down the dock to where a gorgeous, sleek boat was moored. "Wow," she said. "It's beautiful."

"I made it for a client a few years back," he said. "He's gone into town to grab a drink with some friends. He wanted me to take it out and take a listen to the motor."

"I thought Cole was your mechanic."

"Yeah but he's gone, and I'm good, too." While he was speaking, he was giving her the bum's rush down the ramp, his hand low on her back, then lifting her onto the boat with seemingly no effort at all. Before she could recover from the brief but very welcome feel of being held against his chest, he was tossing her a life vest.

She stared down at it. "You planning on dumping me in the water?"

"Only if you piss me off." He came close, and then closer still, and she pressed her hands to his chest to keep her balance.

She wasn't opposed to pissing him off if it would make him kiss her again. "We going now?"

"In a minute." He ran his hands down her spine, over the backs of her thighs, and then up again, copping a feel of her bottom while he was at it.

"Sam." She was having some trouble getting her cognitive skills to fire with his hands on her like that, roaming, his eyes all hot and liquidy, making his intentions more than clear. "You can't be thinking —"

"About taking you on the galley table below? Yeah," he said, voice whiskey-smooth. "That's pretty much exactly what I'm thinking."

She actually looked to the door that led belowdecks. "Really?" she asked breathlessly.

He laughed, low and sexy. "Yes. Later."

She blew out a sigh. "You don't mean it. You're still just a tease."

He checked the clasps on her vest and adjusted them. There were several layers between his fingers and her skin, but her nipples got perky anyway.

"That good?" he asked, hands still on the vest, resting lightly against her breasts.

She had to clear her throat to answer. "Fine. But why —"

His gaze met hers. "I'm not taking any chances with you."

A squishy feeling settled low in her belly. "Why are you taking me with you at all? You've been avoiding —"

"I need a second body on board."

So much for the squishy feeling.

He walked through the cockpit to the bridge. He stood behind the controls, feet wide, the sexiest man she'd ever seen. "You need help?" she asked.

He flashed her a quick grin that affected her pulse.

No, he didn't need help.

"Hang on," he said.

Sam revved the engine, watching as Becca grabbed the oh-holy-shit hand bar in front of her with a cute little squeak of surprise as the boat leapt forward.

He loved that feeling, the power beneath him, the surge of the boat as it roared to life. The very first time he'd stood behind the controls of a boat and hit the gas, he'd felt free, and that had never lessened, not once in all these years.

The wind whipped, the salty air slapping them in the face as he took Becca out to the open water for some speed. A little while later, he slowed at a hidden cove where he'd once learned to fish.

He set anchor there.

The sun was low but not down, creating long lines of fire on the ocean, bisecting the swells. The scent of the early evening was pure, fresh air, and he watched with amusement and not a little amount of lust as Becca stood there and closed her eyes. "You okay?" he asked.

"Shh. I'm giving myself a *Titanic* moment."

He laughed, and she opened her eyes to smile at him. "You've seen the movie," she said.

He had, years ago under duress — a date who'd insisted on watching the DVD. He'd slept through most of it, but he knew the scene Becca meant, where the hero had stood behind his woman, her back plastered to his front at the bow so she could feel herself fly across the water.

Becca was still standing at the front of the

boat just like that, face to the last of the sun, when he came up right behind her. His hands settled on her hips, then her hands, which he lifted out high to her sides as the wind teased and brushed over their bodies, so close together that a piece of paper couldn't have fit between them.

"You did see the movie," she murmured.

He could feel her every curve as she leaned back into him, her sweet ass snuggled against his crotch. She shifted a little, and clearly felt the reaction she got out of him because she let out a shaky breath that went right through him. She shifted again, more purposefully this time, and he tightened his hands on her hips. "Watch it," he warned.

"I'm tired of watching," she said, "and never doing. You once told me not to play with you, but you're playing with me. If you really wanted me, you'd have had me again by now. Stop doing this, stop making me feel things for you."

He pulled her around, stared into her soft, warm, *hurt* eyes, and saw she really meant it. "Are you talking about the fact that I'm not using you for sex?" he asked incredulously.

"Yes," she said. "I *want* you to use me for sex, damn it!"

"Becca." He slid his fingers into her hair

and stared into her face. "I'm not using you for sex because this isn't just sex between us."

"We've only done it once," she said — as if he didn't know, didn't relive it every single night. "*Of course* it's just sex," she said, sounding pissy.

"Okay. That's it." He'd been holding back for . . . shit. None of his reasoning seemed valid at the moment. So he yanked off her life vest and hauled her into him.

"Hey," she said. "Don't I need that?"

"Not where you're going." He tossed her over his shoulder and headed belowdecks.

"Wait — what are you doing?" she shrieked from upside down.

"I warned you."

She was quiet for a beat, either because she was upside down, or because he'd stunned her. "You'd *better* mean it," she finally said, " 'cause last time I ended up in my bed alone, all hot and bothered, and I had to handle my own business."

Now it was *his* turn to go quiet for a beat, imagining just that, Becca in her bed, hot and bothered, handling her own business. It was a really great image. "You hot and bothered now?" he asked.

"Mostly just bothered." Each word was a breathless murmur since she was bouncing up and down with his stride as he brought her into the small bedroom below. "And anyway," she said, "I'm not getting naked with you now. I don't even like you anymore!"

"I'm going to change your mind about both of those things," he said, and slid his hand from her thighs to her ass.

"I'm going to need that in writing —" she started, and ended with another shriek as he tossed her to the bed.

CHAPTER 21

"Hey —" Becca started, but the air was knocked from her lungs upon impact with the mattress.

Sam was kicking off his sneakers, but she, running on pure adrenaline, bounced up off the bed and gave him a little push until he was up against the wall. With an *oomph* of surprise, he let her have her way. For a beat. But then he took control, turning them so that *she* was pinned between his hard body and the even harder wall, her breasts crushed to his chest. He thrust a thigh between hers and rubbed it against her.

And damn if she didn't moan. This made his eyes heat with both triumph and a hunger that took her breath.

"Hold on," he said.

"For what?" she asked breathlessly.

"The ride." And then, still holding her to the wall, he kissed her.

And God. God, he had a way of kissing

like she was his entire world. He was right. She needed to hold on for this. So she did, to him, gripping his hard biceps, his broad shoulders, his back, clutching at everything she could reach because she was starved for this, for him.

When they needed air, he easily switched from her mouth to her neck, licking, biting, sucking, moving against her the whole time. Becca could feel the pressure building inside her, and a wild thrill skittering on the surface of her skin as he drove her body right where he wanted it to go.

She was out of control, and he had plenty of control. Hell, he had all of it, but this wasn't about pressure, or forcing her. She'd been in that position before, and this was different. Like always with Sam, she was fully, definitely, willingly on board, and absolutely willing to take what he was giving.

And in turn give him everything she had.

It was a new sensation, and she wanted to revel in it, the utter feminine power that came with the surrender, but she couldn't do anything but *feel*. He was still moving against her, his hands rough and yet arousing, his mouth taking little love bites as he held her still. She probably should think about being mad at the manhandling, but the truth was, it excited her. She wasn't mad; she wasn't afraid. She was so damn aroused she could hardly stand it. So when he paused, she clutched at him. "I swear," she gasped, "if you're just teasing me again —"

Planting his forearms on the wall on either side of her head, his big hands captured her face for another long, hard, deep kiss as he rocked into her. "Does this feel like a tease?" he asked.

"I don't know yet," she panted. "Depends on what comes next."

"You do. You come next, Becca."

Oh, God. She could feel the quivers start in her body at just the words. "Not on someone else's bed."

"No," Sam said. "Right here. Like this." And then he slid down her body, dropping to his knees on the floor below her. He spread her legs to suit him and then shoved her denim skirt up to her waist. "Hold this."

"Um," she said, but did as he commanded, and held her skirt up past her pink lace, cheeky-cut panties, hoping to God she looked good. She must have, because he let out a gruffly uttered "Fucking hot, babe," scraped the lace to the side, and put his greedy mouth on her. With a soft cry, she sank her fingers into his hair and held on for dear life as he drove her right to the edge, held her there until she mewled his name in entreaty, and then shoved her over. The orgasm broke hard and fast, and she shuddered against his mouth.

"Again," he demanded, and then made it happen.

Still gasping for breath, she opened her eyes as he slowly rose, kissing her hip, her belly, first one breast and then the other on his way to her mouth.

She could feel him pulsing through the thick cotton of his cargo shorts. He needed to get out of the cargoes and work his magic. Of that she was sure. Goal-oriented, she reached for his top button.

He growled deep in his throat as she shoved the cargoes down far enough to spring him free. She wrapped her fingers around him and stroked, eliciting another growl, a wild, primitive sound that vibrated around her body, through her nipples, and into her core as he throbbed and leapt to her touch. She wanted to taste him, but that would mean moving and there wasn't time for that. She wanted him inside her, pounding into her, touching the parts of her body and soul that no man had ever managed to reach.

Except him. "Please, Sam. Now."

Apparently on board with the demand, he rolled a condom down his length. "The condom's not blue," she whispered.

He huffed out a laugh. "No."

"But still extra large."

He snorted. Then his mouth closed on hers, drinking in her moan as he slid up between her legs. His hands came up to tug her skirt, top, and bra away, the material fluttering to the floor. He pulled her panties down her legs and slid his hand between them, his fingers creating exquisite sensations against her wet flesh as he caressed every inch of her. Then he slid his hands around her thighs to cup her butt, lifting her. "Wrap your legs around me, babe — Yeah, like that —" His breath hissed out in a long inhalation as he filled her with one thrust, stretching her to the limit.

The quivers began in her body and echoed in his, letting her know he was as close to the edge as she. Sheathed to the hilt, he began to rock, using his hips and hands to move her as he chose. She tightened her legs around him and met each of his upward strokes, racing for the pleasure, growing frantic for it.

Fisting a hand into her hair, Sam tugged her face up to his. "Look at me."

It was a struggle. She felt drugged, high

on him, but she met his searing, intense gaze and something happened: They synced, and then she was free falling . . .

So was he. One of his hands slapped onto the wall beside her head, palm flat against the surface for balance as he emptied himself into her with a powerful thrust that drove the breath from her lungs. Still spinning, still coming, she felt the shaking of her own body and the tremors in his as he worked to keep them both upright.

His legs gave out and they slid down the wall to the floor, the both of them sucking in air for all they were worth. She lay on her side and Sam flat on his back on the floor, not moving.

"Christ," he finally muttered, and reached over to snag her by the leg. Boneless, she let him haul her in, across the floor to him. Bracing himself on one elbow above her, he tucked her in so that her head lay in the hollow of his shoulder.

Turning her face into his warm skin, she kissed him. "Okay, so maybe I like you a *little.*"

He looked down at her with eyes gone warm and soft. "Yeah?"

Reaching up, she touched her fingers to his smile and he gently rubbed his lips across her palm, his gaze never leaving hers.

With a sated sigh, she traced his lips, the line of his jaw. "Or a lot. Which leaves me hanging out . . ." She smiled a little self-consciously with the irony. "Naked."

Leaning over her, he gently kissed the spots he'd nibbled at only moments before, his hand stroking her hair from her sweaty face, smoothing down the tangled mass. He made a sound low and deep in his chest, which vibrated against her nipples. "You're not alone in that," he said. Bringing a hand up to her chin, he once again turned her face to his.

He let her see what he was thinking. Desire, hot, liquid, consuming desire.

Affection, too. Which made her all warm and fuzzy.

But it was the *need* that reached her. Need wasn't the same thing as desire. It was even more awe inspiring. This big, tough, self-made man *needed* her.

And in a very scary way, she felt the same.

Becca awoke first. It definitely wasn't dawn yet but there was a lightening of the sky. That wasn't unusual. What was unusual was that she wasn't her usual morning chilly. In fact, she was downright toasty. That was because she was cozied up to a furnace.

A furnace named Sam. They were in her

apartment; he'd brought her here late last night, and then surprised her by staying. He was on his back, the blanket riding low. She was plastered up to his side, one arm flung over his chest, a leg hitched over his. He had his arm snug around her, one big hand palming her butt possessively.

His breathing was slow and even. He was still deeply asleep, and at the thought a smile curved her mouth. She'd worn him out.

She liked that. A lot. Awake, Sam Brody was like a cat, all contained energy, controlled, steady. Asleep, he was boneless and completely relaxed in a way she rarely got to see. He had stubble that was at least twenty-four hours past a five o'clock shadow, and she had no complaints because she'd loved the way it'd felt on her skin. Her face heated as she remembered where some of those places were. She was pretty sure she had the marks to prove it.

If she could, she'd keep him here, right here in her bed, forever. And at that thought, she knew the truth. This wasn't casual. This wasn't about easy sex, or friendship, though both those things absolutely existed.

This was about the fact that she was in deep. Too deep. Her head was still cradled in the crook of his shoulder, and she realized she was rubbing her jaw against him like she was marking him as hers. Stilling, she lifted her head.

His eyes were open and on hers, sleepy . . . sexy. "You finished looking?"

She blushed and bit her lower lip. "Maybe. Maybe not . . ." She playfully tugged the sheet down and exposed . . . yay! . . . a part of him *very* happy to see her. "I like to look," she said.

"Good to know." And that's when she found herself rolled flat to her back and pinned by 180 pounds of testosterone.

"Turnabout's fair play," he said, and proceeded to get his fill of looking at her.

And then touching.

And then tasting . . .

Sam barely got to the docks on time. They had a big group waiting — twelve fishermen in from Phoenix. He smiled at the clients as he pushed off, ignoring both Tanner and Cole giving him long looks. "What?" he said, leaping on board.

"You're smiling," Cole said. "In the early morning, pre-coffee."

"It happens," Sam said.

"When?" Cole asked. "When does that *ever* happen?"

Tanner, eyes narrowed, got up into Sam's

space and studied him. "What's that?" he asked, touching Sam's throat. "Is that a *hickey*?"

Sam smacked his hand away. "No."

"Yeah, it is," Tanner said. "You totally have a hickey."

"Let me see," Cole said, pushing close. At the sight, he grinned. "Nice. I wouldn't mind one of those," he said, sounding wistful.

Tanner snorted.

Sam stalked to the bridge, rolling his eyes at their laughter behind him.

It wasn't until that night, kicking off his shoes in the foyer of his house, that he caught sight of himself in the mirror.

He totally had a hickey on his throat.

"Son, you can have the hot tub tonight," his dad said, coming in behind him without knocking as usual. "I'm tuckered *out.*" He plopped himself on the couch.

Sam moved closer and looked him over. Pale. Even a little gray. He knew he'd been taking his medicine; he'd made damn sure of it every morning. But the meds were no guarantee. "You okay?"

"Always," Mark said.

"Dad."

Mark opened his eyes. "I'm fine. I'm just overtaxed, that's all."

"Maybe it's not a great time to be screwing a woman two decades your junior."

Mark grinned. "But what a way to go, right?"

When Sam just looked at him, he sighed. "And that's not what I've been doing."

"What have you been doing then?" Sam asked.

Mark hesitated.

Never a good sign. "Christ," Sam said. "Gambling?"

"No!" Mark shook his head. "Still got a real high opinion of me, I see." He paused. "I've been working."

"Working," Sam repeated.

"Yeah. I took a job at the arcade, running some of the games, okay?"

"That's a teenager job," Sam said.

"Or the job of a man with no résumé," his dad said.

Sam didn't get it. "Why?"

"I'm going to pay my own way," Mark said.

"Since when?"

"Goddamn it, I'm tired of being a mooch off you."

Sam sighed and sank to the couch next to his dad. "Well, if you're going to take all the fun out of my resentment . . ."

Mark laughed, but it was hollow. "You've

worked so hard all your life," he said. "And people here love you. I want to be a better man, son. Like you."

Sam took the unexpected hit to his solar plexus, heart, and gut. "You can't work, not right now."

"Yes, I can. I am. I already have twenty hours. I'm going to pay you rent and get my own car. And you're not the only one who can build shit, you know. I'm going to make you shelves so all your CDs and DVDs aren't on the damn floor all the time."

Sam stared at him, but his dad looked serious. And sincere. "How about you wait until after you get better?"

Suddenly looking older and very tired, Mark closed his eyes again. "Yeah. Okay. Hey, you got stuff for sandwiches?"

"I think so," Sam said. "You want one?"

"You got any potato chips to put in it?"

Sam blew out a breath. "Yeah."

Sam fed his dad, watched him carefully for a while, and determined he really was just tired and not ill enough for a call to Josh.

"Stop hovering," Mark muttered, eyes closed from his position prone on the couch. "I'm not dying tonight."

"That's not funny," Sam said.

"You're right, it's not. It's sad as hell that you're watching me instead of being with your woman. Go be with your woman."

"Dad —"

"Jesus." Mark pulled out his phone and hit a number. "Hey, darlin'," he said. "Yeah, I'm fine, but I've got someone here who's not. I'm sending him to you, okay?" Mark slid his gaze to Sam. "Okay, I'll tell him." He clicked off. "She says to be ready for lesson number five. What's she teaching you?"

Sam managed to keep a straight face, but Christ, she cracked him up. "I have no idea," he said evenly.

His dad shrugged. "Well, when a woman looks like that, with a heart like that, you ignore the crazy, son, and get ready for lesson number five."

Two days — and two extremely long, hot, erotic nights later — Becca was in the hut, opening for the day, when the man single-handedly responsible for the perma-smile on her face walked in. She was surprised, seeing as she'd left him boneless and face-down on her bed only half an hour earlier. Knowing he was leaving today on a two-day fishing expedition, she'd let him sleep.

"You got up early," he said, heading for

the coffee.

"So did you."

"Twice," he said.

She laughed. It was true. And once the night before as well. "Did I wake you when I left? I tried to be quiet and not talk."

"I wouldn't have minded some talking," he said. "I really liked the *More, Sam, oh please more.*"

She threw her pencil at him.

He caught it in midair and grinned.

"I got up thinking I'd try to work on my next jingle," she said.

"You haven't said what your next assignment is." He caught her grimace and smiled. "It can't be worse than your last few."

"Yeah, it can. It's diapers. But at least it's for *baby* diapers." She blew out a breath. "It's because I'm not doing anything spectacular. I keep waiting for my muse to really kick in, but the truth is, I think I've lost my talent." She caught something in his expression. "What?"

"It's not because you're not talented," Sam said. "It's the importance you're attaching to it."

That this was true didn't help. "I need to be successful at something," she said. "At *this,*" she corrected when he opened his mouth. "I'm going to be successful at this if it kills me."

"You know," he said. "It wasn't all that long ago when you got mad at me for blaming shit on myself, like when I got my dad and me kicked out of that apartment."

"You were thirteen," she said. "I'm not a minor by any stretch of the imagination. I run my own life, and I take the fall for it."

He brought her a mug filled with lots of sugar and a little bit of coffee, and that he knew the exact right formula warmed her heart. Not enough to ward off the unease at the intimacy of this conversation, but enough that she didn't make a run for the door. Apparently sharing orgasms was easier than sharing her soul. She stared down into the steaming brew, wishing it held the answers to her life.

"Becca."

With a sigh, she looked at him, and found her gaze locked in his, held prisoner.

"You're successful just as you are," he said.

"If you think that's true, you haven't been paying attention."

"Wrong," he said. "I've been paying attention better than you. You came into this job to answer phones and you've so completely fixed us up that now *anyone* could run our place with the blink of an eye."

"In my past," she clarified. "I want to have

been successful at stuff in my past."

"Fuck the past. Move on to something that suits you right now."

She stared at him. "Fuck the past? Is that how you live your life? Not thinking or looking back at all, just forward?"

"Hell yeah."

She nodded. This was true. She knew it. She'd seen it. She'd just conveniently forgotten it.

Sam's eyes were warm as his hand curled around the side of her neck, where his thumb gently stroked. "You should try it sometime."

What she wanted to try was him. She wanted to try him out for as long as they both could take it. She almost said so, but saying it out loud twice wouldn't make it so. Her life was in flux. She needed to focus, and focusing around Sam was proving all but impossible. Still, she stepped into him, meeting him halfway when he lowered his mouth and kissed her, an effective kiss that shut down her ability to think and cracked through her defenses.

Of course that's when their morning clients showed up — a group of ten fishermen — and just like that, Sam was gone.

Over the next two days, Becca ran the hut and loaned out the rental gear. She finalized Summer Bash plans. She had dinner with Olivia at the Love Shack on Country Night, and even got talked into dancing a little bit. She was having fun — until she realized Lucille was snapping pics.

Lucille told Becca not to worry her pretty little head about it because the pics would only be posted on Lucky Harbor's Pinterest page, and there weren't many followers yet.

Olivia went home shortly thereafter because she had to work early the next day. The crowd thinned considerably, and Jax sent Becca a long look and a jerk of his chin toward the piano.

Like a moth to the flame. There were still a few stragglers in the place but she sat anyway. Only a few weeks ago, she could not have done so. Still, her heart began to thump. She looked around.

No one was paying any mind at all.

So far so good. She set her fingers on the keys, closed her eyes, and began to play.

When she'd finished one song, she drifted into another, and after three, a movement caught her eye.

Mark.

"Hey," she said, startled, jerking her hands back from the piano. "What are you doing here?"

He set down a full shot glass.

She looked at the glass and then into his face, and her heart softened at the inner turmoil she saw there. "You're struggling."

"Seems like I'm not the only one," he said. "Scooch over, darlin'."

She scooted over, and to her surprise he sat on the bench next to her. "You play the same way you make sandwiches," he said. "Like heaven on earth."

She choked out a laugh. "I don't like it when people listen to me play."

"Is that true, really?"

She thought about it and slowly shook her head. "No, actually. The truth is that I don't like worrying about making a fool of myself."

"Honey, the only foolish act is keeping that talent to yourself." Then he placed his fingers on the keys and began to play "Don't Go Breaking My Heart."

Becca laughed and joined in, and when they were done, she heard a single pair of hands clapping.

Jax, and he was grinning. "You two are hired," he said.

Becca looked at Mark.

"Yeah," he said. "I know. Call me a fool, right?"

She grinned. "You play."

"Nah. I dated a woman who taught me

that one, eons ago now. Other than that, I've no idea what I'm doing." He paused, looked at the shot glass. "With anything."

"Me either," Becca said and nudged the shot glass away from him. "But I know that won't help either of us."

"You're right."

"It's not often I hear that," she said. "I like the sound of it. You going to tell me what you're doing here?"

"Maybe I came to make sure I could stay off the booze. But then I saw you and thought to myself that you looked beautiful. And sad. And since you've helped me so much, I wanted to do the same for you."

She met his gaze. "How do you plan to do that?"

"By imparting wisdom," he said. Then he sighed. "Shit's hard."

She nodded. "Really hard."

"But not having shit . . . that's harder," he said. "Know what I mean?"

"Yes." She paused. "No."

"We're still breathing."

"Yes," she said. "Last I checked, I was still breathing. You too by the looks of you."

"Right. And not breathing, that would be worse," Mark said.

She stared at him. "That's it? That's the wisdom you're going to impart?" Becca said. "Keep breathing?"

"And don't sweat the small stuff," he said. "Both good bits of advice."

"True enough," she said, and stood up. "Need a ride?"

"Nah. I want to walk. No worries, I didn't drink."

"You going to?"

"No, ma'am."

She kissed him on his cheek and went home and sat on her bed, which reminded her of Sam, and work. By dawn, she'd sent off a jingle for the diaper campaign, but she wasn't thrilled with it, and she was a little bit afraid she knew why.

She was sweating the small stuff.

She was also sweating the big stuff, but one thing at a time.

CHAPTER 22

By early evening, Becca had closed the hut and was eating ice cream after snorkeling with Olivia when the guys came back in.

She hurriedly popped the last bite of cone into her mouth and pulled on her denim shorts over her still-damp bathing suit.

"Look at you move," Olivia said, amused.

"My bosses are back. They might need something."

"Uh-huh," Olivia said. "Or you want to pull a *Baywatch* and run down the beach toward your man. Or maybe I should say *Babe-watch.*"

Becca ignored her and . . . ran down the beach.

Cole and Tanner were unloading gear to the dock. She didn't see Sam, and thought maybe he'd somehow gotten by her. She slowed her footsteps, and tried to slow her heart down as well.

After all, he didn't owe her a special hello.

He owed her nothing.

"Hey," she said, greeting Cole and Tanner. "Everyone good?"

"Sure." Tanner tossed some more gear to the docks. "We hardly ever kill anyone anymore."

Cole turned to look at him. "Seriously? You're allowed to joke about it, but not me?"

Tanner shrugged.

Cole shook his head and pulled Becca in for a hug. "Everything holding up here?" he asked her.

"Of course."

His gaze said he knew otherwise, but he let her get away with it. "Saw you and Anderson all hot and heavy on the dance floor. You really gotta watch that guy, okay?"

Becca stared at him. "You were there?"

Tanner laughed. "No, he wasn't there. But *please* ask him how he knows."

Becca looked at Cole.

Cole grimaced. "It's not a big deal."

"Then tell her," Tanner said.

Cole sighed. "Pinterest."

Tanner coughed and said "pussy" at the same time.

"Hey, my mom sent me the link to the pin," Cole said.

Tanner grinned. "Gets better and better."

Cole had accessed the pic on his phone and showed it to Becca. It was her and Anderson dancing, and from the angle the shot had been taken, Anderson appeared to be holding her very close and whispering a sweet nothing in her ear. "Okay, that is not what it looks like," she told them, and in the interest of a subject change she waved the iPad she held and went through her list of things to go over. "The decorations for the Summer Bash," she said to Cole as he did something fancy with the ropes in his hands.

"Whatever you want," he said.

She sighed and looked at Tanner, who was straddling the dock and the boat with circus-like balancing ability as he hosed down the bow.

"What he said," Tanner said.

"You guys are too easy," she said.

They both shrugged. "You could ask the boss," Cole suggested, jerking his head toward the figure coming out of the cabin, heading to the helm.

Sam.

He wore no shirt, no shoes, nothing but a pair of low-slung board shorts, a backward ball cap, and dark lenses as he did something with the controls and the engine roared to life.

He took her breath.

"He's not the only boss," she managed.

"No, but he likes to think he is," Tanner said.

"He's not exactly crazy about this whole shindig," she reminded them.

Cole laughed.

"What?" she asked.

"Honey, what he's crazy about is *you.*"

This startled her. She'd really believed that she and Sam had been doing a great job at keeping . . . whatever this was under wraps. Not that she was ashamed of what they were doing, although thinking about it did make her blush.

But there was the unprofessional factor. She was, after all — and despite his best efforts to the contrary — sleeping with her boss. She glanced at Sam, still behind the helm, his back to them. "You really think he's doing this party just for me?"

"Did he not hire you when he didn't want to?" Cole asked.

"Yes, but —"

"And did he let you into his Man Cave without bloodshed?"

"Well, yes. But . . ."

They were both just looking at her.

"Come on," she said. "This is silly. Sam doesn't do anything he doesn't want to. Not unless . . ." She thought about how he did whatever his dad needed done, just to keep the man afloat, even though it'd be easier to walk away. How much he did for Cole's mom, which she knew he felt was payback, just as she knew that Amelia didn't feel he owed her a thing. How much he did for these guys right in front of her, though that was mutual. How much he'd done for her . . .

Tanner went brows-up.

"He cares," she whispered. "He cares a lot."

Tanner touched a finger to the tip of his nose.

Cole nodded.

"Well, I know that," she said. And she did know how Sam felt about her; it was in every touch, every kiss, every word he murmured against her late at night in her bed.

But still, hearing it out loud in the light of day from the two people closest to him in the whole world gave her a warm glow. She smiled at them and turned to go to the hut.

"Hey," Cole said, and she looked back. "Take it easy on him."

"What do you mean?"

Tanner chuckled. "He means the guy

plays at being tough as hell, but the truth is
—"

"I'm tough enough to beat the shit out of the both of you ladies," Sam said from behind Cole and Tanner.

"You're so dead," Cole murmured to Tanner.

Tanner didn't look worried as he leisurely took off toward the hut. Cole followed, leaving Becca alone with Sam.

"So," she said into the awkward silence. "You only *play* at being tough and hard?"

He surprised her by laughing, and then tugged her onto the boat and into his arms. "You tell me." He nuzzled her neck. "Do I *play* at being hard?"

She thought about how deliciously "hard" he'd been the other morning before he'd left and let out a sigh of pleasure.

Holding her close, Sam opened his mouth on her neck. "Love that sound."

"Sam," she murmured, going soft. And damp . . .

"And that," he said, and nibbled. "Come onto the boat; I want to show you something."

She snorted against his chest. "I've already seen it."

"Smart-ass," he said, his hand sliding down her back to lightly smack her butt.

"You've been busy," he said casually as he nudged her into the cabin.

"Yeah." The quarters were tight here but she didn't feel threatened, not with Sam. "Summer Bash is in four days and there's a lot of last-minute stuff. Plus, I've been working with the kids, and we're really nailing down the rest of the song. Sort of." She laughed a little. "Actually, that might be wishful thinking on my part."

"Cute," he said. "But I meant at the Love Shack."

She stared at him. "You saw the pic, too."

"My little sister showed it to me."

"You don't have a little sister," she said.

"Cole."

She laughed. "You should know, the angle of the picture made the dance look a little . . . more than it was."

He nodded. "He ask you out?"

"He did."

"You tell him you're busy?" he asked, pushing her into the galley.

"Didn't know I was," she said.

"You are." His voice was raspy rough and teasingly sexy — a deadly combo. "Very busy."

"Doing?"

"Me."

She tried to look outraged, but the truth

was that the ridiculously alpha statement made her go all warm and mushy. Before she could decide how to respond to the cocky possessiveness, he turned her to face the table. On it were the music books she'd been eyeing online.

"Sam," she said with surprise, and tried to turn to him, but he pinned her still.

"We docked in Seattle with our clients," he said in her ear. "They had lunch downtown, and I picked these up for you." His lips brushed the skin of her neck as deft fingers tugged at the string ties of her bikini top.

With a gasp, she whirled around, holding up her top with her hands. "Hey."

Sam smiled.

Her heart stuttered.

He looked down at the way her nipples pressed against the thin material of her suit and let out a low, very male sound of approval. "Miss me?" he asked.

"No."

"Liar." He slid a hand to the nape of her neck and rubbed the chafed spot where her bathing suit ties had made her skin raw. When her lips parted on a soft moan, he tangled his fingers in her hair, tipping her face up, his lips inches from hers. He had really great lips.

"Okay," she said. "Maybe I missed your mouth." *And the things you do with it . . .*

He kissed her again, then used his hips to shift her legs apart. "Only my mouth?"

"Mmm," she said, as if she needed to think about it.

He gripped her hips and rubbed her against a most impressive erection. She dug her nails into his back as he rocked into her.

"Mmm. Maybe some other things, too," she managed.

That made him laugh as he slid his hands down her back to her bottom. "I missed *you,*" he murmured against her lips.

The statement was unexpected, and made her melt into him. She looked into his eyes and found herself looking into pure desire. Maybe she had no idea what the future would bring for them, but the next few minutes would be damn good. She slid her hands up ripped abs and around to his warm, sleek back. "Now, Sam?"

"No," he said, surprising her. "Much as I'd love to know if this table would hold, I've been thinking all day about the things I want to do to you. I'm going to need a while. Hours."

She quivered, and felt herself get wet. "Hours?"

"All night."

"Tonight then," she agreed.

"And maybe tomorrow night, too," he said.

She quivered again. "As many as you want."

CHAPTER 23

Sam nudged Becca back above deck, his eyes on her sweet ass as it moved up the narrow stairs in front of him, his mind on how she'd smiled at him when she'd first seen him. She'd been happy to see him.

He'd had women be happy to see him before. He'd had women want him. But that wanting had usually been purely sexual in nature, and although he'd reciprocated, he hadn't spent too much time delving deeper.

Becca was different. He liked her in a bathing suit, no doubt. He also liked her with their clients. He liked her with his partners.

He liked *her.*

He was so lost in thought that he didn't realize when Becca stopped, frozen in her tracks at the sight of the guy standing on the docks staring at them.

"Jase," he heard her whisper.

Jase had gone still as stone as well. "Hey, sis."

Becca glanced back at Sam, a look on her face that he couldn't quite interpret. "Sorry," she said softly. "But I've got to talk to him."

Sam got that she wanted privacy for this reunion, and he should have left the area.

But fuck that. He didn't get off the boat, but instead busied himself with the ropes, an ear cocked to the conversation behind him.

That was the thing about water. Sound carried. Voices carried. From the middle of the harbor on a still day, he'd once heard a conversation between two illicit lovers in a cove, clear as a bell.

"How did you find me?" Becca asked.

"Remember how you made me upload that Find Your Friends app so you could always see where I was?" he asked. "That thing goes both ways."

Becca stared at him. "So all this time I thought I was free, you knew exactly where I was. Why are you here, Jase?"

"Maybe I missed you," he said.

Becca stared into her brother's face, looking like she didn't buy that excuse one bit. "Your eyes aren't yours," she finally said.

"What the hell does that mean?" Jase asked.

Becca stared at him for another beat, then took a step back, her voice shaky. "Damn you, Jase. You promised."

At this, Jase shoved his hands into his pockets and hunched his shoulders, staring out on the water, mouth grim. "Yeah, well, you know I've never been good at keeping promises."

She made a sound of disbelief. "So that's it, your whole explanation?" she asked. "You're not good at promises, so that frees you up to not keep them? For God's sake, Jase, grow up!"

Sam couldn't help but think of his dad. Becca had been nothing but accepting of his dad. It told him there was much more to this story.

Jase closed his eyes, like looking at her was too painful. "I've never been as strong as you," he said. "You expecting different from me is like . . . believing in Santa Claus until sixth grade."

Becca let out a mirthless laugh. "I didn't believe in Santa that long," she said. "I only pretended — for you."

Jase's gaze snapped to Becca's.

"Yeah," she said. "You wanted to believe so bad, I kept up the pretense. For you. You idiot." She gave him a shove that might have landed him in the water if he hadn't been on his toes.

"Jesus, Bex."

"You promised me," she said fiercely with another shove. "You promised me you could do this, get through rehab, stay clean. You wanted a life, you said, your *own* life. You weren't going to need me, lean on me; you were going to do this on your own."

"And *you* said you were drowning from trying to save me," Jase snapped, just as fiercely. "You said you couldn't breathe. Christ, Bex, what was I supposed to do with that?"

"So you lied to me?"

"No. *No,*" he repeated when Becca made a sound of soft angst, and then he reached for her.

She evaded, stabbing a finger into his chest. "I tried to save you," she said. "God, I tried. For years, Jase."

"I know," her brother whispered.

Another sound ripped from Becca's throat and tore Sam in two. This was killing her slowly, and he wanted, needed, to fix it for her.

"So why are you here?" Becca asked her brother. "Why now?"

Jase looked away.

"Truth, Jase," she implored. "You owe me that."

He nodded, a muscle twitching in his jaw. "My concert's tonight, in Seattle. I was hoping to get my big sis to play with me."

"Oh, my God. You're kidding, right?" She stared into her brother's face and let out another mirthless laugh. "You're not kidding. You actually think I can —" She laughed again and bent over at the waist. "My throat's closing up," she said to her knees. "Hopefully I'll suffocate quick."

Jase actually smiled. "Still dramatic."

Becca whipped upright, eyes flashing at him. "Don't do that. Don't you dare make me feel like it's all in my head."

"It is all in your head," Jase said. "That's what stage fright is. Ignore it."

"You can't ignore a panic attack," she said through her teeth.

"Bex —"

"No. Damn it! See, *this* is why I left. Look, I get that you don't believe in panic, that you never even feel nerves before a show at all. I don't know if that's because you truly never get nervous or if you've been self-medicating so long that you can't feel it!"

Jase took a step back like she'd slapped him, and brother and sister stared at each other.

"I'm sorry," Becca finally said. "That was out of line."

"No." Jase shook his head. "I deserved it. And I'm the sorry one. I'm sorry I upset you by coming here without warning. Besides the concert, I wanted to see you, and for once make sure you were okay, the way you always used to do for me." He hesitated. "Mom and Dad are flying in. I promised I'd come get you and bring you to the concert tonight."

Becca shook her head slowly. "You shouldn't have promised that."

"No doubt, given how all my other promises have turned out." He let out a long, shaky breath. "I guess you also think I shouldn't have come."

"You shouldn't have, no," she said. "I asked you for time. It's the only thing I've ever asked of you."

Jase stared at her for a long beat, and then nodded.

Becca rubbed the heels of her hands over her eyes, which were filled with a hollow, haunted devastation that just about killed Sam. He had no idea how Jase could even look at her without doing everything in his power to fix this.

"I'm sorry," Jase whispered, but it wasn't enough; it didn't change Becca's expression. If anything, it made it worse. "I'm sorry I wasn't there for you after . . . Nathan —"

Becca snapped upright, eyes glossy. "Stop."

He didn't stop. "I didn't get what happened. I honestly thought you two were back together, so I didn't think —" He hesitated. "I'm sorry I wasn't there when you needed me most. I know that's why you really left —"

"You're sorry I'm gone."

Jase stared at her for a beat. "Yeah. I'm very sorry you're gone. I wish I'd paid more attention, that I'd really listened —" He broke off when she made a sound like a soft sob and covered her mouth. "Too little too late?" he whispered.

"No, I . . . I don't know." She closed her eyes. "Yes."

Jase closed his eyes. "I shouldn't have come," he said again, and when Becca didn't contradict this, Jase blew out a breath. "I'm going to text you the venue info for tonight, okay? Please, just think about it."

Becca unlocked the hut and stared at nothing, vibrating with so much energy she didn't know what to do with herself. She couldn't get her mind to wrap around anything, but surely there was plenty to do. Their Summer Bash was in a few days. There were a *million* things she could be doing.

She didn't do any of them.

Footsteps sounded behind her, and she forced herself not to move. She knew Jase wouldn't follow her in here, not after the things she'd said to him.

He'd run tail.

That was what he did. He'd wait her out and eventually come back, not referring to their fight or the things she'd said. He'd smile charmingly, sweet-talk, give her the I-can't-help-myself eyes, and she'd sigh and forgive him. Help him. Whatever he needed. She'd seen Sam do this with his father, and she could do the same.

She strode to the counter and busied her hands, forcing a friendly smile so she could greet their customer. But it wasn't a customer at all. It wasn't Cole or Tanner, either. It wasn't anyone she could fool with her friendly smile at all.

It was Sam.

She didn't say anything. She didn't trust her voice, plus there was nothing to say. She figured he'd heard a whole hell of a lot more than she'd wanted him to, but she couldn't change that. She could, however, do her best to brush it under the table. She was off the clock, in fact. She could go home and lick her wounds in private.

Normally when he showed up, he strode in with that innate, almost cat-like grace, always looking completely in control and completely at ease. But this time, he was still by the door, not moving toward her until she made eye contact. Then he walked to her, took her hand, and tugged her into him.

"I'm not going to talk about it," she said, muffled against his shirt. "There's only one thing I will do, and it is *definitely* not talking."

Lowering his head, he brushed a kiss to the top of hers, and she braced for rejection. But he kept ahold of her hand as he closed the big, sliding front door with his other, even though it always took her two hands and *all* her weight.

"You'd better not be teasing me," she said, as he took her to his warehouse. "Because that'd be just mean."

The big hanging door was closed. He bypassed the front and took her to a side door she'd never noticed before, guiding her down a hallway she'd also never noticed. The first door there was his office. He unlocked it, gently pushed her in, then shut the door behind them.

"Sam —"

"Shh a second."

Oh, hell no. She'd been quiet for most of her life — *all* of her life. She'd been good, and a people pleaser, and all sorts of things she could no longer be because they made her sink. So she opened her mouth to tell him what he could do with his *Shh,* but he kissed her.

Softly.

Gently.

She didn't want soft and gentle, so she did what he'd done to her not all that long ago. She pushed him against the wall, trapped him there with her body, and tugged his face down to hers.

His hands came up to her hips, his fingers tightening on her. He was going to push her away, let go of her, but if he did, she'd go under for the count and drown. She could feel it. "Sam," she whispered, unable to say more.

He must have heard it in her voice. That or he knew her well enough to read her mind because his arms immediately came around her, hard and warm. But his eyes. Damn it, his eyes weren't filled with heat. They were worried and concerned.

For her.

The very last two things she wanted. "Hold me," she said. Demanded. "Just for right now, hold me."

"Becca," he said, and oh, God, it was in his voice. So solemn. Sliding a hand up her back and into her hair, he fisted the strands, pulling her head up to look into his face. He stared down at her, searching her expression, his own steady.

"I'm not fragile." She kissed a corner of his mouth, moving along his rough jaw to his ear, which she nipped, liking when he sucked in a harsh breath. "Don't you dare treat me like I am. I'm not going to break, Sam."

"Maybe you should."

No. Hell no. "I just want to feel something good for a change," she said. "Please, Sam, make me feel something good. Make us both feel something."

"I can't."

She froze for a beat and then tried to shove free but he held on with a grip of inexorable steel. "I can't do good," he said softly, his mouth against hers, "but I can do *great.*"

As payback, she nipped his throat. And then the crook of his neck.

He let out a shuddery groan, lowered his

head, and played her game. He took her lower lip between his teeth while she wrapped a leg around him and tried to climb him like a tree.

He slid his hand beneath her other thigh and hoisted her up with ease.

Then he turned and dropped her on the couch, following her down.

"Now?" she whispered hopefully, flinging her arms around his neck.

"Yeah. Now."

And he kept his word. He wasn't good. He was great.

CHAPTER 24

It took a while, but when Becca finally retained enough muscle memory to move, they dressed, and Sam brought her into the small kitchen. Kicking a chair from the wood table, he gestured for her to sit and strode to the fridge.

Still a little shaky — the aftershocks of emotional trauma compounded by really great sex — she sat and looked around. "You're being awfully generous with the Man Cave today."

"Maybe I like the sight of you in it." He brought her a soda and a cup of ice, setting them on the table in front of her. Then he kicked out a chair for himself. "Drink," he said.

She looked at the soda. "You got anything stronger? Say, a hundred proof?"

She expected a smile but didn't get one. "No," he said. "I don't keep it here anymore."

She opened the soda and poured it over the ice. "Anymore?"

He held her gaze. "I used to like it too much."

"AA?"

"No. Cold turkey."

She let out a breath and gulped down some soda. She set the glass to the table and wiped her mouth. "You decided to quit, and you quit. Problem solved. Why can't everyone do that?"

"You have to quit for the right reasons," he said.

Her gaze slid back to his. "What were your reasons?"

"I decided I wanted to stick around for the rest of my life."

She huffed out a breath. "That's a good reason." She played with the condensation on her glass until Sam nudged it out of the way, hooked a foot around the leg of her chair, and dragged her in closer so that she was caged between his thighs.

"Talk to me, Becca."

"I'm not going to Seattle tonight to play in the concert with Jase."

"I got that," he said.

"I'll have a panic attack if I do."

"I got that, too." His hands came up to her arms. Gently. Softly stroked up and down. And the gesture made her open her mouth and say more. More than she wanted to.

"The first time it happened," she said, "I was seventeen. I'd just grown about eight inches in six months and was so awkward that my fingers didn't work. I embarrassed everyone. My parents, Jase . . ." She shook her head.

"Stage fright at seventeen sounds perfectly normal," he said. "Stage fright at *any* age is normal."

"Maybe." She blew out a breath. "I fought it. I managed to keep playing for ten more years, and though I loved it, it was a really difficult time. I used to take anxiety meds to play." She paused. "Jase started stealing them. I let him. And then he moved on to . . . other stuff. Pain meds that he got from one of the other musicians. He got addicted."

"Not your fault," he said quietly.

She stared at him. "I stopped playing when he needed me most. I missed playing, but not enough to get over my fear."

He covered her hand with his, entwined their fingers. "The Becca I know isn't afraid of shit. Well, except for spiders."

"And things that go bump in the night," she added with a low laugh. She stared at their hands, his big and capable.

He squeezed her fingers gently. "Who's Nathan?"

The question startled her — or maybe it was the sound of Nathan's name on his lips. She pulled free of him too quickly and spilled her soda. "Oh, shit, I'm sorry!" She jumped up but Sam grabbed her hand.

"It's nothing," he said and, ignoring the mess, pulled her into his lap.

Becca curled into him and pressed her face to his throat. He cuddled her and let her settle, but not for long because this was Sam, and he never ran from a problem. Nope, he faced it head-on, however he felt was best — and that was never the easy way, or the fast way.

It was the *right* way.

She usually admired the hell out of that. "He was our manager," she finally said, "and then, when I stopped playing, Jase's manager."

He stroked a hand down her hair. "He's the one who hurt you," he said.

She pressed her face harder into his throat and concentrated on just breathing him in. He smelled like the sea, like the wood he'd sanded earlier. He smelled like her, too, and that actually made her smile, but then suddenly she was all choked up.

Sam merely tightened his hold on her in a way that made her feel safe and warm and cherished, and gave her the moment she so desperately needed.

"He was a longtime family friend," she said. "I had this big, fat, painful crush on him. Always did, from the time I was seventeen. He was the one who talked me into staying in music when I had that growth spurt and kept fumbling."

"How old was he back then?"

"What?"

He gently pulled her face from its hiding zone and looked into her eyes. "You were seventeen, and he was . . . ?"

"Twenty-seven."

"Big age difference for a crush."

"Maybe that was part of it for me," she said. Compared with Jase, or the boys her own age, Nathan had been a grown-up. He'd been smart and funny, and so damn handsome . . .

"He went for you," Sam said. Not a question, a statement of fact.

"Not until I turned twenty-one. We . . . dated, a little bit. Nothing serious." That hadn't come until later.

"He kept you playing."

"Yes," she said. "Until after we broke up. After that, not even God could have kept me playing. But Nathan gave it his best shot."

"Tell me," he said, his dark, mossy-green eyes never leaving hers.

She drew an unsteady breath of warm, protective Sam and found the courage to keep speaking about it. "We'd been dating again," she said. "More serious then, much more. We were exclusive. And I did try to play. I tried for Nathan, for Jase, for everyone. But I couldn't do it."

"Let me guess. Nathan didn't like that."

"It frustrated him. I frustrated him," she admitted. "He got . . . different. Unhappy." Mean, she thought. "I left him," she said. "And it got a little ugly."

Sam gently tilted her face and looked down at her, his expression quiet, steady. "How ugly?"

She closed her eyes, the memories she'd managed to mostly bury over the years coming back to her. She swallowed hard. "*Ugly.* I refused to give in to pressure and stay with him. But he was a family friend, and our paths continued to cross. A lot. He was big in my parents' life, in Jase's life, and he was important to his career as well, so I did my best to keep things as friendly as possible."

"It's bullshit that you had to do that."

She opened her eyes. Sam's gaze wasn't

362

his usual calm now. "I don't know a lot about family," he said, "but I do know that the loyalty should have gone to you."

"Yes, but you don't understand. We were all like family. Nathan's mom and dad had gone to college with my mom and dad. All of us were tight, real tight —"

"Still bullshit," Sam said. "Tell me more about the ugly business."

She stared at his chest. His broad chest. There was a lot of strength in his body, and he'd honed it well, both on and off the water with physical labor. And yet she wasn't afraid of that strength because he knew he'd never use it against her. He'd never push her around in anger and try to take what he wanted, especially if it wasn't what she wanted. He'd never —

"Becca," Sam said, cupping her face, drawing her attention back to the here and now.

"There were a lot of family gatherings," she said. "My parents throw a big shindig on Sunday nights, and everyone goes. After I left Nathan, I stopped attending so he wouldn't have to."

Sam's mouth tightened, telling her what he thought of her family allowing *that* to happen, but he didn't say a word, just waited for her to continue.

"Last year, on my twenty-eighth birthday," she said, "Mom and Dad and Jase talked me into having a party at their house."

"Tell me they didn't invite your ex to your own birthday party."

"Like I said, he was a family friend, a really good one."

"Shouldn't have happened, babe."

They were the words she hadn't realized she needed to hear, and she let out a shuddery breath. "Nathan came. He said he wanted to hook up again, but I knew what he really wanted."

"Which was?"

"Jase had been floundering since the last rehab attempt. He'd been showing up late to gigs, missing some altogether . . ."

Sam dropped his head, swearing softly beneath his breath before looking at her again. "Nathan wanted you to keep Jase in line."

"Yes."

"Not your job."

"But it was. It *was* my job, Sam," she said when he swore again, not so softly. "That's been my job my whole life. But Nathan also wanted me to try to play again. He thought that would help."

"And you couldn't," Sam guessed.

"Neither one," she said. "I tried to explain

this to Nathan at the party, but he was drunk."

Sam went very still. "So you kneed him in the nuts and left him singing soprano on the floor, right?"

She shook her head. "I'd like to say yes, but no, that's not what happened."

"What did happen?"

Her breath hitched, but she kept it together. "He didn't get that we weren't going to be a thing again. He wasn't listening, all he was seeing was me standing between him and the success he wanted —" She closed her eyes at the harsh memory, but that was unwise because then she saw it happening again, so she opened her eyes and kept them on Sam. "He said I owed him. He said that if nothing else, I needed to pretend to be together with him in front of Jase so Jase would feel we were all just one big, happy family again. He said he was going to kiss me and I was going to kiss him back."

"Becca," he murmured, with far too much understanding.

Again she pressed her face into his neck, and realizing she hadn't said any of this out loud to anyone except her family. "I said I'd do it, I'd kiss him in front of Jase. I couldn't do anything else, Sam. I was worried sick about my brother, and feeling all this pressure from my family. I —"

"Babe," he said, moving his hands up and down her back. "*Not* your fault." Calm hands, calm voice, royally pissed-off eyes. "Can you tell me what happened?" he asked very softly.

Could she? She had no idea, but she gulped in some air and tried. "Jase saw us kissing and toasted us, and then went inside. So I thought it was over. But Nathan pushed me into the pool house, which was really just a storage room for the pool equipment. And he — We —" She broke off and shook her head. Nope. As it turned out, she couldn't tell him.

Sam's fingers tightened on her for a beat. Then he let out a long breath and loosened his fingers with what felt like great effort. "He raped you."

She lifted her face, her mouth open to say it wasn't rape because she'd known Nathan. Hell, she'd slept with him many times before, but she'd been to counseling and knew the truth. It had been rape.

Sam had kept his hands lightly on her back, stroking up and down. "I don't hate men," she said inanely.

Sam's arms tightened on her in a bear hug as he brushed his mouth to her temple. "For which I'm eternally grateful," he murmured, voice a little gruff, like he was still fighting his own emotions. "Though I get where your distaste for closed, tight spaces comes from. Where's Nathan now?"

"I was stupid," she said into his chest.

"Where is he now?"

She shook her head. She wasn't sure he understood. "I tried to tell my parents what had happened, but they didn't really get it. They knew I'd been intimate with him before, so —"

"Are you telling me that they didn't want you to press charges?" he asked incredulously.

"He was the son of a family friend. His parents —"

"Fuck that," Sam said harshly.

"I underplayed it, Sam. I did. Jase was so fragile then. If I'd pressed charges and put Nathan in jail, I'd have taken away even more from Jase. I didn't want to make things worse, and I just kept thinking it was true, I *had* willingly slept with Nathan before, so I could handle this. I'd just stay away." She closed her eyes, because she knew that she'd been weak and cowardly to go that route and didn't want to see the disappointment in his eyes. "I just wanted it to go away, Sam. I wanted that so much."

"Becca, where is that asshole now?"

"He's dead. Nathan's dead."

"You killed him," he said, his voice and eyes reflecting no judgment at all as he ran his hands up and down her arms.

"No," she said with a horrified laugh. "I didn't kill him. A Mack truck did." She gulped in more air and tried to breathe calmly. Sam's hands on her helped. "He was out on the freeway on his motorcycle, and he got hit. He died instantly."

"That's too bad." Sam said this almost wistfully, like he'd really have liked the opportunity to kill Nathan himself.

Becca choked out a laugh but it backed up in her throat when Sam slid his fingers into her hair, lifted her face to his, and stared into her eyes. "You're pretty damn incredible," he said fiercely.

"Not really," she said, trying to joke. "Just your average screwup."

He didn't smile. He didn't look away; he just stared into her eyes. "Incredible," he repeated, softly but with a fierce intensity that made the knot in her chest loosen for the first time in . . . as long as she could remember.

He took her home, and to bed, where he made slow, sweet love to her. And then not so slow, or sweet. But after, as she drifted off to sleep, she was absolutely sure of two things. One, Sam might indeed think she was incredible, but she thought the same thing about *him.*

And two, she wasn't just falling for him. She *had* fallen. She'd fallen deep.

The next morning Becca woke up alone. This wasn't unusual after a night in Sam's arms. Despite him not being a particularly great morning person, he liked to get up before dawn and run with Ben, or surf.

She showered, her mind whirling with images from the night before. Sam in her bed, his erotic whispers in her ear, the small of his back slick with sweat as he took her right out of herself, over and over again . . .

All really great memories, but she had to shove them from her mind because she had a lot to do at work today, much of it Summer Bash–related. She crossed the alley and headed to the hut.

Normally at this time of morning, the only sounds were the waves hitting the shore with a rhythmic, soothing regularity that had become as familiar to her as breathing. The seagulls usually had something to say as well, and once in a while the guys were out there on the dock or boat, their low, masculine voices carrying over the water.

But this morning she heard a familiar

woman's and man's voice, and Becca rounded the corner to stare in shock at Sam talking to . . . her parents.

CHAPTER 25

Becca took in the sight of Sam and her parents, clearly in the middle of a very intense conversation, and went still with shock. "Mom? Dad?"

Evelyn and Philip Thorpe whirled around and stared at her.

"What's going on?" Becca asked. "What are you all doing here?"

"We got your address from Jase," her mom said, taking in Sam's move and the way he brushed a kiss to her temple. "But we got lost trying to find your apartment." She moved forward, arms reaching out, and Becca stepped into her for a hug. Her father pulled her in next, but it felt awkward and stilted. What didn't feel awkward or stilted was the way Sam slid an arm around her waist afterward, holding her against him.

Surprised at the public display, she looked up into his face. He'd either just gone swimming or surfing or was fresh from a shower because his hair was wet, curling along his neck. His T-shirt stretched taut across his shoulders. He looked alert and tough as hell, his arm around her saying he was in protective mode.

There was a definite tension in the air, making her wonder what the hell had been said just before she'd arrived.

"Jase had really hoped you'd come to the concert last night," her mom said.

Becca met her mom's gaze. "I . . . couldn't."

"I know." Evelyn glanced at Sam. "Or I know better now."

Sam remained silent, keeping his own counsel as usual. Becca narrowed her eyes at him, but he didn't respond to that, either, just held her gaze, his own steady and calm. Damn it, he was good. She'd never once been able to beat him in an eye contact contest.

"We rented a car from Seattle," her mom said. "We wanted to see you before our flight out." She glanced at Sam again. "Sam was just . . . chatting with us," she said carefully. "You didn't tell us you had a boyfriend." Her smile faltered, and her eyes got misty. "I wish you could've told us, Becca. I've been so worried about you being out here alone, with you saying you didn't want

372

anyone to visit you, that you needed time. If I'd known you had a boyfriend, I'd have felt so much less worried about you."

"Mom." If she said the word *boyfriend* one more time, Becca was going to have a stroke. "Sam's my boss."

"*And* your boyfriend," Evelyn said, turning to Sam for confirmation. "Right?"

Sam gave a single nod, and when Becca stared at him, his eyes smiled. Not his mouth, just his eyes.

She didn't know exactly what to make of that, but, definitely feeling a warm fuzzy, she turned to her mom. "I'm sorry you've been worried, but I'm fine. And a boyfriend — or not — doesn't change that." As she said this, Becca realized that for the first time in a very long time, the automatic *I'm fine* statement was actually true. She *was* fine. In fact, she'd truly never been better. She smiled and caught Sam's gaze, which touched over her features possessively, and then warmed.

So did her heart.

"Sam said maybe we could get some breakfast at the diner," her mom said.

"Oh," Becca said, not sure she wanted to commit to an hour of being grilled about Jase.

"Honey." Her dad took her hands and

squeezed gently. "Please? We have some things to say to you, your mom and I, things we hope you'll hear."

Becca stared into his eyes, saw pain and regret, and steeled herself against the wave of guilt. "Okay," she said. "Breakfast."

So they went to the diner, an unlikely foursome.

It was early, but the locals were a hard-working bunch, and some were breakfast regulars. Becca found herself being waved at by a few.

"People know you," her mother said, sounding surprised.

Becca understood the sentiment. Her mother had never lived in a small town, either, and had a healthy respect for privacy. But there was no privacy in Lucky Harbor. As Jax had told her one night, you could leave a pot of gold in your backseat and it wouldn't get stolen, but you couldn't keep a secret. "I like it here," she said, and caught Sam's eye.

He smiled at her.

She smiled back, knowing that this was going to be okay. Somehow.

"Jase had a fantastic show last night," her mom said. "He went out with the promoters afterward and stayed up late. He has a second show tonight, or he'd have been here."

There'd always been excuses for Jase, and Becca had long ago accepted that. But she couldn't do it anymore. "Mom, Jase has a problem. He needs rehab." She'd said this in the past, and it had gotten her nothing but more excuses and arguments. But this time her mom didn't rush in to dispute the fact that Jase did indeed need rehab. This time her eyes filled with tears, and she put a shaky hand to her mouth.

Her father hugged her. Evelyn gave him a watery smile but shook her head and reached for Becca's hand across the table. "I know," she said simply.

"You . . . do?" Becca asked in surprise.

"Yes." Her mom swiped at a tear that slipped and looked around the café self-consciously. She didn't like to show a lot of emotion unless she was on stage. "I've known for a while," she went on softly. "I just didn't want to accept it. After you left . . ." She stopped to blow her nose. "It became more clear."

"You protected him, Becca," her dad said. "We didn't realize how much because you were also protecting us, when we should have been protecting you."

Becca gave up staring into her water like

it held the secrets of life and looked at Sam. "What did you say to them?"

"Don't be upset with him," Evelyn said. "Everything he said was true. Painful to hear, but true. And last week, the Seagals came to us."

Nathan's parents.

"They confessed their knowledge of how . . . terribly he'd treated you in the end —" She broke off, her eyes filling. She reached for a napkin from the table's dispenser, but she couldn't get one out. "Damn it."

Sam opened the dispenser and handed her a huge stack.

"I'm . . . devastated," Evelyn said, dabbing at her eyes. "I didn't understand —" She shook her head. "Honey, I need to know something."

Becca had to swallow the lump in her throat to speak. "What?"

"That you'll . . . you'll forgive us. Can you? Forgive us?"

"No," her father said to Evelyn firmly. "We don't get to ask that. Remember, actions, not words. We just want her to be okay."

And from the way he looked at Sam as he said it, Becca knew exactly where those words had come from. She hesitated and felt his hand gently squeeze her thigh, infusing her with strength. Not his, which he had in spades, but her own, and it welled up from within her. "Mom," she said softly. "I'm okay." She marveled that it was the utter truth, thanks in no small part to Lucky Harbor. To her friends here. To the peace and joy she'd found here.

To Sam himself . . .

"I know it's late for this," her mom said, "but I promise you I won't offer any more excuses for Jase. Ever. We did you wrong, Becca. We let you suffer rather than rock our boat. I can't ask you forgiveness for that, but . . ." She sucked in a breath along with a short sob. "But we are sorry, baby. So very sorry."

Becca felt her throat tighten, her eyes burn. "Thank you," she whispered.

Her father cleared his throat, his own eyes suspiciously red. "In realizing our mistakes," he said, "we realized something else — we've done Jase wrong, too. We've enabled him. That will stop. We came out here to talk to him, to see if he'd go to rehab."

"How did that go?" Becca asked.

Pain crossed her dad's features. "He's not ready. And we don't know if he will be. All we can do now is stand back and let him come to the realization himself."

"We've lost you both," Evelyn whispered.

"Our own fault. Love you, baby. So much."

Beside her, she felt Sam stiffen. She didn't know what that was about, but she took her mom's hand. "You haven't lost me. I'm still yours, Mom. Always."

Sam tried to watch over Becca as much as he could, but he must not have been too subtle about it because by noon she'd told him that if he was going to hover around like a protective mama bear, she was going to call in Lucille and the rest of the geriatric gang for snorkel lessons and book him as the instructor.

That's when he figured Becca wasn't in danger of having a meltdown. That she was dealing in the only way she knew how — by burying her shit deep and moving forward. And he left her to it.

So he was relieved when, at the end of the day, she poked her head into his warehouse, looking good. "I'm off to the rec center," she said, and was immediately on the move.

He barely caught her, snagging her wrist and pulling her back inside. Gently he pushed her up against the wall and cupped her face, tilting it up to his.

She met his gaze, hers clear and remarkably calm. He slid the pad of his thumb across her full lower lip, and it tipped into a smile.

"I'm really okay," she said.

"Yeah?"

"Yeah," she said, and pulled him down for a quick but very hot kiss before shoving at him. "Gotta go."

Not budging, he pulled out his phone and looked at the time. "You've got half an hour."

"Ten minutes of that is drive time."

"Twenty minutes then," he said. "You've got twenty minutes."

Her eyes softened. "For?"

"For whatever comes to mind," he said, and kissed her neck "What comes to mind, Becca?"

When his mouth got to the sweet spot beneath her ear, she moaned. "Everything that comes to mind takes more than twenty minutes," she whispered.

"Let me prove you wrong," he whispered back, and ran his hand from her hip to the underside of her breast, his thumb gliding over her already hardened nipple.

Eyes closed on another moan, her head thunked back against the wall as she arched her back, pressing herself into his palm. "Here? Against the wall?" she asked hopefully.

"No," he said with a laugh, mouth open on her throat. "Last time I nearly killed you when my legs gave out."

She pointed to his worktable across the vast expanse of the room. Then she began to pull him toward it. Halfway there she apparently gave up on trying to walk and kiss at the same time because she threw herself at him. He carried her to the worktable, where he kicked the stool out of his way and, holding her with one arm, swiped a hand across the surface, sending the tools, everything, to the floor.

"Sam," Becca gasped on a laugh, a thrill racing through her entire body as he lifted her to the table. "It'll hold, right?"

"Yeah." He stepped back to look at her sprawled out on the table. "Oh, yeah," he said, voice thick. "It's perfect." He yanked his shirt over his head, as always rendering her stupid with the sight of his bare torso. He made quick work of her shirt as well, and then her shorts and her senses with equal aplomb. Between his mouth and his hands, she was quivering from head to toe in two minutes flat.

She knew she was supposed to be keeping track of time, but honestly she couldn't do anything except melt over what he was doing with his tongue between her legs. In fact, she might have fallen right off the table with all her writhing but Sam had a firm grip on her thighs, preventing her from moving anyplace but closer to his mouth. "Sam —" She stopped when he swirled his tongue over an exceptionally good spot. "Oh, my God. I love that."

He did it again.

And then again.

And then he added a well-placed stroke with the pad of his callused thumb, and she just about screamed his name. "And *that,*" she gasped. "I love that, too."

"How about this?" He slid a long finger into her, timed with another swirl of his tongue.

"Yes! God, Sam — I love that so much —"

"And this . . . ?" Another finger, and another pass of his tongue, all of which melted her into a puddle of desperation. "Tell me, Becca," he commanded.

"Yes," she whispered, shuddering. "I love it when you do that —" She'd been trying to last, straining to hold on, but she couldn't. She came, just as he'd intended.

When she could breathe again, she realized he'd set his head in her lap and was pressing a soft, hot, open-mouthed kiss low on her belly.

"In me," she whispered. "I love it when you're in me."

Lifting his head, he looked right into her eyes as he pulled a condom from a pocket and protected them both before sliding into her. "This?" he asked, voice thick with his own need.

Half-delirious with desire, on the edge of yet another orgasm, her mouth disconnected from her brain. "Yes," she gasped. "That. I love that. And you, Sam. God, I love *you*."

CHAPTER 26

Becca heard the words escape her but she was too far gone. With one of Sam's hands fisted in her hair, the other possessively on her ass holding her close, buried deep inside her as he was, she felt it when every inch of him froze.

Felt it, but couldn't stop the freight train of the orgasm hitting her full blast. She rocked into him, clutched him hard, and let go.

From some deep recess of her mind she was aware that she took him with her, felt him shudder in her arms. She let herself get lulled by that into a puddle of sated bliss.

But then Sam didn't lift his head and flash his sexy smile, as he usually did. He didn't press his mouth to her temple, or drag it along her throat. Or cuddle her in close.

He didn't do any of things he normally did postcoital. In fact, he slid out of her, pulled his jeans back up, and vanished down the hall, presumably into the bathroom since she heard the click of the door shutting.

Letting out a breath, Becca hopped down off the worktable. It took her a moment on shaky legs to straighten and fix herself, not to mention gather her wits. Scratch that, she couldn't gather her wits, not even a little bit.

She opened her eyes and startled. Sam was there, right there in front of her, big and silent. Too silent. "I didn't hear you come back," she said inanely.

He held out her keys, which she'd clearly dropped.

Taking them, she stared up into his face, which was utterly cool and composed.

"You've got to get to the rec center," he said.

"What's wrong?"

He didn't answer. Or move.

"Sam," she said, heart in her throat. "I said I love you, and you . . . well, I don't know what exactly, but one minute you were right here with me, and now you're gone."

He slowly shook his head. "You shouldn't say things that you can't possibly mean."

She stared at him. "And how do you know I don't mean it?"

"Look, I get it," he said. "You were in the

heat of the moment. But you need to be more careful."

There were so many things wrong with those two sentences, she wasn't sure where to start. "And you weren't in the heat of the moment?"

"I was," he said. "You know I was."

She moved onto the more problematic statement. "And . . . careful?" She was as confused as hell, and hurt because he was maintaining his distance with a cool ease she couldn't begin to match. "I just told you that I love you. Love isn't *careful*, Sam."

He looked at her for a long beat. "You called Lucky Harbor a pit stop. You don't fall in love with a pit stop."

"Are you kidding me?" she asked. "When did I say that? When I first came here? I wouldn't have recognized love then if it'd hit me in the face. But you know as well as anyone that things change. *Feelings* change. And you said you weren't a commitment-phobe."

"I'm not."

"Just as long as the L-word doesn't come into play?"

Turning his back to her, he shoved his hands into his pockets and looked out the window. "I'll ruin this," he said softly.

"This?"

He shrugged. "I've ruined a lot of relation-ships. Just about every one of my father's while growing up. And then my own."

She stared at his tense shoulders. "You can't possibly believe that." But clearly, he did. Shocked, she shook her head. "Sam, any woman your father was seeing while you were growing up, whatever happened was on them. You were just a kid; you don't get to be blamed for adult relationships going bad."

"My own then," he said. "I'm not good at long-term relationships. They don't work out."

He was grasping at straws now, and she knew it. "It only takes one," she said. "The right one."

Unable, or unwilling, to believe her, he shook his head, and then walked out.

Sam woke up and stared at the ceiling of his bedroom. *I'm not good at long-term rela-tionships,* he'd said, and here he was alone.

A self-fulfilled prophecy.

He rolled out of bed and went for a long, hard run with Ben. The problem with run-ning, especially predawn, was that it allowed a lot of thoughts to tumble through his brain.

So he cranked his iPod higher and did his

best to drown those thoughts out.

They leaked in anyway, and at the forefront was the memory of the sweet, open look on Becca's face when she'd said it. *I love you.* He knew she'd expected to hear it back, but he hadn't been able to say it.

Christ.

Why she'd had to say it at all was beyond him. Love wasn't in the damn words. Love was in the showing. And if he'd gone there with Becca — which, he could admit, he maybe had — then she should know it without him saying it.

And actually, her using those words, especially when she had, was selfish. Thoughtless.

Because now it was over.

He and Ben normally didn't say much on their runs but after running to the pier and back, Ben stopped and looked at him.

"What?" Sam asked.

"You tell me what. You're talking to yourself."

"The fuck I am."

"You said you don't need this shit."

"I don't," Sam said.

Ben nodded, and looked a little bit amused. "What shit are we talking about exactly?"

"Nothing."

"This have anything to do with the pretty new music teacher?"

When Sam narrowed his eyes, Ben shrugged. "Hey, man, you know Lucky Harbor. There's no need to bolt your door at night, but you've gotta keep your secrets under lock and key. And anyway, you being into the pretty music teacher isn't much of a secret."

Sam shook his head. "Don't you have your own problems to worry about? Seems to me it wasn't all that long ago that you made news when a certain blonde stood outside your house yelling all of *your* secrets for the world to hear."

"Yeah." Ben smiled. "I was pretty sure I didn't need that shit, either. I was wrong. You're wrong, too." And with that asinine, ridiculous statement, he turned and walked away.

"I don't," Sam said to the morning. "I don't need that shit."

The morning didn't answer.

He walked into his house to shower, and found his dad at his kitchen table on the laptop.

And Becca at his stovetop cooking breakfast.

Sam stopped short. Hell, his heart stopped short, despite the possible hostility in her gaze. He started to smile at her, so fucking happy to see her that it had to be all over his face, but she gave him a blank face and turned away from him.

Yeah. Definite hostility.

"I felt sick," his dad said. "Weak. I called you, but you didn't answer."

Sam pulled his cell phone from his pocket. No missed calls.

"So anyway," his dad said, not meeting his eyes. "My blood sugar was low or something."

Sam gave him a long look.

"*Real* low," Mark added.

"So you call Cole," Sam said. "Or Tanner."

"Uh . . . they didn't answer, either."

Becca brought a plate over to Mark, nudging Sam out of the way to do so. Actually, it was more like a shove. "Leave him alone," she said to Sam. "He has low blood sugar."

"He always has low blood sugar in the morning," Sam said. "That's why I've got a fridge full of food for him. All he had to do was take a bite of something, and in less than sixty seconds he'd have been fine."

Becca turned to him, hands on hips, face dialed to Stubborn, Pissed-Off Female. "It's no bother for me to help him."

"Of course it's a bother," Sam said. "You had to get up even earlier than usual, which

389

you hate. You had to drive here. He's not your responsibility, Becca."

"I didn't mind," she said.

"Well you should have."

"Why?" she asked, eyes narrowed. "Just because *you* don't feel anything doesn't mean I can't."

Okay, there it was. The two-ton elephant in the room. Finding his own mad, he stared at her, hard. "You don't want to go there with me right now."

She lifted her nose to nosebleed heights. "You're absolutely right."

"I mean it, Becca."

Mark started to rise with his plate. "You know what? I'll just go eat in the other room —"

"You'll do no such thing," Becca said, and pointed her wooden spoon at him like she meant business. "Sit," she commanded. "Eat."

"Go in the other room, Dad," Sam said.

Mark gave them a look like *You're both crazy,* grabbed his plate, and walked out of the kitchen — but not before bending to drop a kiss on Becca's cheek.

She sighed, softened, and gave him a quick hug.

And then Sam and Becca were alone. Perfect. Just where he didn't want to be.

Becca looked at him for a moment, shook her head, muttered something to herself that sounded suspiciously like "jackass idiot," and then walked out of the kitchen.

He followed after her just in time to catch the double doors as they closed.

In his face.

"Damn it." He managed to catch her in the living room by the front door — barely. She was ticked off, and she was quick.

But he was quicker.

"Knock it off," she said, pushing at him. "I'm only here to check on him, not to see you. You're here now, you can take over, I'm out."

"You're out," he repeated.

"Yep," she said, popping the *p.* "Out. As in all the way out."

He pinned her to the front door. "Not before we discuss this like adults."

"Seriously?" she asked incredulously, fighting to free herself, nearly catching him in the jaw with her elbow until he leaned in and flattened her to the wood.

Panting, she blew her hair out of her face and glared up at him. "Is *discuss like adults* what you did yesterday when you flung my own words back in my face? *Damn it,*" she said, struggling. "Let me go!"

"I didn't fling your words back in your face."

"You basically said I didn't mean them," she said. "Same thing. I mean honest to God, Sam, you reacted to my *I love you* like I'd tried to kill you!"

"You don't tell your summer fling in the town you just happened to 'pit-stop' in that you lo—" He fumbled over the word that she seemed to have no trouble with at all.

"My God, you can't even say the word?" She shoved him again. "And you're not a pit stop, not for me, and you damn well know it so stop saying it."

"*You're* the one who said it in the first place."

"I say a lot of things, especially when I'm pissed off," she snapped. "In fact, I have another thing to say to you — I quit."

Well, hell. "Becca —"

"Don't worry, I won't leave you in the lurch, that's not how I operate. But I'm giving you notice, Sam. I'll spend the next two or three weeks finding my replacement and training them before I go, because it turns out you were right, we can't work together, and do . . . whatever it was that we were doing."

The past tense killed him. "You're not quitting."

"I need to," she said. "It's for me. And you're going to let me go, because you didn't want me to work for you in the first place."

Christ. She was killing him.

The soft knock on the other side of the door galvanized them both.

"Sorry," came Cole's sheepish voice. "I kept waiting for a good time to interrupt, but it never came. I missed a call from your dad, wanted to make sure everything was okay."

Becca wriggled out from between Sam and the door, but he caught her hand. "We're done here," she said, trying to pull free.

He held on and studied her face, taking in the misery and pain he'd caused her. "I don't think we are," he said quietly.

"Think again." And without looking back, she tore loose and headed back to the kitchen. A minute later, he heard the back door slam as she made her escape.

Sam swore as he hauled open the front door.

Cole was arms-up on the door frame, and gave him a long look. "She said *I love you* and you flung it in her face?"

Sam started to shut the door on Cole's nose but Cole was quicker than he looked, and stronger too, and shoved his way in.

Sam turned to ignore him and go after Becca, but Cole got in his way and in his face.

"Don't," Sam warned him.

"You going to say it back?" Cole wanted to know.

"We're not discussing this."

Cole stared into Sam's eyes and saw the truth: No, he wasn't going to say it back. "You're a fucking idiot," Cole said, but he wasn't done. Hell, no. Cole always did have plenty to say, and no one, not man, woman, or God himself, could shut the guy up when he had something on his mind.

"You're not good with letting people in, I get that," his oldest friend said. "We *all* get that, but —"

"You don't get shit," Sam said.

Cole ignored this, because he knew, as did Sam, that no one knew Sam better than Cole himself.

No one.

"You go so far with trust and no further," Cole said, "and I get that, too. You got it from your dad. He let you in and then let you back out again how many fucking times? I can't imagine it, going through all that, except I can, since I watched you go through it."

"Drop it, Cole."

Of course he didn't. Cole was incapable of dropping a damn thing. "But," he went on as if he hadn't been interrupted, "you landed at a damn good home when you needed one, and we never threw you away, not once. So you do know real trust, and that it can be good." He paused, waiting for his words to sink in. "That woman you just chased out of here, she's got eyes for only you. And she's the kind of woman that loves down to her toes, with her entire heart and soul. You're safe with her, Sam. You get me? You're as *safe* with her as she is with you."

"Shut up or I'll shut you up."

"You know, it's funny," Cole said casually, unperturbed by the threat. "We all think of you as the guy always willing to risk whatever it takes. And it's true. Physically."

"Gee, thanks, Dr. Phil."

"But the one thing you never risk is your emotions. You hold them close to the vest," Cole said. "I think it's because you're afraid they'll be taken away. You're too stubborn to realize otherwise, and now after listening to your conversation with Becca, I think you're also a little bit stupid as well."

Sam shoved free without a word, mostly because he was fresh out of words, and maybe a little afraid that Cole was right —

about everything.

"You want to be an idiot, be my guest," Cole said, lifting his hands like he surrendered. "It's certainly your turn after all these years of keeping our shit together for us. But if that's your plan, you've got to stop reeling her in, man. She deserves more than that from you. Hell, *you* deserve more from you."

Before Sam could respond to this, Cole added one more thing. "And if she really quits because of you, I'm going to kick your ass. I might need Tanner to help me, but I will do it."

CHAPTER 27

Sam actually agreed with most of what Cole had said. Becca deserved more from him. As for what *he* deserved, the jury was still out on that one. So he went to work. He opened his shop and stood in the middle of it, wondering when the hell he'd stopped enjoying the solitude of his warehouse, instead looking forward to the moments Becca spent in here with him. But he'd blown that one.

I love you, Sam . . .

The words mocked him. He'd heard those exact same words from his dad throughout his life, and they'd never meant a damn thing. Those three words had never gotten him anywhere, not once. The only thing to do that was hard work. He had a lot to show for hard work, and absolutely jackshit to show for love.

But at the thought, he felt only a sense of unease. Because it wasn't strictly true. Cole

397

and his family had taken him in every time he'd needed it. They'd fed and housed him. That had been love.

Without the words.

He liked it a whole lot better that way.

He needed to talk to Becca. Make her understand that they didn't need the damn words. But, typical of the season, the day was crazy, and she was swamped, giving him the stink eye every time he showed up in the hut.

A busy business was great, he told himself. After the way he'd grown up and the long years on the rigs where he'd worked 24/7 in conditions he wouldn't wish on an enemy, he knew more than anyone just how good he had it. He enjoyed chartering, enjoyed the work — which didn't really feel like work at all — enjoyed the people, and their bottom line had been more than decent. He'd made sure of it.

But today, he didn't enjoy shit. By mid-afternoon, he was over pretending to work and headed back to the hut. He had no real plan. He was hoping one would come to him.

Becca was in denim shorts, a halter top, her little name tag pinned to it, a straw hat on her head, with her hair loose and tumbling around her shoulders. It'd gotten sun-streaked over the past weeks, and her shoulders and toned arms were tanned, as were her mile-long legs. She had a few freckles, too. She hated them, but he didn't. In fact, he enjoyed connecting the dots.

With his mouth.

As if she could feel his presence, she looked up. She was busy with several clients, but as she gave him yet another Come-closer-and-die look, he realized that beneath her temper, she was hurt as hell.

That was all on him.

"Ouch," Tanner said, coming up beside him, slipping an arm around his shoulders. "Looks like you've been served."

Sam gave him an elbow to the ribs that Tanner returned.

Normally Sam would've been ready for it but he'd caught sight of a guy skulking off to the side of the hut, just out of Becca's sight. Waiting. And because Sam was concentrating on that, Tanner's elbow to the ribs nearly sent him sprawling into the water.

Tanner started to laugh, but the smile died on his face at the sight of Sam's expression. "What?"

"Keep Becca occupied," he directed, and strode for Jase.

Jase saw him coming and straightened.

"Hey, man." He lifted his hands. "I just want to borrow your employee for a minute, that's all."

"She know you're here?" Sam asked.

"No."

"Good. Get the fuck off my property."

Jase's good-natured smile slipped. "What?"

"You heard me."

"Hey, wait a minute," Jase said with a shake of his head. "I need to talk to my sister."

"Yeah? You ever think about what *she* needs?"

Jase blinked. "What the hell is this?"

"It's me telling you one last time to leave," Sam said. *"Now."*

Jase shoved his hands in his pockets. "Listen, I don't know what she's told you about me, but we're cool, her and I, so —"

Sam grabbed him by the collar. "Are you? Cool?"

"Yeah. I mean . . ." Jase closed his eyes and shook his head. "Okay, so we're not cool, but it's not what you think."

"You know what I think?" Sam tightened his grip on Jase to make sure he had his full attention. "I think you let her take care of *you* all your life, and then when she needed the favor returned one time, you failed her.

You let her get hurt. You let her feel guilty for being raped." Christ, he wanted to squeeze until Jase stopped breathing. And indeed, Jase choked and brought his hands up, but Sam was beyond giving a shit. He heard Cole and Tanner calling his name, felt them trying to pull him off Jase, but he held on.

Until he heard her voice. Becca's.

"Sam! Sam, let go!"

Shocked, Becca clutched at Sam's cement biceps. "Please, Sam," she said, heart in her throat, but as if *please* had been the magic word, Sam did indeed let go.

Jase slid to the ground, gasping for air. Letting out her own tense breath, Becca dropped to her knees at her brother's side, running her gaze over him. Realizing he was indeed mostly in one piece, she tilted her head to Sam's. "What the hell?"

Eyes shuttered now, Sam took a step backward and said nothing.

Becca shook her head and turned back to Jase. "What are you doing here?"

Still holding his throat, Jase slid a cautious look up at Sam.

Becca couldn't blame him. Sam had backed up, but he still had a feral look of fury in his eyes. He was breathing steadily,

401

calm even, but his hands were in fists. On either side of him stood Cole and Tanner. Probably to back up Sam, but maybe also to keep him from killing Jase. Hard to tell.

"I was trying to see you," Jase said, "but then I was assaulted."

Tanner made a sound from deep in his throat that should have been a warning, but Jase had never been good at warnings.

"I mean, Jesus," he went on. "I didn't do shit; he just came after me."

This time the growl came from Cole. Clearly, neither he nor Tanner had any idea what this was about, but it didn't matter. Brothers of the heart, they stood united with Sam. "Jase," she said softly. "This isn't the time or place. I'm at *work*. Go home."

"I . . . can't."

She stared into his eyes, saw shame and guilt, and felt her heart clutch. "Why, Jase?" Oh, God. "What have you done?"

"I . . . need your help." He clutched at her hands and held her gaze in his own red-rimmed one. "This one last time, Becca. *Please.*"

At his words, the years fell away. She could see him at age five to her seven, needing her to chase away his night terrors after he'd been bullied at school. At age twelve needing her to hide him after he'd stupidly shoplifted a metronome from the music store. Then over a decade later, coming out of rehab and still looking broken. And she felt herself waver. "Jase —"

"Just this one last time," he promised in a broken whisper.

She pulled her key from her pocket. "Go to my place. I'll be off in a few hours. Wait there."

He took the key.

"Jase," she said. "Promise me."

"I promise," he said woodenly.

She rose and watched him do the same. He straightened his shirt, gave her three bosses a very wide berth, and left.

She let out a breath and turned to the small crowd gathered. "Show's over," she said briskly. "We've got a sale on water equipment for the next hour only, twenty-five percent off. Who wants to snorkel or kayak? Line up, first come, first served."

A murmur rose from the crowd. Lucky Harbor was filled with good people, but they were also hardworking and loved a bargain.

"Does the snorkel gear come with a hottie instructor?"

This came from Lucille. She had her hand raised, her gaze on Tanner. "Because I wouldn't mind getting . . . instructed," she said.

Tanner winced but everyone else laughed, dispelling the tense atmosphere.

Satisfied that things would go back to normal, or as normal as it got around here, Becca started back around to the front of the hut.

"Becca."

The softly spoken single word was from Sam. She considered ignoring him, but the problem with that was she'd never been able to ignore Sam. Not when he'd been her Sexy Grumpy Surfer, not when he'd become her boss, and certainly not now that he'd become so very much more. She was going to have to do something about that, and she knew it. It was one thing to put herself out there and fall in love with someone. It was another entirely to be the only one of the two of them putting herself out there. "I've got work," she said.

And then she got to it.

Becca sat in the reception room of the "recovery" center in Seattle and watched her brother walk away from her toward the nurse who'd just called his name.

She'd gone home after work and found Jase pacing, looking more than a little crazed, and in desperate need of a fix.

"I fucked up," he said straight off. "I stole Janet's Vicodin."

She blinked. "Who's Janet?"

"Someone I met after last night's concert."

Becca just stared at him. "Are you crazy?"

"Yes, apparently. She could've called the cops on me, but she didn't. Jesus, Becca." He shoved his fingers into his hair and looked at her wild-eyed. "I *stole* from her. I sneaked out of her bed and into her purse and I took her pain pills." He dropped his hands to his sides, leaving his hair standing on end. "I'm a fucking thief now?" he whispered.

"Actually, you've been a thief for a while," she said, desperate to lighten his mood. "Remember when you stole makeup from the department store at the mall? They called Mom and Dad, and you gave them the story that you were thinking of becoming a drag queen. Which," she went on, "was bullshit. You'd just already spent your allowance on pot, and wanted the makeup for your girlfriend."

He stared at her, then scrubbed his hands over his face, letting out a half laugh, half groan. "Christ, Becca. I'm trying to be dramatic here and have a moment, and you're making light of it all."

She'd opened her laptop then, and they'd looked up rehab centers together. Jase had settled on one in Seattle. And now, there in the Seattle waiting room watching him go, her eyes filled. "I love you, Jase," she said. "Be safe."

He was too thin, very pale, and maybe a little bit terrified to boot, but there was one thing Jase had known since birth, and that was how to put on a show. He smiled and blew her a kiss.

She rubbed her aching chest but smiled, keeping up the brave pretense until he'd vanished behind the door of the thirty-day rehab center.

Besides her, Olivia grabbed her hand. "He'll be okay."

"He will," Becca said, because she wanted to believe it.

"No, I mean really," Olivia said. "He had a really determined look."

Becca decided to put her faith into that being true. She squeezed Olivia's hand in return and, for the second time in her life, walked away from Jase.

Halfway back to Lucky Harbor, Olivia said casually, "You going to tell me why you're over there crying while pretending not to cry?"

Becca sniffed. "It's smoggy. My eyes are

burning."

Olivia looked out at the clear blue sky and raised an eyebrow at Becca.

"Okay, well, then I have allergies."

"To what?" Olivia wanted to know.

"Your nosiness."

Olivia laughed. "That I could almost buy." She glanced over at Becca. "I'd bet my last dollar that you're not crying about Jase anymore. That you've moved on to crying about something else. Someone else. Sam."

Becca stared out the window. "Don't ever bet your last dollar."

"What did he do?"

"He didn't do anything." Which was the problem. "I just thought I knew him, but as it turns out, I didn't."

"Yes you do," Olivia said. "Guys are simple. There's only three things you need to see a guy deal with to know exactly who he is."

"Like?"

"One, slow Internet."

Becca thought back to her first day on the job when she'd first discovered the slow Internet in the hut. Sam hadn't lost his collective shit as her old boss would have. Nope, he'd simply gotten around the problem by writing things down on napkins, pieces of wood, whatever was handy. Not patiently, exactly, because Sam had a lot of great qualities, and patience wasn't one of them. But he had a depthless reservoir of steady calm. After the craziness of her family and her life, that never failed to bring *her* to a steady calm.

Well, until very recently.

"Two," Olivia said, "untangling Christmas tree lights."

She remembered the tangled strings of white lights she'd found, the ones Sam had replaced, and smiled despite herself.

"What?" Olivia asked.

"I had a bag of tangled dock lights, and Sam handled the situation." She shook her head. "By buying new ones."

Olivia laughed out loud. "Honey, that man's a keeper."

Well, she'd tried to keep him . . . "That's only two out of three things you need to see a guy deal with," she said. "What's the third?"

Olivia slid her a look. "How he deals with overwrought female theatrics."

Oh, boy. Becca had seen this, too, the night she'd heard a noise outside her door and gone into a full-blown panic attack. Sam hadn't thought her ridiculous or made her feel stupid. He'd been too far away for his own comfort and had sent Cole to stand in for him until he could arrive. And then there'd been the unexpected visit from her parents. Whatever she'd faced, Sam had been there for her.

Two hours later, Becca came home and found a stack of boxes waiting for her. An assortment of brand-new instruments for the kids, including a horn, a percussion set, and a bass.

For your new music program, the card read. Nothing else, no name, no address, nothing.

An anonymous donation.

But there was nothing anonymous about how she felt. Overwhelmed. Cared for.

Loved.

And as she sat there, surrounded by the boxes of brand-new instruments, she realized something. She didn't need a card. She knew exactly who the instruments were from. Damn, stubborn, stupid, wonderful man.

CHAPTER 28

On the morning of their Summer Bash, Sam got up extra early, knowing the day would be crazy. He was an hour earlier than usual, but he wasn't the only one. Standing in front of his warehouse door, waiting for entry, were both Amelia and Mark.

They'd squared off and were glaring at each other, Amelia with her arms crossed over her chest, Mark looking guilty as hell.

"What's going on?" Sam asked.

"Just making sure you don't need anything today, honey," Amelia said, tearing her hard gaze from Mark and moving toward Sam to hug and kiss him. "Summer Bash has taken over town," she said, "and everyone's so excited. I thought I'd come offer to help."

"Me too," Mark said.

Amelia snorted.

Mark frowned at her. "What the hell was that?"

"Dad," Sam said.

"No, I mean it," Mark said, staring at Amelia. "You got something to say?"

"I sure do," Amelia said. "I came here to give whatever I could. Time. Encouraging words. Whatever it takes. And you —"

"I what?" Mark asked, eyes narrowed.

"Coffee," Sam said. "Clearly, we need coffee."

"You think I didn't come to help," Mark said to Amelia. "You think I came to take."

"Isn't that your MO?" Amelia said.

"Breakfast even," Sam tried. "From the diner —"

"Shut up, Sam," Mark said. "The lady's got something to say."

"Don't you tell him to shut up," Amelia said.

Sam moved to step between them but Mark pointed at Amelia. "No, son, I want to hear what she thinks of me."

"You know what I think of you," Amelia said. "I —"

"Caffeine," Sam said. "The hut's got —"

"Sam, baby," Amelia said, eyes sharp on his father, "shut up."

Sam opened his mouth, but Mark pointed at him. "Do what she says, son."

Christ. Sam rubbed a hand over his jaw and wondered if this is how Cole and Tanner felt dealing with his grumpy ass in

411

the mornings. "You know, usually I'm the one snarling at people before sunrise," he said.

This didn't lighten the tension.

"Maybe things change," Mark said to Amelia. "Maybe people change."

The words hit Sam. They were close to what Becca had said to him. He stared at his father. "What did you just say?"

"Maybe it's not just my liver I'm working on healing," Mark said, but he was speaking directly to Amelia. "I know what I've got here, Am. You've got to trust me on that. He's given me everything. I know it, but I'm trying to give back now. Trying to be what he needs."

Wait a minute. "I don't need anything," Sam said.

"You're wrong, son."

"Very wrong," Amelia agreed, but she hadn't taken her eyes off Mark. "What is it that you think he needs?"

"Nothing," Sam said. "I don't need shit."

"He needs to learn to be happy, let people in."

"And depend on people," Amelia piped up.

"Becca could make him happy," Mark said to her.

"Which brings us to love," Amelia said.

"I didn't do a great job there," Mark said. "I admit it. I'm trying to remedy that."

"I said I don't need anything," Sam said with a frown, but no one spoke to him. Hell, no one looked at him.

"It's a work in progress," Mark said to Amelia. "It's taking time. It took time to get him this screwed up; it's gonna take time to unscrew him."

"Hello," Sam said, waving his hands. "Right here. Am I invisible?"

Amelia didn't move an inch, but there was a very slight lessening of the grim set to her mouth. "You're starting to get it," she said to Mark.

Mark nodded.

"I wonder if I should use my invisibility for good, or for evil," Sam mused.

At that, it was Mark's turn to snort.

Amelia let out a very reluctant, very small smile and hugged Sam again, hard. "It's going to be okay," she said. "It's all going to be okay. Assuming you don't do anything stupid."

"Wait — me?" Sam asked.

"You," Mark said.

Sam pointed at them. "You've lost it. Both of you, cuckoo for Cocoa Puffs."

"Like I said," Mark muttered to Amelia. "Work in progress." He hugged Sam, too.

"I'm proud of you," he said. "Love ya, son."

Sam waited for the usual anger over those words, so casually uttered, to hit. It didn't. Because suddenly the words didn't feel so casually uttered.

He wasn't sure what to make of that. "Cuckoo," he repeated, and tossed his dad the keys to the warehouse. "I'm going to check on the setup. Don't kill each other."

Becca was already at the beach when he arrived.

She was a tyrant in white shorts and a white tank top, whistle around her neck, clipboard in hand, a visor on her head, and a militant finger pointing out where she wanted what. She'd hired high school kids to help set up, and they were carrying out the equipment she'd rented. Benches. Trash bins. Awnings.

She'd gotten the Eat Me diner to cater, and they were setting up a food tent.

Cole arrived just behind Sam and watched along with him. "She's really something," he said.

Just then, Becca glanced up and met Sam's gaze from across a stretch of a hundred feet of organized chaos. He stared into those fathomless eyes and felt a piece of him that he hadn't even known was loose settle into place. "Yes," he agreed. "She is

414

something."

"Something that you're going to get back," Cole said. "Right?"

He'd like to say yes, but the truth was, she was a woman who believed in the words, needed the words. She deserved a man who could give them to her. "Stay out of it," he said.

Tanner came up beside them. "Stay out of what?"

"Nothing," Sam said.

"He's being a pussy," Cole said.

"What's new about that?" Tanner asked.

Sam blew out a breath and pushed past them both.

"Where you going?" Cole asked.

"Work. You oughta try it sometime."

"He definitely didn't get laid last night," Tanner said. "He's always an asshole when he doesn't get laid."

Ignoring this, Sam strode out to the beach. Becca was now on top of one of the tables, messing with the umbrella over it.

It shut on her.

He was grinning even before he heard the colorful swearing from beneath the canvas. All he could see of her now was her bare feet and a bit of her shapely calves. He reached beneath the umbrella and got two good handfuls of warm, pissy woman.

She squeaked.

He let his hands slowly glide up the entire length of her body to reopen the umbrella.

Becca turned to face him and stared down at him from her perch. "Did you really just feel me up in front of all these people?"

"It was beneath the umbrella."

"That's not funny."

His smile faded at the pain on her face. "You're right. It isn't funny. Becca —"

"You bought me instruments?"

"I bought the kids instruments," he said.

"Why?"

"Because watching you teach those kids music, anyone can see how much it means to you," he said. "And knowing it makes it mean something to me." He tried to reach her with his gaze but she was closed off to him completely. "I was in a position to help," he said. "So I did."

"It had to be thousands of dollars," she said, sounding worried.

"I had it," he said simply. "And now you have a music program."

"But —"

"Stop." He put a finger to her lips. "Becca, you give your time to the program. You give your heart and soul. You give everything you have. Why can't I give what I have to give?"

She shook her head, muttered something

beneath her breath that might or might not have been a well-thought-out commentary on his ability to out-stubborn even her. Then she jumped down, strode to the next table, and climbed up.

Sam followed and leapt on the table with her just as she opened the umbrella. Reaching up, he closed it around them and whipped a still-sputtering Becca to face him.

Now they were nose-to-nose, chest-to-chest, thigh-to-thigh, pressed tight together inside the umbrella like a banana in its peel.

"What the hell are you doing?" she demanded.

"Helping."

"I don't need your help. And FYI — people I fall in love with who don't love me back don't get to cop feels, beneath an umbrella or not."

"Let's talk about that," he said.

She stared at him incredulously. "You have five hundred people pouring onto this beach today. I've got a list of stuff to do a mile long, and —"

"I've had the words all my life," he said quietly. "It was always *I love ya, Sam, go get me my booze.* Or *I love ya, Sam, get lost for a few hours, will you?* Or *I love ya, Sam, where's that money you got from Grandma for your birthday, Dad needs a little loan.*"

417

Becca let out a long, shuddery breath and put her hands on his chest, her eyes not so closed off to him now. "Sam —"

"I'm sorry for how I reacted," he said. "I was a total asshole. I —"

"Ms. Teacher?" came a little girl's voice somewhere near their feet. "Is that you?"

Becca's eyes flew open, and she stared at Sam wide-eyed. "Pink?" she called out.

"Yes, ma'am. You sure have pretty toenail polish. My daddy just brought me here, along with some of the other girls. The boys are coming soon, too. We're gonna play the games you talked about. Who's that with you? It's a boy. I can tell 'cause he's got hair on his legs, and his toenails aren't painted."

Becca tried to jump down, but Sam held on to her. She gave him a long look. "It's my . . ." She hesitated. Narrowed her eyes at Sam. "Boss."

"The drummer?"

Sam grinned at Becca, who rolled her eyes. "Yes. The drum player."

"Whatcha doing in there?" Pink wanted to know. "Kissing?"

"No."

"Are you *gonna* kiss?"

"No! We're just —"

"We're totally gonna kiss," Sam whispered

in her ear.

Becca gave him another long look, but as they were sandwiched together, he didn't miss her shiver. And it wasn't because she was cold.

"— Setting up the umbrellas," she said to Pink. "I'll be right there." Then she shook her head at Sam. "We're *not* going to kiss."

"Gonna eat those words, babe."

She didn't smile at him, or soften in any way.

His fault. He wasn't done fixing this with her, not by a long shot. He skimmed his hand up her back and into her hair. "You threw me the other day," he admitted.

"I didn't mean to," she said. "The words, they just sort of came out. But I felt it, Sam," she said, the pain in her voice tearing his guts out. "I meant it."

"Becca —"

"No. I need you to hear this," she said. "I was touching you, looking at you, and thinking, All I ever want is to feel like this, surrounded by you, consumed by you, warmed from the inside out by *you.*" She punctuated each word with a finger poke to his chest. "I've never felt that way before, and I thought, I honestly believed, you felt the same." She dropped her hand. "And looking back, I can't even say I regret letting you know. I still believe you felt it, too, I saw it in your eyes. I still believe that you'd have gotten there, that you'd have said it to me, too, eventually."

Sam closed his eyes until he felt her body go still and then opened them again to see a look of defeat on her face.

"You were never going to get there," she said flatly. "You were never going to say it."

CHAPTER 29

Heart pounding, eyes stinging, Becca started to climb down off the table, but Sam caught her. He wrapped one arm low on her back to hold her against him, the other tilting her jaw.

She did her best not to be moved by his proximity, and failed spectacularly.

"It's true," Sam admitted. "I never intended to say the words."

Oh, God. Face burning with humiliation, she began to struggle in earnest, knowing only that she had to get away.

Between them a phone began vibrating. Hers. She slapped a hand down to it, hitting IGNORE. The moment she did, Sam's phone began ringing. He hit IGNORE, too. "Becca —"

"I let you in," she said. "All the way in. I told you everything, things I've never told anyone, and you held back. You kept yourself distant — God forbid anyone walk into the

Man Cave."

"You didn't walk in," he said. "You blasted your way in."

"Well, I'd have waited to be invited, but I'd still be waiting!" She drew a breath with what appeared to be great difficulty. "And you telling me to stop living in the past is bullshit, Sam. Your entire present is lived the way it is because of your past. And you know what?" She got right up in his face. "That's just as bad as me being unable to get past my own past. Which means we're *both* screwed up!"

She began to fight the umbrella to get down, completely ignoring the six-foot-plus of testosterone and bad attitude still trapped inside the umbrella with her. And then all that testosterone and attitude spoke, and his words stopped her cold.

"I'm not good with trust."

Like a knife to the heart, she thought, and dropped her head to the pole of the umbrella, squeezing her eyes shut at the pain in his voice. "I've never given you any reason to doubt me," she said softly. "I was yours before you even knew what you had." She looked at him. "I'd never have stepped out on you, Sam."

"I don't mean that," he said, and drew in a deep breath. "I —"

422

"Hey," Tanner said, his voice floating up to them from below. "Trust me, this conversation is fascinating, but you need to shelve it for later. We've got other problems."

"Problems can wait," Sam said, eyes still on Becca.

"Becca isn't going to think so," Tanner said.

Crap, what now? Becca ducked low, beneath the umbrella, hopping off the table to face Tanner. "What is it?" She was aware of Sam hopping down behind her and standing at her back, but she ignored him. She planned to ignore him until forever. Or until the time she got over him, whichever came last.

"That was fun," Tanner said. "Four legs, two female, two male, poking out beneath the umbrella. Lots of yelling. I think Lucille got video of it if you want to revisit it later."

Sam gave him a hard look.

"No? Okay." Tanner shrugged. "The band Becca hired just canceled."

Becca gasped. "What?"

"Yeah, apparently they went out last night and had all-you-can-eat sushi. They're currently in the B and B puking their guts out."

"Oh, my God," she said.

Sam shook his head. "It's going to be okay."

She stared at him. "How?" she demanded. "How is not having music at the Summer Bash going to be okay?"

"We have games, food, and the ocean right here," he said reasonably. "Trust me, Lucky Harbor knows how to have a good time. There's no need to panic."

"It's a party, Sam." She could feel her voice rising along with her anxiety. "A big one, the biggest of the year. I set this whole thing up, I strong-armed you guys into having this party in the first place, and I want it to be perfect. So of course I have to panic. Join me, won't you?"

He had the nerve to smile at her, like her hissy fit was cute.

"We need music, Sam," she said tightly. "Music makes the damn world go around."

"I thought that was love."

She narrowed her eyes. "So you *can* say the word."

Tanner snorted, then turned it into a cough when Sam gave him another hard look. "Maybe I should give you two a moment," he said, and flashed a grin at Becca. "Give him hell, sweetness."

When he was gone, Sam put his hands on her and turned her to face him. "Babe, seriously, it's going to be okay."

Shaking her head, she looked away, to the

424

sand. Her kids were out there — not the entire class yet, but many. Playing in the sand, chasing each other, having a ball. She felt a pang for the simplicity of youth.

"Becca."

When she looked at him again, he was no longer smiling, but his eyes were gentle. Warm.

Fierce.

"I know how much this means to you," he said. "And that you've had a lot of shit dumped on you —"

"I'm fine," she said, not enjoying the reminder of her shitty week. "This is my problem. I'll take care of it." *Somehow.*

He slid his hands to her hips. "I want to ask something of you."

"What?"

"I want you to trust me to help," he said. "Trust me to fix the bash for you. And then after, I fix us," he said, voice low. Determined.

Still fierce.

Her heart caught. "Sam —"

He slanted his head and gave her one quick, hot kiss, and then he was gone.

She stood there a moment, then realized the beach was filling quickly. The air was hot, salty, and ringing with the laughter and sounds of people fully enjoying themselves.

It seemed that all of Lucky Harbor had come.

She let out a breath and went back to supervising the setup. An hour later, everything was going amazingly well. The food was plentiful; the drinks were flowing. The younger kids were playing games near the water, supervised by the teens from the rec center whom Becca had hired to do exactly that.

A little later, the pyrotechnic team arrived and set up for the night's show. The crowd thickened some more. There was face painting and a hula-hoop contest. Older kids were bodyboarding, or flirting with each other. Adults were eating, drinking, relaxing in the late-afternoon sun.

There was music after all. It came from Sam's quick-thinking setup with his iPod, a speaker, and a long extension cord from the hut. As night began to fall, Becca walked through the crowds for the umpteenth time. She was hot and tired and exhausted, but exhilarated as well.

She'd pulled it off.

Well, everything except the live music. That was still needling her. It was the only thing lacking. But then she saw movement in the area that she'd originally blocked off for the band. Sam was there, directing the high school boys she'd hired to help set up. They were dragging chairs onto the make-shift stage, and . . .

"Oh, my God," she whispered to herself.

Instruments.

From her classroom.

The instruments Sam had bought. And more than that, there was her keyboard as well. She started walking over there, ended up running, and skidded to a halt behind him. "What the hell are you doing?"

"Not supposed to swear in front of the kids," he said, waving them in.

"But —" She broke off as the kids sat with their instruments.

Sam smiled at them.

They beamed back.

"Sam," Becca said, her heart rate accelerating to near-stroke levels. "What's going on?"

Sam moved closer to her, pulling her into him.

"Don't," she said.

"Don't what?"

She pushed free. "I can't think when you touch me."

He just looked at her, like she was still cute but also a colossal pain in his ass. "Or look at me," she added.

So what did he do? He tightened his grip,

stepped into her, and cupped her face up to his. "Couple of things we have to get straight," he said.

"Now isn't exactly the time —"

"You were right before," he said over her. "I never intended to say the words to you."

She went still, absorbed it, decided she hated it, and tried to back away.

He tightened his grip. "I never was going to say them," he went on, "because they'd never meant anything to me, never gave me anything but a headache. They've always cost me one way or another. I thought this, with you, was different, that somehow my actions would be enough."

At that, she stopped fighting him and stared up at him. "Oh, Sam."

"I've had the words all my life and they meant nothing. I thought love was in the showing." He let out a low laugh and shook his head. "But then you came out of nowhere. I didn't expect you, Becca."

"I know, I —"

He put a finger to her lips. "I'm still getting past the surprise that I was willing to go there with you at all."

"There," she said, needing a translation.

"*Here.* You've become a part of me," he said. "As important and basic as breathing. I feel things for you that I can't even name."

His lips twitched. "And a few that I can."

She sucked in a breath and looked around to see if anyone was listening. When the kids had gathered on stage, the crowds had shifted in and were settling around the stage. Her keyboard sat up there, mocking her, and a new pit of panic gripped her, but Sam took her hands in his.

"You can do this," he said softly.

"Do what?"

But he let her go and moved to the edge of the stage, facing the crowd. "Welcome to the first annual Lucky Harbor Charters Summer Bash!" he called out.

The crowd cheered.

He grinned at them, and Becca could hear the collective hearts of every woman in the place sigh.

"Here at Lucky Harbor Charters," he said, "we've appreciated your business all year. We appreciate your *future* business as well. And today is mine, Tanner's, and Cole's thanks to you. But first, I'd be remiss if I didn't ask you to help me thank Becca Thorpe for . . ." He met her gaze. "Well, everything."

Everyone whooped and hollered for her, and Becca found herself staring at them all, cheeks hot as she gave a little wave.

Sam nodded to the pyrotechnic guys waiting for their cue. "We hope you enjoy the show —"

"Sam!" Becca whispered.

Sam held up a finger to the crowd, grinned at them again, effectively paralyzed them with the gorgeousness of his good humor, and then stepped close to Becca, as if they were alone instead of with every single person in town.

"What are you doing?" she hissed.

"Getting ready to start the fireworks display."

"Why are all my kids sitting in those chairs holding their instruments?" she asked, already knowing the answer as the blood began to roar in her ears.

"You can do this," he said again, so damn sure. Of course he was sure; it wasn't *his* ass on the line here.

"*What do you mean?* Why do you keep talking in some language that I don't understand! I can't —" She broke off and put a hand to her chest, which was pounding, pounding, pounding. "Oh, my God. I'm going to have a stroke; I'm not kidding. I can't do this. Sam, you know that I can't play in front of strangers."

He ran his hands up and down her arms. "They're not strangers, babe. They're your friends."

She looked out at the crowd. She saw Cole and Tanner. Mark. Jack, and Ben. Jax. Lucille. Amelia. Lance. Mark. Olivia . . .

Sam was right. These were her friends. They cared about her. And she cared about them. "But . . ." She swallowed. The lump in her throat — the one the size of a regulation football — didn't go anywhere. "We haven't practiced anything for this."

"Yes we have, Ms. Teacher!" Pink called out, bouncing in her seat so hard her little-girl legs swung with each word. "We've been practicing for weeks, remember?"

" 'God Bless America,' " Becca whispered.

Sam nodded. " 'God Bless America.' " He nudged her to her keyboard.

"You sneaked into my apartment for the keyboard?" she asked.

"Nope," he said. "I used a key."

"You don't have a key."

He smiled.

He had a key. He had a key to everything, including her heart. Damn it. "Sam —"

"Just try it, Becca, I promise you'll do great. And afterward, I've got ranch-flavored popcorn waiting."

She paused. "You bought me more ranch-flavored popcorn?"

"A brand-new tin," he promised, and then lowered his voice. "And more condoms.

431

None of them blue." He gave her another nudge, gestured to the pyrotechnic guys, and a hush came over the crowd. "We welcome our own Lucky Harbor band," he called out. "Give them a hand as we start the show!"

The crowd hooted and hollered, and Becca gave one last panicked look in Sam's direction.

Tanner was standing with him now, beaming. "I can't believe you bribe your woman with popcorn," he said to Sam.

"And sex," Sam said, his voice low and serious. "Don't forget the sex."

Becca stifled a half-hysterical laugh and turned to her kids. They were all grinning widely, excited, and she could only hope to God they actually remembered the song this time. "One, two, three," she prompted, and waited for them to jump in.

Silence. As if suddenly overcome by shyness as one, the kids had gone suddenly still as stone, staring out at the audience like a pack of deer caught in the headlights.

"One, two, three," she repeated.

Nothing.

Oh, God.

The crowded shifted but remained quiet. These people were mothers, fathers, friends . . . they *wanted* these kids to achieve their dreams. Which meant that there was no sense of impatience or irritation that the ticket price was too high for the value of the show or that she was disappointing anyone. Lucky Harbor wanted this, them, *her,* to succeed. Becca drew a breath and spoke softly. "Hey," she called to her precious class. "Guys, look at me."

The anxious faces turned her way. God. God, she knew just how they felt. The panic was clawing its way up from her own gut to her throat, choking her until it was all but impossible to breathe. But they were looking at her, eyes wide. Counting on her. She walked to the keyboard.

You can do this, Sam had told her. And Sam was always right. She ran her gaze over the kids, taking in each and every one of them, and smiled. "Just me," she said softly, for their ears only. "Just me and a few friends and family. That's all. Everyone knows this song. If we start, they'll join us, okay?"

Like bobbleheads, the kids nodded in unison.

And she smiled at them again, feeling her heart warm and fill with love and pride. "One, two, three," she prompted, and this time she began to play first, an intro, not taking her gaze off the kids.

Just her and the kids . . .

As she played, she settled. Her heart still threatened to burst out of her chest, but the fear receded a little bit, replaced by a familiar tingle that was so old she hardly recognized it.

Excitement.

She ran the intro again and held her breath, but the kids joined in this time — though not exactly smoothly. Several of them were half a beat behind, and Pink and Kendra were at least half a beat ahead.

Just like in real life.

The fireworks began as they entered the chorus. The town indeed joined in, and by the end of "God Bless America," everyone was in sync, and Becca could hardly keep in time herself because the lump in her throat was back.

I thought my actions would be enough.

The entire song, Sam's words floated in her head, and in her heart. He'd never said he didn't love her, only that he'd hoped his actions would be enough. And his actions did speak pretty loudly. He'd given her a job. He'd supported her, encouraged her to follow her heart, whether that be music or whatever floated her boat. He'd helped her get over the past. He'd backed her up with her family. He'd come running when she'd gotten scared. He'd been there for her, through whatever she needed, at the drop of a hat.

His actions *had* spoken for him — loud and clear. He'd *shown* her he loved her, with every look, every touch, every move he made.

The song ended, the fireworks ended, and everyone burst into a roar of applause. The kids bowed. Becca started to bow, too, but was pulled into a brick wall.

Sam's chest. "So proud of you," he murmured in her ear.

She was shaking. Adrenaline, she knew. But Sam had her, his arms locked tight around her. "Look at me," he said, voice low and serious.

She tilted her face to his.

"I hold people at a distance, I know it. I do it because I also know that anyone or anything can be ripped away from you at any time. But you, Becca . . ." He shook his head. "I can't — you're in, babe. You're past my walls, past my defenses. If I have to deal with that, so do you."

The crowd was still cheering as she stared up at him. "What are you saying?"

He got serious. Very serious, very intent, his eyes focused on hers. "It means I'm in love with you." He slid his thumb over her jaw in a gesture so sweetly powerful that she had to close her eyes at the sensation. "It means I love you so fucking much I ache with it. All the time. It means I want you to stay here in Lucky Harbor and be with me for as long as you'll have me, which I'm hoping is a damn long time because I've carved out a damn fine life for myself and I want you in it. All the way in it."

She stared up at him. "You . . . you said the words."

"I did," he agreed.

"You said the words," she whispered again, marveling. "Right?"

From the front, Lucille leaned in. "Honey, yes," she called up to her. "He said he loves you. You might want to see Dr. Scott on Monday about that hearing problem."

Becca wasn't about to be distracted from Sam. "You didn't want to say them, but you did. For me."

"Always for you," Sam said, and, ignoring their avid audience, he bent her over his arm and kissed her, a long, slow, deep one that meant business. It was there in his kiss how much he loved her, and it had been all along.

When he was done, he lifted his mouth from hers and slid his thumb over her wet lower lip. "We good?" he asked.

Lucille cupped her hands around her mouth and shouted to Becca, "Honey, he wants to know if you're good!"

Becca gave her a thumbs-up before turning to Sam. "Considering all I want is you, we're perfect."

EPILOGUE

One month later, Becca got a call. Her agency had been steadily sending her new assignments, and she'd done well on all of them. This time they were offering her one of their largest accounts, an American car company.

Finally.

Becca hung up and laughed, and then did a little dance right there on the boat.

The guys were sprawled out enjoying the last of the Indian summer as September came to a close.

After a crazy summer, the best summer of Becca's life, they'd all taken a rare day off and were fishing. Or at least making a semblance of fishing, as in the lines were cast. But she doubted any of them, slouched in various positions on deck, each with a beer, dark sunglasses on, bodies relaxed and still, was worried about his catch.

It'd been Sam's idea to take Becca out

today. He'd been unhappy when Cole and Tanner had tagged along without invitation, but he'd given in to the inevitable invasion, and they'd had a great day.

Cole was smiling at her little dance. "Probably you shouldn't ever teach dance classes," he said.

"I think she dances kinda cute," Tanner said. "It's white-girl rhythm, but it's the enthusiasm that counts. Although I could tell better if you'd do it again, in a bikini this time," he said with some hopefulness and a sidelong glance at Becca's tee and shorts. "Maybe we should instill a new uniform code. A bikini code."

Sam smacked him upside the back of his head. "My woman," he said. Then he tugged Becca onto his lap.

"Hey," Cole complained. "No PDA on this boat."

"You tagged along," Sam reminded him. "Deal with it." He smiled at Becca. "What's up, babe?"

"I got a big assignment."

His smile was slow and sure. "Proud of you," he said, and leaned in for a warm kiss.

She cupped his scruffy jaw. "Do you have any idea how much I love you?"

Sam nipped her bottom lip and slid his palm to the nape of her neck to hold her still for another kiss. "Show me," he murmured against her lips.

"Christ," Tanner mumbled to Cole. "They're like bunnies."

Cole sighed, rose to his feet, and headed for the helm. "Time to head in." He pointed at Sam. "And that wasn't one of those double entendre things. You can wait until we get back."

Sam smiled into Becca's eyes. "I'll try."

She smiled back. It'd been a great month, maybe the best month of her life. She was teaching, writing jingles, sometimes still playing late at night at the Love Shack . . . when she wasn't sleeping in Sam's arms. They stayed at his house sometimes, but more often than not Sam left his place to his father and stayed with Becca in her warehouse apartment.

She loved it.

She loved him.

She loved life.

As a bonus, Jase had just gotten out of rehab. She'd talked to him the day before, and he sounded good, real good. He wasn't going to go straight back out on the concert rounds but was going to stay with their parents and do some studio work and see how things went.

She was hopeful about that, and as Sam

440

pulled her sunglasses off and kissed her, she realized she was hopeful about a bunch of things.

Thirty minutes later they pulled up to their dock.

Becca had placed an ad in the paper for help at the hut, freeing her up to teach music classes to the rest of the grades in the district. She'd hired someone who was perfect for the job.

"Hey, son." Mark caught the ropes Sam tossed him and helped tie down the boat.

Becca looked him over carefully. He'd had a rough month health-wise, and they'd had to change up his meds, but he was looking good today at least, and she'd take that. She knew he was happy to be working, and that he loved feeling helpful, and most of the days he was even on time.

"You do it yet?" Mark asked Sam.

"Do what?" Cole wanted to know.

Mark blinked at Cole, then looked at Sam. "I thought you were going to do it today. How did you do it with these clowns with you?"

Sam's mouth tightened.

"She didn't like it?" Mark asked. He turned to Becca. "You didn't like it?"

"Dad, drop it," Sam said. "Jesus."

Becca grabbed her small backpack and the

441

tin of ranch-flavored popcorn Sam had given her that morning as she'd boarded. Clutching all her stuff, she stepped off the boat. "Like what?" she asked Mark.

He tapped on the tin.

"Oh, I *love* it when he buys me the popcorn," she said. "I just didn't get a chance to eat any yet. Sam distracted me every time I tried."

Sam looked pained.

Becca stared at him, wondering what the odd tremor in her belly was. She couldn't help but feel like she was missing something.

Something big.

Mark looked at Sam and laughed. "You poor, dumb bastard. I almost feel sorry for you."

Sam scrubbed a hand over his face and let out a sigh.

Becca set her backpack down and opened the tin.

Popcorn.

"Becca," Sam said, and reached for the tin.

She shoved a handful in her mouth, and the delicious flavor exploded against her taste buds. Cole reached into the tin as well, but she smacked his hand away. "Mine."

"Man, never get between a woman and her popcorn," Tanner told Cole.

Becca shoved down another few bites, leaving enough room to push the popcorn aside. At the bottom was a little velvet black box, dusted with popcorn crumbs. She stopped breathing.

"I knew you'd get hungry enough eventually," Sam said. "I was just trying to avoid a crowd when it happened." He leveled the guys with a look. "I should've known better."

She just stared at him, her heart pounding.

Sam reached into the tin.

"Hey," Cole bitched. "You'll share with him and not me? I thought we were friends."

Tanner wrapped an arm around Cole's neck, clapping a hand over his mouth.

Sam pulled the small black box from the tin. He nudged a gobsmacked Becca to the dock bench and then crouched at her side. "I might be a little slow," he said, "but luckily I learn from my mistakes." He opened the box and revealed a diamond ring that dazzled her and left her speechless.

It spoke of forever and stability and calm acceptance. It was a testament to his life, proof of his love and commitment. "Oh, Sam," she breathed.

"Is that *Oh, Sam,* you done good?" Mark asked. "Or *Oh, Sam,* you're an idiot? 'Cause there's a big difference, darlin'."

Tanner wrapped his other arm around Mark's neck and muzzled him as well.

"It's so beautiful," Becca whispered, throat tight, eyes misting.

Sam smiled at her. "I love you. Be mine, Becca. Marry me."

Mark tore Tanner's hand from his mouth. "Son, you're supposed to ask, not tell."

Sam slid his dad a dark look.

Mark grimaced. "Right. Don't butt in. I almost forgot that part, sorry." He then lifted Tanner's hand back to his own mouth.

Becca let out a laugh and stared down at Sam, the big, tough, stoic man who was so good at coming in under the emotional radar that she'd never seen him coming at all. He had his heart out on the line, and she knew he wasn't all that patient about such things. So she touched his face, feeling the rough day-old stubble beneath her fingertips as she leaned in. "Yes," she whispered against his mouth. "I'll be yours. And that makes you mine as well, you know. You ready for that?"

He grinned. "It's all I ever wanted."

The employees of Thorndike Press hope you have enjoyed this Large Print book. All our Thorndike, Wheeler, and Kennebec Large Print titles are designed for easy reading, and all our books are made to last. Other Thorndike Press Large Print books are available at your library, through selected bookstores, or directly from us.

For information about titles, please call:
  (800) 223-1244

or visit our Web site at:
  http://gale.cengage.com/thorndike

To share your comments, please write:
Publisher
Thorndike Press
10 Water St., Suite 310
Waterville, ME 04901